SAVAGE SCREAM

BREAKING THE SILENCE
BOOK TWO

SARAH JD

PAPERBACK ISBN-13: 978-0-6456492-3-9

PA: Obsidian Author Services (Bibiane Lybaek)

Cover by Simply Defined Art

Formatting: DAZED Designs

Cover Model: Trista Duncan

Many thanks to my Beta Readers: Alana, Anoesjka, Kathy, Melissa, and Tamarra.

For Jaz Flowers
Such an inspiring role model you have been to my daughter,
helping her grow creatively through dance,
and to become a more resilient woman.
You have a truly spectacular creative mind.
Your ability to choreograph such unique and captivating
dance routines will never cease to amaze me.
Thank you for some of the best and most
memorable years of my daughter's life,
And for still being there for her
as she moves on with her dance career.

CONTENT WARNING

Savage Scream is the second book in the Breaking the Silence duet.

Please note: This is a dark contemporary MF romance that contains subjects that maybe triggering to some readers, including, but not limited to: Detailed violence, killing, bullying, harassment, dub-con, non-con, explicit sex scenes, blackmail, and issues relating to crimes against children.

JARED

A slow, steady, consistent beep irritates me enough to drag me to consciousness. As my hearing increases, the sound of someone crying close by forces my lids to blink open. Light floods my vision painfully, and I snap my lids shut again as I release a groan.

"Oh, my goodness. Jared."

The voice is my mum's, filled with relief as I recognise her gentle touch on my shoulder.

"Mum?" I croak, confused about what the hell is going on.

"Gregory, he's waking up. Get the nurse."

I hear feet shuffling, followed by my dad's voice calling to a nurse before it fades, and I can only assume it's because he left the room, or wherever it is I am.

I try to crack my eyes open again, but the light is too much, and I cringe as pain slices through my head.

"Muuum." I groan. "Can you turn the light off, please?"

"Oh. Of course." She rushes out, the touch of her hand disappearing from my shoulder as I hear her moving. "Oh wait. Please don't go. I'm sure Jared would like to thank you for helping him."

My eyes snap open at my mum's words, thankful that the light over my head is now off, the only glow coming from a back light somewhere behind me.

I quickly take in my surroundings. I'm in a bed. A hospital bed. The annoying beep that won't fucking let up is coming from a monitor next to me, but it's now beeping faster as I ease my head to the side to see my mum standing near the silhouette of another person at the side of the room.

I'd know those curves and short stature of my little pocket rocket anywhere.

"Dee?" Her name flies from my lips as she steps closer to the door.

Her feet halt, her shadowed form becoming clearer as my eyes push away the haze, but she doesn't turn to me. She stays angled towards the door, her head covered by the black hood she's wearing, shielding her face from me.

"Her name is Dee?" my mum asks, glancing back at me, before sending her gentle eyes towards my girl.

Yes, she is *my* fucking girl. I don't care what Dee thinks about it. She owns my fucking soul, and I'm not going to keep lying to myself about that. Not after everything we've been through. Not after I thought I was never going to see her again. My life nearly cut short not too long ago.

Dee doesn't respond to my mum, which is nothing new since she doesn't talk to anyone, keeping her voice to herself.

My mum darts a worried glance at me, so I offer her a warm smile.

"Mum. Could you give us a few minutes?" I ask, my throat feeling scratchy and dry.

"But honey. You were in a car wreck a few hours ago. The nurse will want to see you. The doctor too. And you need to rest. You've had another bad concussion." A sob flies from my mum's lips on the last word, and she presses her hand to her mouth, trying to stifle her cries.

My dad steps back into the room at that moment, his concerned gaze locking onto mine.

Shit. I feel bad for scaring them like this. Here I was thinking they didn't care, when obviously they do. They just don't know how to deal with their grief over losing Tim. Both of them are worried sick right now. Hell, I've probably brought their past trauma back to the surface from the day my brother died.

I fucking love my parents, and I'm going to tell them exactly that, right after I speak to my girl.

"I just need a few minutes with Dee, please." I basically beg, and Dad glances with confusion between me, my mum, and Dee, whose stance is slight, her head angled down as if she's trying to hide.

Clearing his throat, my dad approaches me, leaning down to block my view of the two women that mean the most to me in this fucked up world.

"The girl won't speak to us," he whispers. "She won't speak to anyone. Wouldn't let anyone touch her or look over her for injuries, and at the mention of separating the two of you, I was almost certain she was going to kill anyone if they tried just by the look on her face."

I fucking smirk. "Dee doesn't talk, Dad."

His brows shoot up. "Oh. At all?" he asks, and I give my head a small shake, although the action makes me a little lightheaded. "Do you know who her parents are? They really need to be called."

When my dad shifts back, my eyes land on Dee, still standing curled into herself, unmoving.

"Dee is Principal Rogan's new foster daughter," I explain, and my mum steps into the line of sight of my little deranged mute girl.

"Oh good. I can give Cynthia a call." My mum preens, shooting an awkward smile in Dee's direction, even though

3

Dee doesn't see it.

"Great idea. That will give me some time with Dee." I remind my parents that I want to speak with her alone, and they nod, eyeing both me and Dee as they reluctantly exit the room.

Finally alone, I use the bed remote next to my head to sit me more upright, trying to ignore the dizziness. Dee still doesn't move, standing in the shadows, just like I know she prefers.

"Come here," I rasp, but she doesn't move. "Dee, please come here." Still, she remains where she stands, unmoving.

Stubborn little pocket rocket.

"Dee, you can either come here, or I'm getting out of this bed to come to you, which I'm pretty sure will result in me passing out."

That gets her moving, but she's in no hurry as she walks at a snail's pace, stepping out of the shadows. Her head is still tilted down, her brown hair tumbling out from the black hood as she slowly steps towards me, like she is... scared?

I wish she would look up or pull that fucking hood off so I can see her face. The only skin on her body I can see right now are her fingers, which are fidgeting at her sides.

She stops a few feet from the bed, and that's when I see it. A droplet of water falls from her hidden face.

Shit.

"Dee? Are you crying?"

She doesn't respond, and I feel the telltale signs of anger and frustration gnawing at me, but then a sob escapes her, and the anger disappears as my need to comfort her consumes me.

"Fuck, baby. Come here." I sit up in the bed, reaching my hand towards her, and the moment she sees it, she takes it and lets me pull her to the bed. "Get up here," I demand, and she obeys, still keeping her head ducked low so I can't see her face.

She climbs up on the bed with me, straddling my lap and wrapping her arms around me as another sob escapes her, and then she falls apart in my arms.

I can't hold back my own damn tears, my eyes heating and spilling over as I soak in the heartbreakingly painful cries flowing from my dancing assassin.

"I'm ok," I whisper against her hood, over and over, wanting to comfort her in some way, and each time I say the words, she squeezes me tighter.

The door to the room cracks open and my dad pops his head in, his brows shooting high as he takes in the scene. I shoo him away with my hand, and he gives me a nod before closing me back in the room with Dee.

As I hold my girl, my mind goes back to the events that led me here. We had been on a job for Griffin Marx, at a farmhouse a little way out of Fox Pines. It should have been straightforward. Well, as straightforward as it can be when you send Dee, AKA Hush, a seventeen-year-old girl, into a house in the middle of the night, to assassinate some predators.

Everything went wrong, though. She was ambushed. Black-clad figures creeping through the dark and entering the house after her. Griffin had ordered me over the phone to go in and help, giving me a ten second lesson on how to use the gun that was hidden under the driver's seat of the car he has me drive Dee around in for these jobs.

I would have gone in to help regardless of Griffin's order. There's no way I would have let some arseholes kill my girl. I'd never killed anyone until last night, though. I'd never pulled the trigger of a handgun, something that is crazy to think I held in my hand given the strict gun laws here in Australia.

I guess I am dealing with some kind of Australian mafia now though. The Marx family is clearly a big fucking deal in the Aussie underworld, and because of Dee and her brother Travis, I'm now balls deep in that world, too.

Flashes of blood splatter whip past my vision as I remember how I killed a man last night. If I hadn't pulled the trigger on the gun, Dee would be dead right now. I'm glad I could save her, but fuck. I killed a man. Ended his life. His existence.

The whole fucking incident had been too much for me to deal with. I'd lost my mind after that, driving erratically out to Ebony Falls where I had screamed like a madman at the one person that owns my heart.

Dee.

I was shaken to the bone about what had gone down in that farmhouse. Not just because I killed someone, but also because of how shocked I was at my reaction to seeing Dee kill.

I fucking enjoyed watching her slaughter those men.

She executed them so seamlessly. The way she moved with such precision and grace made it look like she was dancing one of the dances she does in her classes. She was fucking breathtaking.

Which is wrong for me to feel that way. I shouldn't feel like that about watching someone kill another person. It was those confusing thoughts that had helped send me past my ability to control my anger. What sort of person am I to think like that? So, I took it out on Dee. I lashed out at her, trying to get her to react and fight back, but she wouldn't. She wouldn't even give me the one thing I've basically been begging her for since day one.

Her voice.

I had totally planned to leave her there at the falls. I

wanted out. I felt like if I couldn't have her voice that I'd rather fucking die.

How fucking pathetic am I!

Dee had other plans though, getting into the car even though she knew how reckless I was in that moment. She knew I was unstable and ready to end things, yet she got in with me.

Did she want to die too?

I don't think so. Not with how scared she looked. And fuck, when she reached out and squeezed my thigh, something in me snapped. It was like the veil of anger lifted, and I could finally see that I'd been wrong.

I didn't need to hear Dee's voice.

I just needed her.

My attempt to stop the car still ended badly, though, despite trying to avoid a wreck. I guess I should be thankful there was a guardrail there since it stopped the car from rocketing over the edge. For a few minutes at least.

And those few minutes were everything.

Finally, with the fear of the situation, Dee showed her true colours.

She cared.

About me.

Fuck, and that kiss. The willing kiss that I didn't have to force or coerce from her made me both elated and heartbroken.

Heartbroken because I was sure I was about to die and I'd never get to taste her lips again. But I accepted it, in that moment. I accepted that I was about to die, and I only knew one thing.

I had to save Dee again.

So I pushed her out of the open car door, and fuck, I can still see the untamed fear on Dee's face as she watched helplessly as the car slid over the edge.

But mostly, the thing I remember as if the volume of the world turned up to maximum, was the scream that ripped from her as the car slid, rolled and crashed down the steep embankment into the thick bushland near Ebony Falls.

Everything after that is a bit fuzzy. I must have come in and out of consciousness multiple times, so my brain could be conjuring up things that didn't really happen, but I'm almost certain that what I heard during a couple moments of consciousness, was Dee's voice.

2

DEE

I can't seem to bring myself to let him go. I thought I lost him for a bit there. I thought I'd never get to feel his arms around me again. The pain was unimaginable. Excruciating. Something I never want to feel again.

I watched the black Audi slide down the embankment before it rolled a couple of times, snapping through thick scrub and finally coming to rest on its side in the gully, surrounded by dense Australian bush. I didn't hesitate once it stopped, leaping over the edge of the incline, gripping bushes and exposed roots as I half slid, half stumbled down to the mangled car.

Everything was silent. It's like even the birds didn't want to make a noise. But then I realised there was noise. There was someone screaming.

Me.

"Let me look at you." Jared rasps as he pulls back from our embrace on his hospital bed. I should have left him with his parents hours ago, but I couldn't bring myself to leave. I needed to see him awake and talking. I needed to know he was going to be alright.

As Jared eases back from me, he cups my hood covered head and tries to tilt my head up, but I keep it down, not wanting to show him the mess I'm in.

"Stop hiding from me." He rasps again, his voice sounding scratchy, like he must have a sore throat. "Let me see those beautiful chocolate eyes."

Reluctantly, I lift my head just enough to peer up at him from beneath my dark lashes. My eyes lock onto his blue pools, the honest care flowing from them almost too much to bear.

I don't deserve you.

"Fuck, Deranged." He tugs my hood off, exposing my head, and I know the moment his eyes find the dried blood on my skin by the way they widen. "Shit. You're hurt."

Shifting his hand under my chin, he tilts my head. And as always, I don't say anything. I just stare at this boy.

Wait, no.

Not a boy.

This man.

There's a rare beauty to him. I've never studied his face this closely before, and even past the paleness left behind from his concussion, I can see strength. I don't mind the way he looks right now. A little dishevelled. His blonde hair is sticking out all over the place, and he even has a dusting of blonde stubble framing his jaw. His lips are dry, but not too bad, and he has a scar on his upper lip from an old injury.

Probably left behind from Lexi's now dead brother.

If that guy wasn't already dead, then I would bathe in his fucking blood and let Thana dice him up.

"Do you need to see a doctor?" Jared asks, as my eyes shift from the scar above his lip to return to his blue gaze framed by thick, dark lashes.

I shake my head, reaching up with a trembling hand to

press my fingers to his cheek. There's a slight graze there, and when he doesn't flinch away, I know it mustn't hurt.

Fuck... I want to keep him.

I want to call him mine and have him call me his and face this fucked up world together.

But I can't.

I have to leave soon. My birthday is exactly two weeks away, and then I'll be gone.

Pain slices through my chest at the thought of leaving Jared. Why did I let myself react to him? Why did I open my heart to him when I know it's only going to break?

"Shit." Jared whispers, his eyes glassing over as he presses his forehead to mine. "I thought I was gonna die and never see you again."

More tears blur my vision at his words, and my lower lip trembles. Jared's thumb comes up, pressing against my lips before running over them like he is savouring how they feel.

"I heard you," he whispers, and I still, my eyes going wide at his comment. "I heard you scream, Dee."

I don't move or blink or do anything, hoping that's all he remembers.

"And I heard your voice."

I pull back from him abruptly, and the fucker grins, tightening his arms around me to keep me trapped.

I mean, I could get away if I really wanted to, but I don't want to hurt him, so I stay there, waiting to see if he'll elaborate.

"You have a beautiful voice."

My eyes widen, and I shake my head, shooting him an incredulous glare.

He chuckles. "You were on the phone, talking to emergency services." His lips thin. "You were crying, too. I didn't like hearing that part." He presses his forehead against mine again. "But I fucking loved hearing your voice."

Shit.

The need to flee is overpowering, to say the least, yet I stay there on Jared's lap because my need to be near him is even more consuming.

I shake my head, trying to silently say that he didn't hear my voice, but he smirks, pulling back again.

"You can try to deny it all you like. I know what I heard."

Reaching into my hoodie pocket, I tug out my phone and tap out a message to him.

'I think you hit your head a little too hard. You're talking gibberish.'

Holding it up for Jared to read, I watch his eyes scan over it before he throws his head back, laughing.

"Nice try, Deranged." Then he presses his hand to his head. "Ouch. Laughing hurts."

My face falls and I reach out to place my hand over his, and our eyes lock.

I should leave now. I should go and let him recover and figure out how the fuck to explain the car wreck to Griffin, but then my eyes drop to his lips as my inner urges take over.

"If you want to kiss me, then kiss me," he whispers, and my nostrils flare. "Do it, Dee. Put us both out of our misery."

My lips part in a silent gasp as his words egg me on to give into the need racing through me.

I shouldn't.

I lean in a little.

I should leave.

I lean a little further.

I should run.

I close the distance and press my lips to his.

Jared's arms instantly tighten around me, and our lips part as we kiss each other with a longing that has me whimpering. Jared matches my whimper with a growl, and I grip onto his face, needing to hold him captive.

14

We get lost in that kiss. Our lips and tongues saying what words can't as we grapple each other like we can't get close enough. It's everything. I know I shouldn't let myself feel this, yet I'm not strong enough to pull away. The need to kiss him, to feel his tongue brush against mine, feel his moan in my mouth, to get lost with him is all-consuming.

A tap on the door has us pulling apart quickly, and Jared calls out, "Hang on," as he studies me, both of us breathing heavily. "Thank you for helping me."

I offer him a small smile. I want to tell him he doesn't have to thank me, but the words stay trapped inside.

"I wanna ask you something. And I don't want you to run instead of answering me." He states, not giving me an option to refuse when he keeps talking. "Be my girl?"

I stiffen and then try to move.

"Stop, Dee. Don't run from me. Not after everything we've been through."

Shit.

My eyes prickle with heat again, and my cheeks flare to life.

"I get it. You're leaving soon. You don't want to get involved with someone because it will be more painful when you have to leave. But the way I see it, I'd rather say the hardest goodbye to you when the time comes, than to forever wonder what things could have been like if we just allowed ourselves to make the most of our time together."

Fucking hell!

FUCKING HELL!

How the fuck am I meant to say no to that?

A tear pops free and I swallow over and over, trying to dislodge the lump in my throat.

"So this is what's going to happen." Jared smirks even while he wipes away my tear with his thumb. "I'm gonna keep annoying you, because I know how much you like it."

He winks, and I can't hold back my grin. "And I'm going to keep pushing you until I hear your voice again, even if it's just once. And you're going to sit me on my arse ninja style, play hangman with me, let me chase you around Lake Woodall again, and while we are at it, we should definitely re-enact your legs wrapped around my face at the lookout." My mouth drops open and he chuckles. "And we will do all of this while you pretend not to want me as much as I want you."

I'm on fire. All of a sudden, my hoodie is trapping me in an inferno raging inside my body.

Panicking, I slowly shake my head, and Jared quirks a brow.

"Come on, Dee. Why won't you open up to me?"

I drop my eyes to my lap and pick up my phone, tapping out my response before sucking in a brave breath and showing him my honesty.

'I'm scared if I open up to you, it will make it harder to leave.'

His blue eyes scan over my words, and they flare before locking with mine.

"It will be hard, Dee. It will be hard for me to let you go and watch you walk away just as much as it will be hard for you to do it." He takes my hand and presses it to his chest. "But I'm scared if we don't allow ourselves to have this brief time together, that I'll die an old man, never knowing what it's like to have a soul mate."

3

JARED

The arrival of Dee's foster parents abruptly put an end to our little deep and meaningful chat. Dee left in a hurry without looking back, and I have no idea where we stand on my proposal. Or perhaps it was a declaration. Whatever it was, she'd better not think I'm giving up. Not when we only have a short time left before she leaves.

Alone with my parents, they insist I get looked over again by the doctors, who declare that I'm fine but want to keep me overnight for observation.

Just as my parents start questioning me about whose car I crashed, I'm saved by my mates bounding in with worry on their faces.

Shaun and Simon reach my bedside first but nearly end up on the floor by Garrett's feet when Marcus shoves them out of the way and launches himself at me.

"Fuck, man. You gotta stop scaring me like that." He's practically in my lap, not even caring if his big frame might be hurting me anywhere. I keep my mouth shut about it, because I'm just as fucking glad to see him and the other three.

"What were you doing out at Ebony Falls?" Simon asks, as Marcus releases me, standing up.

"Isn't it obvious?" Garrett smirks at me before turning his eyes to Simon. "He was with Dee."

"Umm," my mum steps up to the other side of my bed, her blonde brows furrowing. "What exactly *were* you doing out there at that time of night with Dee?"

Fucking hell.

Obviously, I can't divulge that I was there because I freaked out about killing a man and watching Dee slaughter four others. Garrett's insinuation about me and Dee is also something I don't want to admit to my mum if it were true, but it's all I've got for now.

"I was hanging out with Dee," I state and she frowns.

"Hanging out?" She raises her brows.

"Mum, you *do* know I'm eighteen, right?" I deadpan and her brows shoot up.

"Well, yes Jared. I *do* know that, but surely you can 'hang out,'" she uses air quotes, "at a more reasonable time of day."

"Oh, come on, honey." My dad counters, stepping up behind my mum, turning her to face him as he grins. "Don't you remember how we used to stay out all night under the stars?"

My mum melts into his chest, looking up into his eyes, and I'm about ready to fucking flee.

"Can you not? I've been traumatised enough today," I snap and my dad shoots me a glare before turning his gaze back to his wife.

"Maybe we should do that again?" He grins down at her. "It could be fun." Then he leans in and kisses her.

As much as I like to see them happy, which has been really fucking rare of late, I don't want to see them *that* happy.

"Damn. You learn your moves from your old man, Jar?"
Shaun chuckles and my mum pulls back, blushing.

Fucking blushing!

Fuck my life.

"Don't be gross," I snap, yet can't help but smirk.

"So whose car were you in?" Garrett asks, and my mind
races, trying to figure out what to say to that. I can't tell them
whose car it is, can I?

"It was my car." All eyes turn to the door and the looming
figure of Griffin Marx as he fills it.

"And you are?" my dad snaps, glaring at Griffin.

"My apologies." Griffin steps into the room, letting the
door shut behind him. He's in one of his signature suits, his
dark hair groomed to perfection. "I'm Griffin Marx." He
steps around the bed and offers his hand out to my dad, and I
stiffen.

I don't want the Marx men anywhere near my family.

My dad frowns but takes Griffin's hand for a shake before
Griffin addresses my mum.

"You must be Janine. Jared said you were a beautiful
woman."

"Oh." My mum's hand lands over her heart as she blushes
again, and my dad clears his throat.

"How do you know my son?" my dad asks, wearing a
glare, and I raise a brow at Griffin as he glances at me.

"I'm Jared's new employer. I've hired him to be my driver
occasionally. I asked him to test out the car I wanted him to
drive me in for a few days." His lips thin as he glances at my
parents' gazes before turning his hard eyes to me. "I guess
things got a little out of control."

"Oh. I'm so sorry, Mr Marx. We will pay for the damages
to your car." My mum offers like Griffin is here to tell me off.

He can fucking try.

"No, no. That won't be necessary," Griffin states, shooting

21

her a warm smile. "I just wanted to make sure Jared was alright. His safety is my top priority."

Fucking hell. I bet this arsehole did drama class back in high school. He's a fucking pro.

"Thank you." My dad offers Griffin a nod as his shoulders relax.

"Marx?" Garrett asks, his eyes a hard glare as he death stares Griffin from the other side of the bed. "As in the Marx family? From the city?"

My heart races.

Shit! Garrett must know something about them, and my eyes widen as they dart from Garrett to Griffin and back.

Griffin's jaw ticks slightly, but that's the only sign I see that he's bothered by Garrett's question.

"Correct. We have a big family." The smile he directs Garrett's way is tense, and I realise I need to try to get these people separated as soon as possible.

"Uh, would you all mind giving me a minute with Mr Marx?" I ask, and everyone but Garrett nods happily before turning to leave.

Garrett hangs back for a beat, his icy blue eyes boring a hole in the side of Griffin's head. When he turns his glare to me, I have to fight off a flinch.

"I don't know what the fuck is going on Crowley, but this man here," he jabs a finger towards Griffin, "is not someone you want to be working for."

Griffin's brows shoot up, but he doesn't respond to the accusation in Garrett's tone.

"Thanks for your concern, Cole. I'll talk to you later," I snap, returning his glare.

His lip curls ever so slightly, his shoulders tense and his fists ball tightly at his sides as he stares at me. I start shifting uncomfortably in the bed at the glare Garrett shoots me, but then he turns and leaves without another word.

"Intense guy." Griffin remarks and I turn my glare to him.

"I don't want you or any of your fucking family near my friends or family."

"Well, maybe if you didn't drive my car off a fucking cliff, then I wouldn't have had to step in and cover your arse, not just with your family, but with the cops as well." Griffin snaps back and I frown.

"It wasn't even a cliff. Just an incline."

"Doesn't fucking matter, Crow."

I flinch at his use of my 'gang' name.

Fuck!

"You should be thanking me for stepping in. And fuck, what a mess the farmhouse is. Those two girls will be traumatised for life after what they found."

I scoff. "Maybe if you don't want innocent people to witness shit like that, you won't send Hush in while they are there," I hiss. "Have you figured out who the men were yet? They were there to kill Hush, not the residents of the house."

Griffin's hard glare softens, and he sighs. "I'm working on that. It was definitely a professional hit."

"You think it's Travis' family? Have they found out Dee is here?"

Griffin shakes his head. "I don't think they know she's here. Plus, if it was their crew, it would have been more reckless. Those fuckers are nothing but street thugs."

"So, who?"

"We have a lot of enemies, Crow. But, if I had to guess, I'd say it's linked to Carnal Unicorn. I've just received intel this morning that it may not just be a dark website, but perhaps a secret society of depraved members who prefer their subjects unwilling, or in the most illegal of ways imaginable."

"Fuck," I hiss.

"Yeah." Griffin agrees. "Fuck."

He stands there for a moment, his eyes looking over me, and the silence turns awkward before he speaks.

"I'm glad you and Hush are ok. Just for the record."

I chuckle. "Your ability to show compassion is over-whelming."

"Shut the fuck up," Griffin snaps before a smirk tugs at his lips.

"So, what happens now?" I ask, because I have no idea how this fucking underworld shit operates.

"Now, you and Hush stay out of trouble for a bit while my guys investigate."

I nod, happy with that idea. Mainly the part about Dee staying out of trouble.

I can get behind that.

4

DEE

Griffin doesn't stir as I slowly and carefully step up onto his bed. He looks peaceful in sleep. Happy. Maybe it has something to do with the blonde-haired goddess lying next to him. I can tell they care about each other by the way they are angled towards each other, even in sleep.

Placing a foot on either side of Griffin, my movement disturbs the blonde goddess, and as she stirs, I lean down and press Thana to Griffin's throat.

The half scream, half gasp that comes from the woman startles Griffin awake, and he moves to sit up, only stilling just in time when Thana's sharp edge breaks his skin.

"Get away from him!" the woman cries, and my eyes shift from Griffin's dark pools, which are wide with shock, to the woman's. Her caramel eyes are filled with terror, her mouth snapping shut when I direct my glare at her.

Then she lunges from the bed to her bedside drawer.

The action has me pressing Thana deeper into Griffin's delicate skin over his throat and he growls through clenched teeth.

"Stop, Aggie!"

I smirk at him, and he tries to gulp, so I let up a little on the knife. Because you know, I'm caring like that.

Aggie halts quickly by the bedside, her hand on the knob of the drawer, her eyes wide with disbelief.

"What? But-."

Griffin cuts her off. "Aggie, this is Hush."

Confusion contorts her face before something like recognition flits over it and her expression softens.

"Hush?"

"Yes. You remember what I told you about *Hush?*" Griffin rasps, his eyes remaining on me.

"Yes, but she has a knife to your throat," Aggie snaps and Griffin grins.

"Trust me, little elf, if she wanted me dead, she would have killed me already."

Aggie's brows shoot up, and she does the smart thing and steps away from the bedside table.

"To what do I owe the pleasure, Hush? You seem to have no problem getting past my security measures."

I scoff and roll my eyes, and Griffin chuckles.

"You mind removing your blade?"

I bare my teeth and hiss at him, pressing Thana harder again, causing him to flinch.

"Please don't hurt him," Aggie cries. "I don't want to hurt you, but if you hurt my man, I will fucking kill you. I don't care that you are a child."

Slowly, a smirk spreads my lips wider, and I tilt my head towards Aggie. I can see she means what she says. I mean, she wouldn't be able to kill me before I got to her, but she thinks she can pull it off.

It's good to see Griffin has found a woman that compliments him.

"Aggie, stop, honey. It's ok. Hush won't hurt me."

I roll my eyes with even more dramatics and snap Thana away from him before leaping off the bed.

As I stroll out of the room like I didn't just threaten one of Australia's biggest players in the crime world, I hear Griffin release a relieved breath as his woman leaps for him.

Are they kissing?

At least they waited until my back was turned. It's too early for that shit.

While I wait for Griffin to get dressed, I make my way through this ridiculously sterile house and sit my arse down at the table. My stomach growls as I eye the bowl of fruit in the centre, and I try to remember when I last ate.

I spent the first part of Friday watching over Jared in the hospital before Cynthia and William came to get me. They tried to feed me when I got home, and I nibbled on a sandwich, but I think that was it.

It's now 5am on Saturday morning, and the sun is starting to rise, so it's definitely been a while since I ate.

With my sights set on a big green apple, I lean forward and jab Thana into it, holding it up to inspect on her tip before bringing it to my mouth to take a bite.

Mmm, juicy.

"You want a plate for that?" Griffin snaps, and I shrug, not looking at him and his woman as they join me with caution.

Griffin chuckles and pulls a chair out opposite me, while his woman moves to the kitchen and starts making coffee.

"Wanna tell me what this little visit is about?" Griffin asks, and I sigh, laying Thana and the apple on the table and take out my phone.

When I tap out my message, I hold it up to Griff.

Do you wanna tell me who the fuckers were that tried to take me out at the farmhouse?'

"I'm working on finding out." Griffin sighs. "Like I told

Crow, I have my suspicions that it's the Carnal Unicorn Secret Society."

I frown and tap out a response, holding it up again.

'When did you speak to Jared?'

"I went to see him in the hospital yesterday. I needed to make sure there were no questions as to why he was driving my car. I told his parents that I've recently hired him as a driver and had asked him to test out the car."

Shit. I hadn't even considered that. I was too distraught with making sure Jared was ok. Thank fuck Griffin helped to cover up the blurred lines.

Cynthia and Will still have no idea what happened since I did my usual thing and didn't tell them shit. The problem is, I feel bad about that. They are such nice people. They deserve an explanation as to why I wasn't home in my bed, and why I was in a car with Jared outside the Fox Pines town limits.

They have been patient with me through all of this. Surely their patience will run out soon. They can't be that good, can they?

I give Griffin a nod and then tap out another question.

'Carnal Unicorn has a secret society?'

Griffin nods. "So it seems. I only found out yesterday, and if they are suspicious that their members are being targeted, then it makes sense they would try to intervene."

Shit. This isn't good. People like that have a lot to lose, which makes them dangerous.

'They will try again, then. They will try to protect their secrets by any means possible.'

"Yes."

This just got ten times harder.

'Do you have any names yet?'

"I do. I have a list. I will schedule the jobs for you, but you need to be prepared that you're going to be busy before you up and leave."

I shake my head and tap out a response, showing Griffin as his woman clangs around in the kitchen.

'No. Don't schedule anything for me. Print up the information. I will get the jobs done my way and without a trail. It's likely they've hacked into our messages to get the locations of the jobs. Either that, or you have a mole in the crew.'

Griffin grunts. "If I have a mole in my crew, then they will die a very slow and fucking painful death when I figure out who it is."

My eyes flick to Aggie, who grins with excitement at Griffin's comment as she places a plate of croissants on the table before returning to the kitchen.

Jesus, she really is made for him.

Nodding, I tap out another message and hold it up.

'Print up everything you have so far, and while you're at it, get me all the names and details of those working in the Kerr crew.'

Griffin's brows shoot up. "You wanna take them out?"

I shrug. *'Maybe. Taking them out will fast track your takeover of the area, won't it?'*

Griffin eyes me suspiciously. "It will."

'I'll take them out if you release Jared from any commitments to you and your family.'

Griffin's brows shoot high. "This is a negotiation?" he asks, and I nod.

"So you'll clean out all the cobwebs, and in return, I release Jared from working for me?"

I nod again, but turn my eyes back to my phone as I tap out another response.

'Travis too. Let him go, even if he doesn't choose a side. Just let him walk away. With me. Or without me. Just leave him alone.'

Griffin frowns. "That's a lot."

I shrug. *'Those are my terms. Take it or leave it.'*

"Why do I get the feeling if I leave it, I'm going to need extra muscle protecting my back?"

I smirk and shrug before responding with my phone. *'Sounds like you're paranoid.'*

Griffin chuckles. "Too fucking right. Having you on our side is in my best interest."

I sneer at him and hold up my phone after tapping out a response aggressively.

'Then why fucking blackmail me in the first place if having me on your side is in your best interest?'

He shrugs. "Trick of the trade. Maybe you should have called my bluff."

Snarling this time, I stand abruptly, the chair scraping on the floor as it flies backwards, nearly tipping over, and Griffin stumbles to his feet quickly, readying himself for my attack.

"You want to kill me, Hush?" he asks, and I nod slowly as my top lip curls back to reveal my teeth. Griffin nods and relaxes his stance. "Good. If I renounce on this arrangement, make sure you follow through, and then fucking disappear."

A gasp sounds behind me, and I turn to see Griffin's blonde haired beauty standing with two cups of steaming coffee. Her angry eyes locked on her man.

"Take that back, Griffin. You know she will kill you."

He chuckles. "Yes. I do. Which is why she can trust my word with this new deal. I don't want her to kill me, so I'll make sure to honour our agreement. It's how I'll make sure no one gets in my fucking head and tries to convince me otherwise. She's just a kid, like you said, Aggie. She's already given so much of herself. It's time for her to be free of this part of our world, and go and live her life."

I frown at Griffin's words, a little confused why he'd need to make sure no one can change his mind, but then his blonde piece fills in the blanks.

"Your dad?" she asks, and he shoots her a knowing look. "Has he spoken of using her in the future?"

Oh, hell no. I'm not working for Ewan Marx.

"He mentioned what a good asset she is and can be for the family's future. I told him she was working with us on a one off, but he didn't seem deterred by that."

"Shit," Aggie whispered, placing the mugs on the table.

I have to agree with her.

Shit.

Sighing, Griffin sits back in his seat, gesturing for me to take a seat as well, before he lifts his cup of coffee to his lips and takes a sip.

I ease back into the seat and look down at the apple still sitting on the table with Thana protruding from it. I should eat, but my appetite has vanished.

I need all this crap to end. I need to save Travis and Jared from this fucked up shit, and I need them to be free.

"You ok, kid?" Griffin's words startle me, and I realise I retreated into my head there for a moment. "You didn't get hurt in the accident, or at the farmhouse, did you?"

I shake my head and reply in text.

'I only got a small bump on the head from the accident, which was from Jared pushing me out the door to save me. As for the farmhouse. I killed my friend's parents while she slept down the hall. The amateur ambushers I can handle, but hurting a friend doesn't sit well with me. Neither does the fact that Jared had to kill one of the men for me. I'll never be ok with that.'

Griffin nods as he reads my words. "I get that. We want to protect the ones we love."

My brows shoot high as I shake my head and tap out a response.

'Jared and I aren't a thing.'

Griffin throws his head back, laughing. "Sure. Keep telling yourself that, kid."

I glare at him, but he ignores me, and I shift my gaze to Aggie, who is trying to hide her smirk.

FML!

Glancing down at my phone, I tap out a message and hold it up so Griffin can read it.

'Get me the list. I start cleaning house tonight.'

5

JARED

*L*eaving the hospital yesterday was the best fucking news, but now that I'm home, my mum won't stop fussing. I have to wonder if this will be like the last time I was in hospital after Mike West, Lexi's brother, beat me within an inch of my life.

Mum had hovered, fussed, and spoiled me right up until the bruises faded and I appeared normal again, and then she retreated back into her bottles of wine.

I want to ask her why she did that. Why she didn't think to ask if the invisible wounds to my fucking soul were still healing? If she did, she'd know they will never heal.

I keep those thoughts to myself, though. My mum doesn't need my selfish crap, and I'm grateful for this brief attention, even if it is starting to grate on my nerves.

I haven't seen or heard from Dee since she left the hospital with her foster parents on Friday. I sent her a message on Friday night and last night, but she hasn't responded. I've been fighting the urge to send her multiple messages, but I don't want to smother her, not when we had such an honest moment on my hospital bed.

If there's one thing I've learned about Dee, it's that she will be freaking out about the moment we shared. She's used to being a one woman show. Not needing anyone or sharing her true self.

But now she has, and she's likely avoiding me, just like I knew she would.

It's always one step forward and ten steps back with this chick. It should piss me off more than it does. Normally I wouldn't bother with someone that you have to work so hard with.

But Dee is different. I'm not sure why. It's just something I feel deep in the centre of my chest. I'm pretty sure she could try to kill me a thousand times, and I'd still pursue her. Still try to break down her walls and hopefully show her that she doesn't need to be alone. That she can be loved.

Shit.

Love.

That's a BIG four letter word. Yet it feels like the right word where Dee Porter is concerned.

After Griffin left the hospital on Friday, my mates came back in and parked their arses on chairs for the rest of the day and night. Gaz was quiet and broody, which isn't that unusual for him, but the heated glares he shot me on occasion told me that this stuff with him not liking me associating with Griffin isn't over.

I was thankful for my mates' attention, though. They didn't even ditch me for Rhys. Sure there were some phone calls, and at one stage, Marcus handed me his phone where I listened to Rhys tell me how glad she was that I was ok, and even told me that Dee was ok, and resting in her room.

That news made me feel a little more at ease, and I instantly felt like shit for being so shitty at my mates and their relationship with Rhys George over the past few months.

After all, I'm beginning to understand what it's like to be that addicted to another person.

My head is clearer now, and since I spent all of yesterday and most of this morning in bed, I decide to lounge around in the living room, where Mum doesn't have to make such an effort to come and check on me.

She has the radio on today, something she hasn't done in a long time, which means she's doing ok. She shakes her shoulders a little as she cleans to the song playing on the old school station, and I grin.

I really like this version of my mum.

My old man is out in the yard. I can hear him cursing every now and then as he tries time and time again to get the whipper snipper started.

Deciding not to annoy Mum by turning the TV on, I scroll through TikTok with the volume low, chuckling at the ridiculous videos my mate Simon has posted trying to dance.

He's such a funny fucker.

The turmoil of the past few weeks lightens as I get wrapped up in the addictive app, and I have no idea how much time has passed when a breaking news story interrupts Mum's shimmying to an ABBA song.

"Detective Zimora, who has been assigned to investigate the string of murders that have occurred recently in the Timber Valley district, asks that people remain calm. He doesn't believe the recent murders, including that of husband and wife, Holice and Belinda Crawford who were found brutally murdered in their farmhouse in the early hours of Friday morning, or the series of murders that happened across Timber Valley last night, are that of a serial killer. His team believes that the brutal deaths are linked to organised crime that has gone unnoticed in the area for many years."

What the fuck? More murders last night?

"Sources say there is a new player moving in, and they are cleaning shop, so to speak. With the shock of recent events relating to a child pornography ring, this reporter can't deny that I don't hate the idea of these vigilantes taking action. If such depravity has gone unnoticed in the area for so long by local law enforcement, one has to be concerned that they aren't doing their jobs properly. Whoever it is that is seeking justice and cleaning up our streets, I say, thank you."

"Oh, my goodness." My mum gasps, her hand pressed to her chest as she glares at the radio like it's the offender. "I know news reporters aren't meant to take sides, but I have to say I agree with that one."

"Yeah," I mumble, my mind racing.

Shit. Did Dee go out killing last night without me?

With my mum distracted by the news as she unloads the dishwasher, I stand and go to my bedroom, closing myself inside. My finger hovers over Dee's number, but there's no point in calling her. She won't speak, so a voice call is useless.

Unless you're in an emergency. Apparently, she'll speak then.

Or to Griffin Marx when he threatens someone she cares about.

Fuck.

That night at the club, sitting around the table when Dee, or should I say, Hush, leaped onto the table and drew a blade was one of the hottest things I've ever seen.

She spoke to Griffin that night. Whispered something to him that only he could hear.

Am I jealous?

Fuck yes, I am. I want her to whisper to *me*, damn it.

I also want her to kill *with* me.

Wait, no. Not with me, but while I'm there to watch her back and drive her around.

I bring up Griffin's number and hit call, pressing the phone to my ear.

"Crow. There'd better be a good reason why you are interrupting my Sunday afternoon with my woman."

I roll my eyes, even though he can't see it.

"There'd better be a good reason as to why you're sending Hush out to work while I'm laid up." I hiss, and Griffin curses as I hear him whisper something like, *"hold that thought little elf, I'll be right back."*

The fuck?

I hear a door close in the background before Griffin's voice comes back through the line.

"You and your girl are getting rather fucking bossy, Crow. Best you remember who you are talking to."

"Yeah, yeah. Fill me in... *please.*" I smirk as I draw out the word, and I can just imagine Griffin rolling his eyes this time.

"Look. I haven't booked any particular jobs. She wanted to take on the list and then some before she has to leave. I'm pretty sure she would have cut my balls from my body and fed them to a dog if I didn't give her what she wanted."

I smirk, nodding. "Yeah. That sounds about right."

"So you see my predicament. Besides, we've worked out a new arrangement. You should be happy about that."

"What new arrangement?"

Griffin sighs. "Best you ask her about that."

"For fuck's sake, Griffin, if I could ask her about any of this and get a straight fucking answer, I would."

Griffin chuckles. "Not my problem. Now fuck off and let me get back to my dessert."

"Dessert?" I ask, dumbly.

"My woman, Crow. She's my dessert."

At that, Griffin hangs up, and I'm left with more fucking questions than I started with.

Falling back on my bed, I contemplate my options. I probably shouldn't be driving yet, but fuck, I want to see Dee.

Deciding to take a chance, I bring up Dee's number and hit the video call. I know she won't talk to me, but she can still text and I'd still get to see her.

It rings and rings, and just when I think it's about to drop out, the call connects and the screen flickers before Dee's big chocolate eyes come into view.

"There you are," I say, unable to hide my grin.

She shoots me a small smile from her laying down position on her bed and gives me a wave.

"I wasn't sure if you'd answer."

Biting her lower lip, her eyes shift lower on her phone screen as she does something, and a moment later, a text message pops up.

Yes. This is exactly what I wanted.

'I almost didn't.'

My brows shoot up at her response.

"Why?" I ask, and again, she responds in text.

'Habit, I think. I'm not used to communicating with people.'

I nod. "Am I making you uncomfortable?" I smirk and she narrows her eyes at me, a playful grin tilting up her lips.

'I think you like making me uncomfortable.'

I chuckle. "It's true. I do… but." I hesitate and she frowns, sending me another message.

'But?'

Shit, can I be this honest with her over the phone? I should, right? No matter the situation, we have very little time left, so I should just say what I think. What I feel.

"I want to be your safe place to land."

An expression of sad longing crosses her face as she blinks rapidly, and her lower lip quivers slightly before she sucks it in, trying to compose herself.

"Shit, Dee. I want to hug you."

She nods, not responding in text, so I question her.

"Do you want that? To be in my arms."

Her nostrils flare this time, and she nods. And fuck, I want to get in my car right fucking now and go to her.

A knock sounds in the background, and Dee's attention moves to another spot in her room as a voice filters in.

"Dinner will be ready in a few minutes." Rhys' voice gets louder before Dee bounces around, and a moment later Rhys' face comes into view next to Dee's.

"Oh hi, Jared. Did I interrupt you guys having phone sex?"

I roll my eyes, and Dee does the same, shaking her head.

"What do you think, George?" I use her last name and it doesn't even bother her because a huge fucking smile spreads her black lips wide.

"I think you were working your way up to it." She wags her dark brows, and Dee shoves her with her shoulder, knocking her off the bed. "Hey! Not cool, sister!"

Dee smirks, and I love seeing that. Her interacting with her new foster family. I chuckle, because I can't help it. From my point of view, it looked funny to have Rhys there one second and gone the next.

"You should be nicer to me, Dee. I have things that you could borrow that might come in handy for your phone games with Crowley." I can hear Rhys, but can't see her, the camera directed at the only female I ever want to lay eyes on. "Like a ring light stand that you can put your phone in. Frees up your hands to do other things."

Dee shifts and the pillow under her head disappears before I can only assume she throws it, and I hear Rhys cackling like a fucking hyena before a door slams and the background noise disappears.

"She gone?" I ask, still chuckling, and Dee directs her frown back to the screen before her face softens and she nods. "I like the idea of the ring light. You should totally borrow that."

Her chocolate eyes widen at my words before that familiar pink blush flushes over her cheeks, and I beam.

It still blows me away that she can kill and slaughter, yet be so fucking cute and shy when it comes to sex.

'Bye Jared!'

Her message comes through and I chuckle, but shake my head.

"Nope, you're not hanging up yet. Not until you answer a question."

She rolls her eyes, so I take that as agreement and continue.

"Who drove you around last night?"

She frowns.

"You know, when you went and completed multiple jobs."

Her eyes fall lower as she types out her response, and a moment later it comes through.

'I don't know what you mean.'

I shake my head. "Yeah, you do, Deranged. You know exactly what I mean." When her face remains neutral and she makes no attempt to respond, I continue. "Who the fuck drove you?!"

Her brows shoot high at my tone, and a dark expression crosses her face. It's a lethal expression, and I have no doubt that if we were in the same room right now, she'd probably sit me on my arse.

"Look. I'm not trying to be a prick, but I fucking care about you. A couple of nights ago you were ambushed, Dee. You shouldn't be alone on these jobs. It's too dangerous. So please tell me someone drove you. And then tell me who the fuck it was."

Her glare turns to an eye roll before she taps out her response.

'No one drove me. I stole a bike from a house a few streets over and rode it to the locations. I stayed in Fox Pines last night, but I will need a driver when I venture out of this town. It won't be you, though.'

"Like fuck it won't!" I hiss and she shakes her head as if she's fed up.

'I won't put you at risk again.'

"Why?" I snap. "Why is it ok for you to be at risk, and not me?"

She doesn't respond.

"Come on, Dee. Don't hold back on me. Be honest. Tell me."

She worries her lower lip for a moment and then responds.

'Because I fucking care about you, too.'

Then the line disconnects.

Fuck!

6

DEE

*E*xhaustion has its claws in me as I leave the peace of my bedroom and enter the rowdy Rogan house living area for dinner. I don't really feel like a family dinner after the chaos I've been living lately.

Aside from wielding Thana and eliminating some new targets, I've been busy on my side hustle, trying to get that done without anyone noticing, which isn't easy in this house.

I could probably use Jared's car again, but I'm worried if I go to his house that I'll ditch the work I need to get done and end up in his bedroom. And as much as I really want to do that. I can't. Not when I'm leaving soon. Right?

I've barely set foot in the living room when a hard body comes barrelling into me.

An umph flies from me as familiar arms wind around me and hold me close. I'm stiff as a board for a few moments, not used to physical contact without invitation, or in Jared's case, persuasion, but as the familiar scent wraps around me, I relax and wind my arms around my brother's back.

Travis.

"Fuck, Ell. When I found out you were involved in a car

wreck, I..." He trails off, rasping into my hair, his arms tightening even more.

Scanning the room, Cynthia is wiping a tear from her eye while Will rubs her back as they watch. Charlotte still looks as unimpressed as the first day I entered this house, and the twins are grinning, their dark eyes magnified by their glasses.

And then there's Rhys, currently sitting on Shaun's knee, her black lips spread wide with a carrot stick dangling from her lips as she munches on it.

I want to tell Travis that I'm ok, but with the eyes on us, and the fact that the reason I don't speak is because he said he never wanted to hear my voice again, I keep my words to myself.

I ease my grip around him and he does the same, pulling back to look me in the eyes.

"I know I've been a prick, but I don't want you to die, Ell. I just want..." He trails off, shaking his head as he struggles to finish, so I mouth *'what?'*

He shrugs. "I just want you to be ok."

Tears well in my eyes.

This is different. Travis hasn't been very welcoming to my sudden appearance back in his life, which I get. He's still mad at me for killing his mum. He seems to have blocked out the bad shit that bitch did to him when he was little, so of course, I've been the enemy since the day I took her from him.

I do feel bad about that. I blame myself for him being sent to foster care and separated from me. I don't feel bad about killing his mum, though. She killed my dad, and she would have killed both me and Travis that day had I not stepped in.

I pat my chest and then give him a thumbs up to indicate that I'm ok, and he grins. "Why don't you just speak?"

I shake my head as fear creeps in.

When I first started withholding my voice, I did it because of what he said, and because I found it to be a good way to get people to leave me alone. By not talking, I could control things a little more, but now... now I realise I am scared. Scared to let down that wall I've spent years erecting. A wall that has kept me safe until recently.

A wall that Jared Crowley has somehow penetrated.

Travis sighs. "Well, if you won't talk, you know Rhys is going to do all the talking and it will be about all of her fellas."

"I don't see a problem with that," Shaun offers, and Rhys giggles.

"Me either."

Then they start kissing. Or perhaps it is more like eating each other's faces.

"Hey! Not at the dinner table!" Will growls and the twins giggle.

"Kissy, kissy, kissy." They say in unison, doing that weird in sync twin thing.

"I think I just vomited in my mouth," Charlotte adds, and still Rhys keeps kissing her guy.

Cynthia approaches them and tips a cup of cold water over their heads, and they shoot apart quickly, laughing.

This family is so weird.

But also, so nice.

A pang shoots through my chest as I follow behind Travis, watching him take a seat. He's staying for dinner, apparently. Probably something Cynthia arranged, which is just another nice gesture from her and this family.

I wish I could stay!

I should open up to Cynthia more. Explain about the car wreck, but she obviously got information about it from Jared's mum already. They are doing so much for me, and what am I doing in return?

Nothing.

Well, not nothing. If I'm being honest, I'm potentially putting them in danger. My links to the crime world puts anyone close to me in danger, but I have to hope the Marx family wouldn't do anything to hurt these innocent people. I have to hope Griffin will be true to his word.

Still, he's only one of many in that family. A very powerful family.

Throughout dinner I watch Travis. He's more relaxed than the last time he sat at this table, almost as if he's one of the family. He deserves this family more than I do. He should be the one under their roof, getting love and attention. Not me.

After dinner, Travis helps with the dishes, and then he asks to see my room.

I feel awkward as I lead him into the kids' zone of the house, and into my bedroom, for the first time noticing the distance between us and the different lives we've led since being separated.

"Wow, I love what you've done with the space. Loads of personality."

I roll my eyes at his sarcasm, and he chuckles.

"Oh, come on, Ell. Why haven't you turned this room into your own?"

Taking out my phone, I tap out my response and hold it up to him.

You know why. I'm not staying. When I turn eighteen, I'm leaving. With you.'

Travis sighs and drops his arse to my bed.

"I gotta say I like the part about you leaving."

My brows shoot up and he chuckles.

"I didn't mean that the way it sounded."

Really? How did you mean it then?'

Raking a hand through his brown hair, Travis sighs. "I

don't want you around this gang stuff. You need to leave, Ell. Get out now before there's an all out war. Before it's too late."

Frowning, I take in Travis' expression and the tone of his voice. He wants me to leave, not because he doesn't want to see me, but because he's worried. His words are a warning of sorts.

'What do you know that I don't?' I respond, holding up my phone for him to read.

Shaking his head, Travis stands from the bed. "Nothing. It's just normal stuff. You know, and I know that the Marx family is trying to take over. It's going to get worse before it gets better."

He's not wrong about that.

"Is Crowley ok?" Travis asks, changing the conversation as he starts pacing.

I nod, and Travis nods too. "Good. You and I have really fucked up his life, hey?"

I nod again, feeling the guilt gnawing at me.

"You like him?"

I shrug, shifting my gaze out the window, feeling awkward to be talking about this sort of stuff with my little brother. It would probably feel normal if we had finished growing up together.

"I think he has it bad for you. When I didn't know it was you that he had on his radar, I found it funny that he was so twisted in knots about this chick that pissed him off, but also turned him on..." Travis scrunches his face up in a cringe and shakes his head before correcting himself. "I mean, interested him."

I silently giggle at Travis' awkward attempt to brush over the part about me turning Jared on.

I have to admit, if Tillie was talking about Travis, I certainly don't want the intimate details.

Just... no.

We fall silent then, Travis standing in the middle of my small bedroom looking down at me as I stare back up at him. Pain slices through my heart at the time we lost together. Time and connection we may never have again.

Glancing down at my phone, I construct my message and then take a deep breath before holding it up to him.

'I'm sorry for taking your mum away from you. But I'm not sorry for saving you, Travis. I'd do it again in a heartbeat, because you are all that matters.'

Travis chews the inside of his cheek as he finishes reading over my words and quickly shoots his gaze out my window as his eyes glass over.

I stand, getting in his line of sight and sign the words.

I'm sorry.

His lip trembles and his nostrils flare as he tries to fight his emotions, but then big tears spill over, running down his cheeks as he reaches out and tugs me to his chest, wrapping his arms around me.

I cry too then, knowing this is the moment right here that I've dreamed of for so long. The moment he forgives me for the bad things in order to keep him safe.

"I've started remembering." He rasps quietly into my hair. "The way she used to grab my hair in a fist and drag me around the house, shoving me to the floor and then pushing my head all the way down with her foot."

A sob escapes me at the detail of his memory, because I remember it too.

"I remember the day she made me lick the kitchen floor clean after we brought home that stray dog covered in mud that we found in the park on the way home from school."

My sobs come louder as anger flares alive in my veins.

"I remember you looking after me the next day in the bushes at the back of our yard when I was vomiting, and how you snuck into the house three times to get me more clean clothes and a blanket." Travis sobs then. "I got sick because of what she made me do, didn't I?"

I nod, a guttural cry slipping from my lips as my knees nearly give out on me. Travis holds me up, though. This time, he's the one trying to protect me.

"I'm really fucking angry, Ell." He admits, pulling back to look down at me as he brushes my hair back off my face and I swipe at the tears that won't seem to stop. "I'm angry at myself for still loving that cunt bitch after everything she did to us."

Reaching up, I cup Travis' face and shake my head as I mouth *'she was your mum.'*

He scoffs and bats at his tears before puffing out his chest.

"She didn't deserve to be a mother, and she sure as shit didn't deserve our dad. I'm fucking sorry she took him from you too, Ell. She fucking took everything from us."

I nod, trying to hold back on the raging emotions thumping at my invisible walls, trying to break free.

Not yet.

Just wait.

"I know you're here thinking you're going to save me, big sis, but I need you to let me save you this time. You need to leave. Like tomorrow. Just go. When things settle down, I'll find you. I promise."

Travis doesn't let me respond, pressing his lips to my forehead before turning and practically bolting from my room.

Silly boy. There's no force on earth that will make me turn my back and walk away from him.

Ever.

7

JARED

*G*oing to school isn't really something I'm interested in right now given the bigger issues going on, but staying home to have my mum hover over me again definitely isn't something I can endure for another day.

News has spread about me getting in a car wreck, which has morphed into some amusing rumours. None seem to involve Dee, though, and I'm both happy and annoyed about that.

I'm happy because I know she wouldn't want the attention. But it's fucking annoying because I want everyone to know that Dee is my girl, and since they don't, all the girls seem to have me on their fucking radar now, and I can't seem to escape their need to ask me if I'm ok, or if there's anything they can do to make me feel better. Which all sounds like normal human decency, right? Except these girls are too touchy feely, resting their hand on my arm and pressing their tits into me as they talk. Not to mention, a couple of them have been following me around to the extent that they trailed me into the men's room, and the morning hasn't even finished yet. I dread to think how much crazier this shit is going to get as the day goes on.

The rumours range from me competing in drag races and losing control, to me stealing cars and being in a fucking police chase.

Dickheads.

As if I'd be at school today if I'd been chased by the cops. Fairly sure I'd be locked up right now if that was the case.

Unfortunately, the one girl I want attention from is back to ignoring me. It makes me angry, when just last night I thought things between us were good.

Once again, we have taken ten fucking steps backwards.

If it weren't for the small breakthrough we had in the car and at the hospital, I'd probably be walking away by now. But those few *real* moments we had are more than the many fake moments when she pretends not to care. Because I know now. I know she cares and I know she's scared, and I know that when she lets down her walls, even if it's brief, it's the most honest and alive moments I think I've ever had.

So, like an addict, I'm hooked, trying to figure out a way to get my next fix. Trying to figure out a way to get Dee to let me in for another real moment.

Recess has just begun, and I spot my little pocket rocket at her locker, putting her laptop away.

I grin.

If she thinks she is going to keep avoiding me, she's got another thing coming.

"Crowley, we need to talk." Garrett grabs my bicep as I try to pass by, but I keep my eyes on the prize, not wanting her to disappear into the crowd.

"Now's not a good time," I mutter to Garrett as Dee steps back to shut her locker.

"When's a good time?" he snaps and I shrug.

"After school."

"Fine," he hisses, dropping his hold on me in time for me to stalk towards Dee and close the distance.

Reaching her, I grip her hips, spin her and shove her against the locker.

It's an aggressive move, but I've learned that Dee likes aggressive.

Her chocolate eyes flare with fury as her gaze locks with mine, and I crowd her in, one hand on the locker next to her head with the other gripping her hip.

"Wanna tell me why you're ignoring me?"

She doesn't respond.

"For fuck's sake, Dee. We are past this shit. Communicate with me. What happened between last night when I called you, to now? Something must have happened because the last words you communicated were that you cared about me."

Dee's shoulders drop as she gives in, her hand slipping into her blazer pocket to take out her phone. She worries her lip as she types out her words before turning the screen to me.

'You have enough attention from the other girls. You don't need mine too.'

A huge fucking grin spreads my lips wide, and I chuckle.

"Is Deranged Porter jealous?"

She rolls her eyes and tries to shove me back, but I don't move.

I'm well aware that she could move me if she wanted to. She'd just have to do some of her ninja tricks on me and she'd sit me on my arse. She doesn't though, and I pretend it's not because she doesn't want to gain more attention than we are already getting as students pass by, and that it's because she really just wants me near.

"You know, you're the only girl whose attention I care about, right? Just in case you've forgotten everything that happened last week and over the weekend, I'm kinda into you."

A smirk tugs at her lips, but she tries to fight it.

"And I told you that I'm gonna keep annoying you, and keep pushing you until I hear your voice again, and you're going to keep trying to fight it, but really, you want to give in and let down those thick walls you keep up to protect yourself." Leaning forward, I hover my lips an inch from hers as she tilts her head up to me, and I can feel how her chest rises and falls rapidly as I press close.

It's good to know I affect her just as much as she affects me.

"You have me, Dee. For as long as you stay in Fox Pines, I'm yours. So why don't you show all these thirsty bitches who I belong to?"

Just like that, her dainty hand fists my blazer and she drags me in, sealing her lips to mine.

I fucking melt.

M. E. L. T!

Her soft lips are demanding, and I let her have this control, this dominance, so she knows she's the one who holds all the power here.

I hear hoots from my mates behind us, but I also hear disappointed sighs and some bitchy slurs thrown in Dee's direction. I want to turn around and hiss at them, but there's no fucking way I'm tearing my lips away from Dee's.

No fucking way!

The immature reactions from behind me fade into nothing as I let Dee consume me with her lips and tongue. My hands find their way to cup each side of her face, and that's when I feel it.

Her hand, the one that isn't fisting my blazer, grazes over my crotch. I'm not sure if she meant to do that or not, but I moan into her mouth, her kisses swallowing the noise as I press closer.

I'm hard already. It's just a natural reaction to Dee, especially when she responds like this, so when her gentle touch brushes over me again, this time giving a little grope, my cock jerks.

"Fuck," I hiss, breaking the kiss and pressing my forehead to hers. "Do you have any idea how much I want to throw you over my shoulder right now and take you to my car?"

"Ooooh, I'm gonna say very much."

Rhys' voice is like a bucket of water, and Dee and I turn our heads to the side to see Rhys leaning against the lockers next to us, watching intently.

"Don't stop on my behalf. It was just getting good." She wags her dark brows and flashes her white teeth.

"Really, George?" I grunt, and she shrugs.

"I mean, you are in public," she points out, "and I'm totally down with a bit of voyeurism. Marcus is too, in case you didn't already know that."

"Kitten," Shaun steps up to her and takes her hand. "Don't we have a special gym session planned for recess?"

That gains Rhys' attention, and her smile broadens. "I believe we do, Cass. Lead the way."

Shaun chuckles, leaning in to lick her lips, and she growls like an animal at him, before he drags her away.

"Fucking hell. Your foster sister is weird." I glance back at Dee, who slowly drags her eyes from her retreating foster sibling, and she shakes her head.

"She's not weird?" I ask, and again she shakes her head before turning her attention to her phone to tap out a response.

She's one of the most honest people I've ever met. She speaks her truth, the way she sees it. It must be liberating to be that open.

My brows shoot up at Dee's written words. She's right, of course. Rhys George doesn't hide behind what society deems is normal. She may seem quirky and out there to some, but hell, she doesn't hide who she is like the rest of us do.

"That's true." I nod, snagging Dee's chocolate gaze with mine again. "I know it seems scary to be as open about things as Rhys is, but you can be open and honest with me. I'm in your corner."

She chews the inside of her cheek as she studies me. I almost expect her to bolt, something she has a tendency for when things get too real, but then she mouths the word, *'maybe.'*

Damn. I need more time with her before she leaves. I'm nowhere near ready to let her go.

I shoot her a small grin before I link our fingers together and pull her away from the lockers, walking down the passage and out into the yard, holding her hand.

I can feel reluctance in her grip at first, but with each step we take, her grip gets tighter, and she shifts a little closer, and fuck, I can hardly wipe the shit-eating grin from my face as we pass through the quad, all eyes shifting to us.

I know there's a part of Dee that's hating this attention, but there's also the competitive spark in her that comes out in PE class that I sense is helping her through this exposing moment for her.

Right now, she has what the other girls want. Not that I'm trying to float my own fucking boat, or anything.

I don't let go of her hand throughout recess. We eat with our free hand, and as time passes, Dee's hidden smirk turns to a showing grin, and by the time recess is over, she full on smiles at me.

Fuck. It's the most beautiful smile ever, lighting up an expression that normally walks on the dark side. If I can, I'd make sure that smile never drops from her face again.

I'm thankful when we have a PE class next. Not that I'm meant to be getting too physical. I could sit on the sidelines and watch, I guess, but after I reluctantly release Dee's hand so she can go and get changed into her sport uniform, I decide a little physical activity can't hurt. Especially if it means I can interact with Dee some more.

"Ok class. Today we are doing a Jiu-Jitsu taster class." Mrs Bailey, our new PE teacher, bellows, gaining our attention as we file from the change rooms. "Mr Hoberman has come in to teach some basics for today's class."

Standing before the class is a buff guy, not overly tall, but fucking built, his arms and legs covered in tatts. My eyes dart to Dee for some reason, and I see her eyes wide with what I can only assume is excitement as she examines the guest teacher.

My eyes turn to slits as I zero in on Mr fucking Hoberman, and I hold back the snarl that wants to make itself known.

The other few girls in the class are blushing and fluttering their fucking lashes at the guy, so clearly he's some sort of fucking eye candy for them.

Is that why Dee looks so excited?

Is she into this guy?

The Jiu-Jitsu dude starts talking and I can't hear a thing he's saying because I'm laser focused on Dee, and the way she watches on, not even glancing over at me once, like I don't fucking exist.

Looks like we are back to *that* game again.

"Can I have a volunteer?" Mr Hoberman asks, and the handful of girls in the class shoot their hands up. All but Lexi and Dee. That is, until Dee ignores all the hands up and just walks onto the mats.

What the fuck?

"Oh, ok." The dude smiles at Dee. "And what's your name?"

When she doesn't answer, I grin. Mr Hoberman looks confused.

"This is Dee." Mrs Bailey steps in. "She doesn't speak."

The guy's brows shoot up and he nods before turning his eyes back to my girl.

"At all?" he asks her and Dee shakes her head. "Do you sign?"

Dee nods. And then would you fucking believe it? The dude that looks like he kills people for a living, much like my girl, starts moving his fucking hands and arms, talking to her in sign language.

Then, Dee responds to him by signing back.

Fucking hell.

She's shared her voice with Griffin, and emergency services, and now she's talking with her hands to a complete fucking stranger, but all she gives me is words on a screen.

Mr Hoberman laughs and nods, looking fucking pleased about something before facing the class again.

"Looks like we have a skilled volunteer. Dee and I will show you some basic grappling moves."

Heat washes over me as I watch the man put his hands on Dee, like it's fucking ok, and they do a series of moves that I hear no explanation about because all I can hear is my fucking blood rushing past my ears.

"Hey. What the fuck is going on?" Marcus steps in front of me, whispering as he frowns.

"What?" I whisper back.

"You're practically growling, and you look like you're ready to kill. You need to chill the fuck out." Marcus turns a concerned gaze over his shoulder to where Dee has just ninja'd the instructor.

"He shouldn't be touching her like that," I hiss and Marcus turns back, trying to bite back a smirk.

"He's not hurting her, man."

"No. But she... likes it."

Marcus releases a brief chuckle before trying to compose himself. "She likes martial arts, by the looks of it. It's not about the instructor. I'm sure she would prefer your hands on her body."

"Hmmm. Maybe," I mutter, and Grady shakes his head as he steps aside again.

"Ok, so everyone, please partner up and we will try a few basic grapples."

The instructor's words set my feet in motion, my eyes trained on my prize as I weave through the other students.

"Dee is my partner," I announce as I step onto the mat, gaining the instructor's attention.

"Oh, is that ok with you, Dee?" The instructor asks, and I'm about ready to tell him that he doesn't need to ask her, because she's mine, but she nods and offers him a smile.

A fucking smile.

The instructor nods before walking off, and I glare at Dee.

"You'll smile so easily for him, but I have to work for it?"

Her dark brows shoot up and she gives me a 'really' look.

"Yeah, really," I snap and she frowns before I grab her wrist. "You can't use your phone to write me a message and tell me to stop during this class, Dee. Looks like you'll have to use your words."

She tilts her head at me, frowning, before lifting her hand and raising her middle finger.

I smirk.

And then she snatches her wrist free of my grip and plants me on my arse.

The class laughs, even my fucking mates, and the

instructor calls out his fucking praises to Dee, so I roll over and grab both her legs when she turns her back on me and I reef her feet from under her sending her crashing to the floor.

Gasps sound around the room as Dee lands on her tummy. There's a part of me that knows I should be fucking scared of her. I know who she really is. I know she has the skills to kill me before I take my next breath, but when she looks over her shoulder at me with a killer fucking smirk, I feel nothing but primed and ready to take her wrath.

Before I know what's happening, Dee has rolled us both and is on my back with her arms around my neck in some sort of chokehold. The moment I move to get off the floor— because let's be honest, Dee is as light as a feather—she wraps her legs around me from behind like a fucking monkey.

"You know, all this is doing is turning me on," I hiss so only she can hear, and her legs grip tighter. I try to fling her forward off my back, but somehow, I end up the one flung forward, and now Dee is straddling my front as she presses her arms and chin to my shoulders.

I'll give it to her. She's stronger than she looks.

The class is cheering Dee on, and I should be focused on trying to get her off me, but she keeps fucking moving over my crotch, and now my dick is rising to attention for the second time today.

"Dee," I rasp, turning my lips to press against her ear. "I need you to stop."

She presses harder.

"Fuck, Dee," I hiss quietly. "You're making my dick hard. Can't you feel it?"

She stiffens at my words, the pressure on my shoulders vanishing as she releases her hold and sits upright, which only presses the heat between her legs harder against my cock.

Her eyes widen with panic, and she goes to move off me, but I grip her hips.

"She won!" I call, and everyone laughs.

"Ok everyone, focus on your own partners." The instructor calls, thank fuck.

I mean, I don't really care if everyone sees my wood, but I feel like it would embarrass Dee, which is something I don't want to do.

Dee glances down from where she sits straddling me, and as the attention falls away from us, I grin, wagging my brows. "That was close, huh?"

She's still. Too still. Her eyes are on mine, but it's like she's not really seeing me.

Then I feel it. The slightest move of her hips.

My eyes widen, and she bites her lip, her cheeks turning pink as she does it again, and my dick jerks pressing right against her fabric covered core.

Her lips part as a small gasp escapes, and I shift us quickly, rolling so I'm on top of her, hoping that if anyone heard her slight noise, they will think it's because I surprised her with my move.

The new position causes her legs to fall away from my waist, but I'm still pressing firmly between her legs, and her eyes lock with mine.

"What I wouldn't give for every fucker in this room to vanish right now."

She nods.

She fucking nods.

I growl, and that must snap her out of her daze, because she starts doing another grappling move.

Every time she moves her pelvis too far away from mine, I get the urge to lead her right back again. I'm so fucking riled up. My dick is like stone, and my body senses every place we touch as we pretend to Jiu-Jitsu our way through the lesson, but really, it's a session in foreplay and edging, and as soon as it's over, I lean down and whisper in her ear.

"Go into the toilets and touch yourself until you come. I wanna know you're doing that while I jerk off in the men's toilets."

When I pull back, I expect to see an eye roll, or a disgusted frown, so I'm fucking shocked when she gives me a slight nod.

I can't hide my fucking grin, and I leap up from her quickly, ignoring my mates as I watch Dee disappear into the girls' change rooms, and I head to the boys' change rooms and through to the toilets. Those fuckers probably know exactly what I'm doing, but I don't care. Not when all I can think about is her pulling her gym shorts down and pressing her dainty fingers to her needy clit.

As soon as I'm in the stall, I jerk my pants down and wrap my hand around my cock. I squeeze tight, knowing I'm literally only a few strokes from exploding.

That class was hot. Dee's flushed cheeks and the way she responded to me, even though it was slight, was fucking hot. Imagining her naked, wrestling me, fighting for dominance, is fucking HOT!

I pump my dick fast, my balls tightening before I explode hard, a guttural moan leaping uncontrollably from me. It's a short yet intense wave rushing from my toes to my head and leaving me absolutely spent.

Fuck, I wish I could see Dee right now. I wish I could be the one pressing my fingers to her heat and wringing the orgasm from her as she cries out.

Fuck yes. There's nothing like making her come and hearing the husky moans that fall from her lips.

I might not be able to do that right this minute, but I sure as fuck am going to try to make that happen sometime today.

8

DEE

*M*y cheeks are flushed as I work my fingers over my shorts, rubbing the place that ignites me from the inside out. My eyes fall shut and I tip my head back against the stall wall, images of Jared swirling through my head, remembering how hard he was under me when I straddled him.

Then I remember what it's like to press my lips to his dick, and how it feels like silk under my touch.

Intense pleasure builds quickly, and I wish more than anything that Jared was here with me. Touching me. Kissing me. Loving me.

My orgasm crashes over me suddenly, and I slap my hand over my mouth to hold in any sound as it consumes me.

It's a quick and intense wave, which I'm sure would be a thousand times better if Jared had wrung it from me, but it will do for now.

It takes me a few minutes to compose myself after that. I feel like I should be more ashamed than I am that I actually did that at school.

I can't seem to find it in me to care, though.

Jared Crowley is under my skin like a raging inferno, and I don't want to douse it.

When I felt his hardness pressed between my legs, I'd wished our clothes away so he could fill me. Which is fucking insane, right? I'm a virgin. I haven't been filled like that, and I'm pretty sure I should be scared of *that*. But I'm not. Not with Jared. I've never wanted anything more in my life.

I groan inwardly as the memory heats me again while I follow the other year twelve students inside the chapel for the next class. Fuck if ever there's a time for this so-called God we apparently worship to see my impure thoughts and set me on fire before sending me to hell. It's now.

We do some crap about being grateful and lighting candles, supposedly spending the period to reflect, but all I can reflect on is how hot my flesh feels, and the need to touch in between my legs again is more than my need to breathe right now.

Fucking hell. What has Jared Crowley done to me?

Some foreplay and a little masturbation and I'm a horny rabbit.

The lunch break can't come quick enough, and the moment the bell rings, I all but run out of the chapel like there's a fire under my arse, rushing to my locker.

I shove my gym clothes in and lean my head inside my locker, wishing it was a fridge to cool me down.

"Thinking about me?"

I stiffen as Jared's breath fans over my ear before his arm wraps around my front and pulls me back against him.

I nod, unable to keep the truth from him, and he squeezes me tighter to him.

I can feel the hard press of his cock against my back, and a slight moan escapes me.

"Did you make yourself come for me, Deranged?"

I nod, tilting my head to the side as he brushes my hair free of my neck and presses his lips to my blazing skin.

"Excuse me." A stern voice comes from behind us, and it feels like a bucket of water has just been poured over my head, quickly dousing my blazing skin.

Jared eases back, releasing his hold of me, and I turn at the same time as him to see our English teacher, Miss Dice, standing with her arms crossed, glaring at us past her glasses.

"That is inappropriate behaviour for school."

Jared nods. "Yes. Sorry."

She glares at him before turning her eyes to me with raised brows.

A normal girl would apologise, but since I'm not normal, I just stare right back at her.

I like Miss Dice. I really do, but apparently the horny bitch in me is still here and happy to rebel.

"Uh. It won't happen again." Jared adds, and Miss Dice slowly drags her eyes from me and back to him before nodding and walking away, but not too far.

Shit.

She has her eyes on us now.

"Back of the school," Marcus says quietly to Jared as he comes to stand next to us, and they stare at each other for a few beats, leaving me confused. *Back of the school?*

"How?" Jared asks Marcus, who grins.

"We got you."

Glancing back at me, Jared takes my hand in his before shooting Marcus a nod and a grin and leads me out of the passage into the quad.

Did they just talk in code? I have no idea what's going on.

We are only alone for a moment before Marcus, Shaun, and Simon are at our backs, following us. I'm not sure what's happening, so I squeeze Jared's hand to get his attention, and he glances down at me as we walk. Frowning, I gesture my head over my shoulder to his mates behind us, and he grins, shaking his head.

"They're ok. They want to help."

What? Help with what?

Before I can get Jared's attention again, he turns, leading us in the opposite direction of the courtyard.

"Where's George and Gaz?" Jared asks his mates over his shoulder.

"Another gym session," Simon chuckles.

"You mean sex?" Jared asks and Shaun answers this time.

"Nope. More like therapy. There are a few things we've been working on with her to move past... what happened."

Jared nods, and I glance back at the serious faces now worn by three of Rhys' fellas.

Rhys went through some difficult stuff a couple of months ago, towards the end of last year, so it's nice to see that her boyfriends have a serious side.

Rhys comes across as the life of the party, but she has feelings, and she's been through some things that you wouldn't even wish on your worst enemy.

I'm glad her fellas look out for her.

We keep walking, turning up the side of the stadium at the back of the school where it's quieter, no other students in sight.

I should probably stop and question Jared. Ask him why we are here. I trust him, though, so I let him lead me as we listen to his mates banter at our backs.

When we reach the rear of the hall, we round the corner to find Tillie, Bell, Dale and Alister sharing a joint, who smile as we approach.

Ok, that's a lie. Tillie and Dale do. Bell and Alister just stare.

"Hey, guys." Tillie beams, her eyes locking with mine.

She's a sweet-looking girl. I can see what Travis sees in her.

"Hey there, Tills. Do you guys wanna come for a walk?" Shaun asks, and Bell screws up her nose.

"Why?"

"Why not?" Simon adds, and Bell shakes her head.

"Pass."

Tillie looks between everyone, and then her eyes fall back onto me. And Jared. And our intertwined fingers.

"Uh, yeah. We should go for a walk." She sucks back one last drag of the joint and butts it out before turning and whispering something to Bell.

Bell's dark eyes shoot to mine as she stares at me over Tillie's shoulder, and a sinister smirk crosses her face before she throws her head back, laughing.

"Really fucking smooth, Crowley." She cackles, stepping down from the steps before linking arms with Alister and steering him in the direction we just came from.

I glance up at Jared, who is busy shaking his head at Bell, while Tillie and Dale follow their friends before Simon and Shaun turn and leave as well.

Confused, I drop Jared's hand and take my phone out, typing a message and holding up the screen.

What's going on?'

Jared reads it but doesn't respond as Marcus speaks to him.

"We'll make sure no one comes back here."

My heart sinks.

What?

"Thanks, man." Jared fist bumps his mate and then Marcus retreats.

When Jared meets my eyes, I lift my brows and shake my phone again, reminding him to answer my question.

"We can have privacy here," he states and I take a step away from him and mouth *'why?'*

He studies me for a moment as I take another step back and he tries to hide a grin.

"It's not what you're thinking, Dee. I didn't bring you back here to fuck you."

When he doesn't elaborate, I lift my hands in an 'I don't know' shrug to help him understand that I'm still not sure why we are here.

"I want to kiss you." He takes a step towards me, and I take a step back, my heels hitting the bottom step of the stoop that Tillie and Bell were sitting on before. "I want to touch you." He steps forward again, so I take another one back, up the first step. "I want to get lost with you without an audience."

Again he shifts closer, and I rise up another step.

His blue gaze drops to the steps I keep retreating back on, before his eyes dart to the far corner of the building where his friends' voices float from, but who we can no longer see.

"We can just hang out, though." His piercing eyes lock back with mine. "We only have a short time together before you leave. I fucking hate the idea of mundane things like school sucking time from us."

Well shit. I hate the idea of that too.

I take another step up, and he frowns. That is, until I crook my finger at him. Then that frown morphs into a devilish grin as he slowly takes the steps, following me up.

My heart starts pounding like a damn drum in my chest as the anticipation of having his lips on mine again sets my blood on fire.

I don't make it all the way up before Jared lurches forward, tugging me to his chest and claiming my lips. I open for him willingly, my arms wrapping around his neck as he lifts me, my legs latching around his waist. He carries me the rest of the way, and then my back meets the hard surface of the stadium's exit doors as we slink into the small alcove.

"Fuck," Jared hisses, dragging his lips from mine to look into my eyes. "Kissing you has to be my favourite thing to do."

I grin at his honesty.

"I wanna know how you got yourself off earlier." He rasps, and instantly my cheeks heat.

Jesus Christ, Dee. You can slit someone's throat and get showered in their blood, yet you can't handle a little flirting and some foreplay?

I consider that for a moment and realise if there's one person I've ever wanted to share this stuff with, it's Jared.

I push at his shoulders and squirm in his arms, showing him I want to be let down. He gets the hint, easing my legs down until my feet hit the concrete stoop below, and then he takes a step back. His eyes search mine with curiosity, and I suck in a calming breath as I will myself to follow through with this.

"What are we doing?" he asks with a cool smirk, and I let my grin show a little as I hold up my right hand, curl my pinky and thumb in until they touch, wiggling the other three fingers. Then I press them to the centre of my chest and start gliding them down over my school shirt until they reach my kilt, and then I press the tartan fabric in between my legs.

"Fuck, Dee. This is how you got yourself off? Three fingers?"

Nodding, I widen my stance and press my fingers firmly over the sensitive spot and begin to circle.

"Did you slip your fingers into your panties?" he asks, and I shake my head, watching how his blue gaze darts from my face to where I'm fondling. "So you just rubbed over the top of your clothes?"

I nod, biting my lips as the pressure I'm applying starts to build pleasure.

Reaching out with my free hand, I point to Jared, and then his crotch, and his smirk grows.

"You wanna see what I did?"

I nod eagerly, desperate to see how he finished himself off, too.

"You sure you wanna see that, Deranged?" he asks, his fingers working his pants open. "Because you know I had to get my dick out to get over the line. You want me to do that now? Here?"

I nod, knowing that unless someone walks up to the stoop, they won't see us.

My admission makes him growl, his blue eyes turning darker as his arousal consumes him, and he reaches his hand into his pants and jocks before tugging out his hard dick.

"Is this what you want to see?" he asks, fisting it so tight I'm sure it must hurt, but he doesn't seem bothered by it, and starts to pump his fist up and down his hard shaft. I nod, and he hisses, pumping faster. "It didn't take me long to come."

I bite my lip, my eyes locked onto his hard length.

"Lift your skirt," Jared rasps. "Hold it up so I can see your panties."

I don't even take the time to be self-conscious about this, and do as he demands, lifting my skirt, holding it up with one hand and exposing my damp panties.

"Fuck. Can I come closer?"

I raise a brow at him, and when he glances from my panties to my face, he grins.

"I forgot. You prefer me to take instead of asking, don't you?"

I don't answer him, but I lift my brow higher in challenge and he chuckles.

"You know the drill, Dee. I only stop unless you say no. Out loud."

I still don't react to him, my heart racing with anticipation at this game we've been playing since day one.

Launching forward with his hard, exposed cock in one hand, Jared claims my lips in a searing kiss that has more dampness pooling in my panties. I feel his fingers press to my fabric covered heat, and I swallow his moan.

The next few minutes are a combination of his fingers mimicking what I did to myself in the girls' toilets earlier today, and me mimicking his hand pumping his shaft, loving its hard yet silky feeling in my hand.

Desperate need slams into me, and without even thinking, I direct his hard length between my legs to slide over my fabric covered folds.

We break the kiss, both of us releasing a moan, and I don't even care that he can hear me.

"Fuuuck. I can't wait to sink inside there." Jared groans, thrusting his dick forward again, doing exquisite things to my needy clit.

I claw at his shoulders, needing something more, my legs parting further as I urge his cock to my pantie clad entrance. He growls in my ear, biting my lobe and my hips start gyrating, dragging his cock back and forth, causing friction, and a delicious nudge to my opening.

"Dee," he rasps, his hands gripping my arse to lift me a little, and the change in position is just the right angle to press his length a fraction more into my entrance. "I want to sink inside you so bad. Feel your cunt grip me."

I whimper, desperate to feel that too, even though I have no idea what that feels like. The temptation to reach down and tug my panties aside so he can do just that is almost overwhelming, but the moment I open my eyes, I'm reminded of where we are, and I know I don't want to lose my virginity here, at the back of the school during the lunch break.

Instead, I thrust faster, desperately chasing the orgasm I know is only moments away, dry humping his dick until I explode.

A cry escapes me, louder than I think he's managed to wrangle from me before and my internal walls clench and spasm as intense pleasure washes over me. Jared continues thrusting a few more times, his dick going further and further inside my opening each time that I worry he will tear through the thin fabric and penetrate me.

He doesn't though, his climax hitting as he stiffens and grunts loud into my ear, and a moment later I feel the hot spurts of cum jetting from his dick, and into the fabric of my panties.

It's not lost on me how close this is to bare fucking. One stray jet of cum into my opening and I might have to worry about pregnancy.

Shit. This is something I need to figure out. I've never considered having sex with anyone before. I never believed I'd trust anyone enough to be that vulnerable, yet here I am, thinking about birth control and potentially handing my V card to Jared.

9

JARED

*H*er panties are in my pocket. I felt bad for dirtying them up so much when I blew my load, but when we finally pulled apart, after a minute or so of heavy petting, I eased back from Dee and she did something I didn't think she'd do.

She took them off.

Apparently she has some dance undies in her locker, so I lead her past my mates who were all smug as fuck, knowing I'd been doing delicious things to Dee. She kept her head down, a pink blush flushing her cheeks, but my mates were cool and kept their big fucking mouths shut, obviously not wanting to embarrass Dee, because they normally wouldn't have any qualms with embarrassing me.

The last class of the day went fast, and before I knew it, I was driving my girl to her dance class. I went inside with her, intending on watching and not caring what she thought about it, but as soon as we entered, the mood inside was sombre.

Dee rushed off to get changed, and when we went upstairs together to the studios, there were girls crying in a huddle. I pressed my hand to Dee's lower back as she moved, but the moment she stilled, so did I.

Ruby.

Dee stiffened at the sight of her dance friend, and just like that, the farmhouse incident came rushing back.

Dee had been there to kill a husband and wife. They were Ruby's parents, which she didn't realise until after she went inside the house and saw the pictures lining the walls.

It can't have been easy for her to do that, but they were bad people hiding behind the facade of a happy family.

"I'm surprised she's here," I say quietly next to Dee's ear, and she nods before dragging her gaze away from the girl she orphaned to look up at me.

Damn. Dee doesn't need words to explain how she feels sometimes. Her eyes. Her expression says it all. And right now, she's feeling guilty and sad.

"It's ok. You did what you had to do." I try to reassure her, and her chocolate eyes glass over as she sucks in a calming breath before she slowly nods.

"Girls, please come inside the studio." The voice of the older lady that teaches Dee's dance class draws everyone's attention, and the huddle of girls breaks away from Ruby and file in quietly.

I've seen Ruby a handful of times, and never has she looked so drained. Her eyes are puffy from crying, dark circles sitting underneath, and her red hair is pulled back, but not in the neat way it usually is.

When she locks eyes with Dee, a sob escapes her and she lurches forward, throwing her arms around my girl. Naturally, Dee stiffens, not one to like random close contact, but as the girl sobs into her neck, Dee lifts her arms and wraps them around her new friend.

The teacher pokes her head out the door a moment later,

and upon seeing the two girls embracing, she doesn't speak and goes back inside the studio.

"Hey Rubes, you don't have to dance today." A male voice comes from behind me and I turn to see Ruby's boyfriend, Caleb, at the top of the stairs, looking just as frazzled as his girl.

His words break Ruby's hold of Dee, and she glances up at him, tears streaming down her cheeks as she nods and rushes to his arms.

"I know." She sobs, "But I think I need to."

Nodding into her red hair, Caleb presses a kiss to her forehead before pulling back and wiping her tears from her face.

"Ok. I'll be right out here. You can leave at any time."

She nods, and while they have a moment, I glance back to my little pocket rocket to see the pain in her eyes. Without hesitation, I reach out and tug her to my chest, leaning down to whisper in her ear.

"Don't forget why you had to do it. I can only imagine the things Ruby has had to endure and never told anyone about. You've made sure those things no longer happen. To her or her little sister."

Nodding into my chest, Dee tilts her head up, standing on her toes as she tugs me by the front of my shirt, down to her level. Then she kisses me.

I'd always associated kissing with sex, or foreplay, until Dee came into my life. Now, kisses don't have to be leading up to anything. It's another way to express feelings. Feelings that are stronger than I ever imagined.

There's no doubt in my mind that when Dee leaves Fox Pines, I'm going to die inside. A sensible person wouldn't have wanted to get involved with anyone who isn't sticking around, but fuck, it's impossible for me to walk away from her, even if I know we only have a short time together.

Dee and Ruby go inside the studio together, and Caleb and I take a seat in front of the viewing window, watching as the teacher talks to the girls and then plays some music.

I'm not sure what they are doing, because no one is doing the same thing, but they are all moving to the music and I realise that most of them are crying.

Fuck. This is brutal.

"She never said anything."

Caleb's words draw my attention away from the window and I look at how pale his face is as he keeps watching his girl dance. Then he turns his pained expression to me.

"They filmed her. Did things to her." He shakes his head and anger flares across his face. "She said she was only young when it started, and that as she got older, she was scared her parents would do the same things to her little sister, Angela, so she went to them and begged them not to touch her. That she would keep doing whatever they wanted as long as they left little Angie alone." Caleb grits his teeth, a snarl falling from his lips. "They fucking lied to her when they said they would leave Angie alone. Ruby saw some of the footage at the police station when she was passing the investigation room. She saw the sick things her parents were doing to her little sister. Just like they'd done to her."

Leaping from his chair, Caleb starts pacing.

"Why the fuck didn't I know? I knew she wasn't a virgin. She made up a vague story of an old boyfriend and I fucking believed her." He fists his hair then, nearly ripping it from his skull. "Fuck. I thought she was just timid. Shy about sex. Hell, I should have known something was up with the way she reacted the first time I made her come." He stops in front of me, fury reddening his cheeks.

"She told me last night the first orgasm she'd had was with me, and she didn't know it could feel like that. It had shocked her, and now I understand her reaction to it when it happened. Why the fuck didn't I know?"

"Hey." I stand, gripping his shoulders and looking him dead in the eyes. "This isn't your fault. She was obviously scared, which is why she never told you, but the main thing is that you know now, and you can help her start to heal."

Nodding, Caleb's shoulders relax. "I fucking love her. I'd do anything for her."

I grin. "Yeah, I can see how much you care about her. It's not gonna be easy, man. But you two are solid. You can get through this."

Again, Caleb nods, and my head spins with this information. He's clearly struggling and probably didn't mean to tell me their secrets, but I'm fucking glad he did. It's just another thing I can remind Dee of when she feels guilty about what she did.

"I hope they find out who it was that killed Ruby's sicko parents." Caleb snaps, stepping back and pacing again. Meanwhile, I stiffen.

I fucking hope they don't find out who did it.

"I wanna thank them for killing those fucking sick cunts."

I relax.

He wants to thank them.

That's a relief.

My phone buzzes with a message then, so I take it out and check the screen.

Garrett Cole
Did you think I would forget about the talk we need to have?

I grin. He's a moody fucker.

Jared Crowley
I'd hoped.

Garrett Cole
I'm outside the dance studio. Get your arse out here.

I roll my eyes. Fucker stalked me.

I say a quick apology to Caleb and dash out of the building to see Garrett leaning against the bonnet of my car. A small grin tugs at his lips when he sees me, and I shake my head.

"Don't fucking start." I point at him, and he chuckles.

"Where's your tutu?"

"Shut the fuck up." I punch his shoulder and he laughs louder.

"Never thought I'd see you walking out of a ballet studio." He grins at me as I lean back against the bonnet of my car next to him.

"What do you want to talk about?" I snap, and his face falls serious.

"Griffin Marx. Tell me how you *really* know him, and don't give me some bullshit about being his employee."

I roll my eyes. "I am his employee."

"Ok, then. Don't give me some crap about you being his driver."

"I do drive for him," I state, and Garrett shakes his head.

"Who or what do you drive for him?"

I narrow my eyes at my mate. "What do *you* know about Griffin Marx?"

"Don't change the fucking conversation. Answer my question."

"I will, if you answer mine first," I snap and we stare at each other, both as fucking stubborn as each other.

"Fine." Garrett concedes, standing tall and gesturing for me to get into my car.

It's probably a smart move. Standing out on the street where anyone can hear us talking isn't a good idea.

Once inside, I turn on the engine, letting the air con cool the space for us so we can keep the windows up on this hot summer afternoon.

"When my old man got out of prison a couple of months back, he mentioned the Marx family name a few times. Something about them taking over everything. Said he'd have to watch his back."

My brows shoot up. "Your old man was involved in more than just getting wasted, then?" I ask and Garrett shrugs.

"Who fucking knows? I'm beginning to think there's a lot of people we know involved in dodgy shit in this town."

He's not fucking wrong.

"I was curious about who this family was that had my dad scared, so I searched them online." Garrett shakes his head as he thinks over something. "There's only so much you can find with a basic internet search. I'm sure all the really bad stuff has been taken down, but the gist is that they are a notorious crime family, said to be taking over this state, and probably the entire east coast of Australia over the next few years."

I nod, already knowing this. "They aren't as bad as you think."

Garrett's brows shoot high as he whips his head in my direction. "Explain."

"How can I put this…" I tap my finger to my chin before continuing. "You've obviously heard about the illegal stuff happening that involves kids, right? Your girl was caught up in it, wasn't she?"

Frowning, Garrett nods. "Are they part of that? Do they come after kids?!"

Fucking hell, he's about to turn into the incredible hulk, given the lethal expression on his face.

"Fuck no. They are the ones working in the background to take them out. Well, I mean they are working with some others to help do that. They are moving into the area. Will probably take over the organised crime, drugs and whores and stuff. But they aren't bad people."

Garrett's brows shoot up. "That sounds bad to me."

"I mean, they aren't saints, but they do have morals. There's always going to be bad guys trying to rule things. As far as I can tell, they are the better of the evils."

Slowly, Garrett nods. "So, what do you drive for them?"

"A person. An asset of theirs that's helping them."

"When do you drive this... asset?"

I shrug. "When they need the asset to do a job."

Garrett narrows his eyes. "What sort of job?"

I shake my head. I can't tell him the truth. Griffin won't hesitate to kill me or my parents if he finds out I've been blabbing.

"I have no idea, man. I just drive the car."

Tilting his head, Garrett's brown curls tumble over one eye as he studies me.

"Any chance these so-called jobs happen right before another murder is announced on the news?"

I shrug. "Don't know. I don't really pay that much attention."

Garrett stares at me for a few beats, and I can tell he doesn't believe me, but he doesn't press any further about that particular subject.

"How did you crash the car? You're a good driver, man. I don't for a minute think it was an accident."

For fuck's sake. Why does he have to be so fucking... caring?

"I was being reckless," I admit. "Had a bit of a screaming match with Dee. Well, I mean, I was the one screaming. She just stayed fucking quiet, as usual. But the car wreck was totally my fault. I was out of my mind with anger."

"Why?" Garrett asks and I shrug.

"I think it all just got too much. The thing with Mike West. My brother dying and my olds checking out." I look down at my lap. "You guys always busy with your girlfriend." I shake my head. "And Dee. I just wanted her to speak. To trust me enough to share that with me."

I glance back up at my mate, and his face is contorted in pain.

"We've been shitty friends."

I shake my head. "It's not all on you guys. I've been a shitty person in general. Hell, the way I've pushed Dee, I'm surprised she didn't leave me to die in that car."

Garrett chuckles. "I'm surprised about that, too."

We fall into a comfortable silence, both of us stuck in our own heads, and when dancers start filing from the building, I check my phone to see that Dee's dance class is over.

"I gotta get back in there," I state, and Garrett nods.

"Do me a favour and be fucking careful with the Marx family. And call me if you get into any trouble."

I nod, wondering if I should have rang him the night Travis and I were involved in killing that druggo, Pike.

No. I could never have dragged him or any of my mates into that.

Without warning, Garrett leans across the console and gives me a man hug. He's the last person you'd think would do something like that, yet here we are.

10

DEE

*M*y last target for tonight is Tim Ovens. He's a middle-aged, rather round fella that likes to wear a skin tight tiger suit and expose his junk to unsuspecting preteen girls on the internet.

He was also a member of the Vixen's Lodge sex club that my foster sister, Rhys, used to attend as Kitten. All the research I've been given on him screams creepy fucker.

I've already slaughtered three others tonight, not bothering to wait until most neighbourhoods were asleep. That's too predictable, and since so many on this list seem to also be Carnal Unicorn members, I know there's a possibility of another ambush.

I stole another bike, not even bothering to hide my identity as I rode through neighbourhoods where the kids were still playing on the front lawns under sprinklers as the sun slowly set.

I told Cynthia and Will that I was going to see Jared, and I am. Just not before I run some errands.

The first kill was easy since the guy was napping in his recliner. The last two were a little more challenging. One had a big fucking dog, so I had to silently coax it out of the house so I could get close enough to my target to complete the job.

The other had a date over for dinner. I had to wait until she excused herself and went to the bathroom so I could strike without an audience. Once she was out of the room, I didn't hesitate to let Thana do her thing, and I was back on the bike out the front of that house before the dead guy's date must have found him and started screaming.

Now, as the last streaks of pink fade from the sky, I slip through Tim's back door. I hear him before I see him, and at first I think he must have someone here with him, because I hear voices, but as I listen, I realise he's talking to someone via cam on his computer.

This complicates things. I can't risk being seen or recorded by someone outside the house, so I retreat back outside and hug the house as I make my way to the side of the garage where the electricity meter box is.

Turning off Tim's power will ensure his internet drops out too, and will allow me to complete the job without risk. So I quietly open the exterior cabinet with my gloved hands, flick the power switch and hurry back into the house.

I can hear Tim cursing, something crashing to the floor, before he curses again, and I grin. He's disoriented by the sudden darkness.

Closing my eyes for a moment, I press my back to the wall in the passage a few metres from the doorway of the room Tim is in. Taking a steadying breath, I slowly open my eyes and they adjust quickly to the darkness, allowing me to see better.

"Stupid fucking power company. We pay a fortune for electricity, yet they can't keep our power running." Tim whines to himself, and I pop my head around the door frame to see his tubby silhouette staggering around. "Where the fuck did my phone go?"

He bends, huffing and puffing as he searches aimlessly in the dark.

"Ah. There you are." He mutters before I see his phone screen light up, illuminating his chubby face, and the ridiculous tiger suit he's wearing.

Ew.

Just. Ew!

Before he manages to get the phone's torch light on, I pounce, darting forward with Thana raised. She slices through the flabby flesh on his neck, doing her job and severing his kill switch.

I weave out of the way just in time to avoid the spray of blood. His gargled gasps fill the room as he panics, stumbles forward to his knees and then falls face first to the floor.

He's not dead yet, but it won't be long, so I flick my phone's flashlight on and retreat from the room, making sure to avoid stepping in any blood.

I hover in the doorway for a few minutes, waiting to make sure he's dead, and when I know the life has left his body, I pass by the bathroom, wipe Thana clean on one of his towels, and leave the way I came in.

The list Griffin sent me is long. Since Saturday, I've eliminated nine of the twenty-two names who are known local members of Carnal Unicorn. That leaves thirteen, all of which live outside Fox Pines. Which means I'll need to find a different form of transport to get to them.

At the bottom of Griffin's list, he included another thirty odd names. These names aren't related to Carnal Unicorn, but are the people he needs to eliminate in order to take control of the Timber Valley district.

What's interesting about that part of the list is that the majority are Kerr gang members or part of the Kerr family. Travis' foster family.

I have a feeling that Travis' name was originally on this

list, and even though it's not on this one that Griffin gave me, I know that he's still in danger. If Travis doesn't stand down, they won't hesitate to kill him, unless I can complete marking names off this list before my eighteenth birthday.

That's less than two weeks away now, so I have my work cut out for me.

Riding back through the streets of Fox Pines, I ditch the bike in the creek and walk the two kilometres to the train underpass where I stashed my backpack earlier. I get changed in the dark, removing my kill clothes and stashing them in a plastic bag, before slipping into my black short sleeve cropped t-shirt, and my black denim shorts.

I feel a little anxious about what I'm wearing. I don't usually wear short sleeves in public, but tonight I'm forcing myself to step out of my comfort zone, because I'm about to do something I've never done before, and part of that is letting down some of these walls I've kept up for so many years.

After burying the plastic bag in the messy scrubland nearby with my kill clothes inside, I make my way to middle class Fox Pines until I find myself outside Jared's house.

He sent me a message earlier, asking what I was up to, trying to spark conversation. I didn't respond, and no doubt he'd be pissed about that, but I needed to focus on the kills.

It's nearly 10:30pm now, and as I sneak into his backyard, my heart starts thrashing in my chest like it's preparing to leap out.

Why the hell am I so nervous about this, and not the four kills I did earlier? I'm definitely wired wrong. That's for sure.

I glance in through the glass doors that show Jared's parents in the living room. It appears that his mum is asleep on the couch, a half empty bottle of wine on the side table next to her, and his dad is reclining in the armchair, his head tipped back with his mouth open, probably snoring.

I shift my focus to another window, back further, and the warm glow coming from it.

Is that Jared's room?

Taking out my phone, I open Jared's message and respond.

Dee Porter
I'm outside your bedroom window.

I hit send, my heart thrashing even more now, and I'm certain I'm about to have a fucking heart attack.

A moment later, the blind on the window where the warm glow is coming from shifts, and I see the silhouette of a head peeking through before it disappears.

Shit.

I should go.

This was a bad idea.

What if he doesn't want me here?

I shouldn't have just shown up uninvited.

What the fuck was I thinking?

I spin on my heel and freeze when I hear my name.

"Dee?"

Shit. Ok. He's definitely seen me.

I have two options.

Run, or grow a pair of lady balls and turn around.

"Dee." His voice comes again, closer this time, so I find those lady balls, and turn back to face him.

Biting my lower lip, my cheeks flush as I offer him an awkward half wave, and his lips spread wide in a grin.

"Are you ok?" he asks, stepping closer, away from the glass door that he must have shut behind him. He isn't wearing a shirt.

Fucking hell, why isn't he wearing a shirt?

It's a warm night, I guess. And he's also in *his* house, so that's totally normal, right?

I bite my lower lip as my eyes wander down his taut abs, down past his navel, to the grey sweat shorts he's wearing.

Fuck me. That should be illegal.

"Dee?"

His voice snaps me out of my trance, and my eyes dart back up to his.

"Are you ok?"

I nod, so he nods, too.

"Do you need me to drive you somewhere?" he asks, clearly unsure why I've shown up like this.

I shake my head.

"Do you want to come inside?" He points his thumb over his shoulder and I worry my lip again and shrug. He chuckles. "Come on. Come inside."

I lean to the side, peering back into the living area through the glass doors to where his parents remain in the same position.

"Don't worry about them. They're asleep, and will probably stumble to their bed at some point in the next hour or so. It's a nightly ritual." He glances back over his shoulder at his parents before turning back to me. "I can wake them if you like? Tell them to go to bed. Would that make you more comfortable? We can watch some TV."

I shake my head quickly, and again he smiles.

"Do you want to come inside... to my bedroom?"

He sounds both cocky and nervous as he asks, and I have to wonder how he manages to do that.

I glance back to the window I now definitely know is his bedroom, before returning my gaze to his, and I nod.

"Yeah?" he asks, his brows shooting up, and I nod again, to reassure him.

"Ok. Come on then." He offers his hand, and I take the four steps to close the distance, placing my hand in his.

I'm expecting him to turn and lead me inside, but he doesn't. Not yet.

He tugs me closer, his free hand delving into the hair at my nape, and he kisses me.

If I were butter, I'd melt right now. There's just something about the way Jared Crowley kisses me that is all-consuming. The moment his tongue glides against mine, I'm lost. I press my hands to his bare chest, feeling his smooth hot flesh, and I moan into his mouth.

He breaks the kiss then, pressing his forehead to mine.

"Shit Dee. The things you do to me."

I want to tell him he does the same things to me, but as usual, I keep my words to myself. It's something I hate myself for more and more each day, wishing I could just speak the words I want to share with him out loud.

Turning, Jared slides open the glass door and tugs me inside behind him before closing it again. I don't get a chance to look around, his hand squeezing mine as he leads me past the kitchen, down a passage, and into a bedroom where he closes us in.

I glance around the space. It's a touch bigger than the bedroom I have at the Rogans', but it's definitely more lived in, feeling homely with a couple of football posters, a pin board with a heap of polaroid pictures of him and his mates, a messy desk, and a double bed.

And best of all. This room smells like Jared.

"Sorry, it's a bit messy," he states, glancing around his room, but I shake my head when he turns his focus back to me, and I mouth 'it's fine.'

He smiles down at me before his eyes drop lower, and I see the moment he realises I'm not wearing long sleeves. Lightning fast, his eyes dart back to mine, so I tug him towards his bed, turn him before pushing him back so he sits on his mattress.

"Has something happened?" he asks, looking concerned, and I can tell he's trying not to look at my arms.

I shake my head, digging deep to find those lady balls again, and I stretch my arms out in between us. His eyes drop to them and he watches as I slowly turn them over to the underside, where faint scars can clearly be seen.

"Dee," he whispers, his eyes going back and forth from my arms to my face. "Did... you do this?"

I'm not annoyed by his question. It's the first thing everyone thinks when they see the scars. It's really only those people who have worked with cutters or are cutters themselves that recognise that these scars are not from self-harm.

I shake my head and run a finger over one of the raised lines. It's too thick and jagged to be from self-harm, but Jared doesn't know that.

Frowning, Jared examines my arms again before glancing back up. "Did someone else do this?"

I nod, and he sucks in an audible breath as anger flares across his face.

"Who?" he demands.

'Travis' mum.' I mouth, but he doesn't clearly read my lips.

"Your mum?"

I shake my head and re-mouth the words, slower.

'Travis' mum. My step-mum.'

His brows shoot up. "Your step-mum? Travis' mum?"

I nod and he shakes his head.

"Why?"

I do the universal sign for crazy next to my head, and he nods.

"Is this something you want to talk about? Is that why you came here?" he asks, genuinely interested, but I shake my head, and he frowns, not really understanding why I'm showing him my arms.

I could get my phone out and write out what I want to say, but it's such a mood killer, and I like communicating with him like this.

Slowly, I shift, reaching for the hem of my cropped t-shirt, and I tug it up over my head.

When I drop it to the floor, Jared's eyes flare and he licks his lips as his eyes travel over the black bra I'm wearing. I shift my hands to the button of my shorts next, but his hand stops me, his eyes connecting with mine.

"I wanna take them off," he rasps, his voice huskier than it was a minute ago.

I nod, my chest rising and falling as my nerves ramp up.

He tugs me closer, between his parted legs, which brings his head to chest height. His gentle fingers graze up the backs of my thighs, over the globes of my arse and up my bare back to find the clasp of my bra.

His face is close now, his blue gaze dark with lust as he peers up at me while he slowly unclasps my bra and eases the straps down over my shoulders.

I'm so nervous I'm nearly trembling, and I'm worried if he notices that he'll stop, but the moment the bra tumbles to my feet, Jared's warm hands reach up and cup my breasts, his thumb grazing over one nipple before his lips close over the other.

Just like that, I forget my damn name, my head falling back at the feel of his lips on my bare skin. I'm no longer nervous. I'm hungry. Hungry for him. For Jared Crowley.

His tongue flicks over my nipple and need clenches between my legs, causing a whimper to escape me.

Pulling back, Jared glances up at me, sucking his lower lip in, even as he grins.

"Remember the rules, Dee. If you want me to stop, you

have to say the words." He winks. "Out loud. With your voice."

I wonder which he wants more, for me to say the words so he can hear my voice, or for me to remain silent so he can keep going.

I want to give him my voice, but not in this way, so I give him a nod to let him know I understand, and he nods back.

"I'm gonna fuck you tonight, Dee. You know that, right?"

My nostrils flare at his words, and my heart pounds in my chest with both anticipation and fear, but I push aside my virginal worries and smirk. He growls in response, his hands pressing into my back as he nips at my other nipple.

Things move fast then. His hands working my shorts open as he devours my nipples, giving each good attention. By the time my shorts are pooling at my feet, my sex is ravenous, and before I realise what's happening, Jared lifts me and has me on my back on his bed. He stands over me, his dark gaze darting to mine every few seconds as he unlaces my Docs and tugs them, my socks and my shorts off before staring down at me splayed out on his bed in only my black panties.

"You're fucking beautiful, Dee."

I can't help but smile, and I point to him.

"What? I'm beautiful?" he asks and I nod. "I'd rather be hot."

I nod again.

"I'm hot?" he asks and I nod again as he smirks.

"You know what's hot, Dee?" He leans down to hover over me, one hand holding him up on the mattress next to me as his other hand glides up the inside of my thigh. "It's hot when you make those little noises you make." Then his fingers graze over my panties.

Another of *those* noises he's talking about escapes me, and he grins wickedly.

"So fucking hot."

He stands back up, quickly hooking the band of my panties with his fingers, and drags them off me.

Suddenly, I feel extremely exposed, but Jared doesn't leave me hanging, his eyes remaining locked with mine as he tugs off his shorts and jocks, freeing his hard cock.

My mouth waters when I catch sight of it, almost angry looking as it stands tall, the head tinted a shade of purple. I want it inside me. I still don't understand how I can want that when I've never had that before, but I just feel like I need to be filled.

"You want this?" he asks, fisting his cock and giving it a couple of pumps. I nod eagerly, and he grins. "You have no idea how much I want to sink it inside you."

Of their own accord, my hips lift off the bed as I moan, and Jared's smile falls away to be replaced with something I can only describe as carnal.

Growling like an animal, Jared falls to his knees, and I watch as he grips my thighs and pries them open.

I should feel embarrassed about being so exposed to him, to have eyes on a part of me that has never had anyone else's gaze fall upon it before. Just his. Only his.

"Fuck, Deranged. I'm gonna devour this pussy."

And he does. Lurching forward, he claims it with his mouth, his lips latching on, and his tongue assaults me in the best way.

I want to keep my eyes on him as he eats me, but the feelings are too intense, and my lids close as I fist the sheets at my sides and writhe with building pleasure.

I let myself go completely, my hips moving, thrusting, as his tongue lashes my clit, through my folds before sinking inside me.

I need more.

I almost say the words, desperate and hungry, but he

must be able to tell, and a moment later, I feel his finger press to my entrance. Immediately, I part my legs wider, desperate to feel his digit sink inside, and a moment later he slowly eases it in.

"Fuck, you're so tight," he rasps against my clit, even as he inserts another finger.

Is that two? I don't really know or care as the familiar sensation of ecstasy builds deep in my core, my back arching off the bed as I release the sheets and grip his head, holding him there as I come apart in a rush on his tongue and fingers.

Jared stays between my legs, sucking on my clit as I ride the waves, and when I finally fall lax, he lifts his head and chuckles.

"I fucking love making you come."

I fucking love him making me come, too.

Slowly, he eases his fingers from me, and our gazes lock as he licks one of his fingers clean. Then he holds the other one up.

"You want some?"

Shit. Do I want some?

He made me suck myself off his finger up at the lookout that night after we met with Griffin and the Angels. It was different then. We were playing a different game. One where I pretended not to like him or the things he did to me, so he didn't *ask* me to taste myself that night. He demanded it.

Now though, things have changed, and he's asking me.

It's easy to pretend I did it last time because he forced me to, but now he wants me to admit I want to.

I bite my lip, unsure if I want to do that, even though he's watched me taste myself before. He loved it then, and I enjoyed pleasing him, so I nod, pushing up on my elbows and parting my lips.

"Fuck," he whispers, reaching forward with one of the glistening fingers before easing it into my mouth.

I close my lips around his finger and swirl my tongue over it, all while keeping my eyes on his face. He looks like he's in a trance right now, and it makes me feel powerful knowing I have some sort of control over him.

Slowly, he eases his finger free with a pop. A grin spreading his lips wide.

"You're fucking perfect. You know that?"

I shake my head at his question, and his eyes narrow.

"It's time for you to learn that about yourself, Dee," he states, his eyes travelling from mine and all the way down my body as he stands. "I can't wait any longer. I need to be inside you," he admits, leaning down to his bedside drawer, reaching in and pulling out a foil packet.

Suddenly, anxious nerves race my heart as it hits me that this is really happening. He's going to put that big dick of his inside me, and I'm not sure it will fit. It's going to hurt. There's no way it won't.

"Hey. What's wrong?" Jared's voice draws me out of my spiralling and I realise I must be showing my fear on my face.

I shake my head, and he frowns.

"Dee. Don't lie to me. Something just changed. What was it?"

I should tell him, right? He should know I'm a virgin before we have sex. Right?

My breathing increases and I shake my head, trying to calm myself.

If you can kill people, you can take a fucking dick, Dee!

"Dee?" Jared says my name like a warning, so I dig deep and find those lady balls again.

Reaching out, I point to my exposed pussy and shake my head.

He frowns. "You don't want to fuck?"

I shake my head quickly, sitting up and biting my lip.

Say the fucking words, Dee. Just speak to him.

I open my mouth, ready to speak, and Jared's eyes widen. *Shit. I can't.*

Snapping my mouth shut, I growl out loud and slap my hands to the mattress on either side of me.

"Hey." Jared falls to his knees on the floor and takes my hands in his. "Do you want me to get a pen and paper?"

Shit. He's been begging me to speak to him, yet he offers me an out.

I shake my head, licking my lips as I lean forward and reach for his hard cock. He gasps when I wrap my hand around it, gliding my hand up and down its silky hardness.

"Shit, Dee. I can't concentrate when you do that." He grins, and I grin back.

Releasing his cock, I point to my chest and then mouth the word *'virgin.'*

He frowns, shaking his head, not understanding. "Sorry what?"

Again, I point to my chest and then mouth the word, *'virgin.'*

When he doesn't say or do anything, I point to the bare flesh between my legs and mouth, *'virgin.'*

His eyes widen. "Virgin?"

I nod, and he goes pale. "But how? You... you're..." He shakes his head and goes to stand, but I grab his wrists, keeping him in place and mouth *'I want you.'*

His shoulders relax as he understands my silent words, but again, he shakes his head.

"Fuck. I'm a fucking prick. The way I've been treating you. I-I... Shit, Dee. I'm so sorry. I assumed that because of what you do that you must..."

I grin.

I get it. I kill people. I work with those deep in the world of organised crime. It would be natural to think I'm experienced.

"Why are you grinning?" he asks, sounding mortified.

I grip his dick again and mouth. *'Fuck me.'*

He stares at me, clearly having an internal battle with himself before he speaks. "You want me to be your first?"

I nod, and he shakes his head. "I don't know if I deserve it."

I roll my eyes and do the only thing I can think of to try to get his head back in the game. I lie back, parting my legs and run my hand down my body until I get to my heat.

His eyes flare, darting from mine to my sex and back again, and I mouth again *'fuck me.'*

With a hiss, Jared bares his teeth before using them to tear the foil condom wrapper open and pulling it free.

"You want me to fuck you, Deranged?"

I nod, and he presses the latex covering to the tip of his dick.

"You want me to break through that barrier and take your virginity?"

Again, I nod, and he rolls the condom over his hard length.

"It's gonna hurt for a bit," he states with no shame, and I nod, already knowing that, but not caring as I circle my clit and bite my lower lip.

"It's gonna feel consuming, Dee. My dick is way bigger than my fingers. It's gonna fill you and stretch you until you can't think straight."

I nod again, my chest rising and falling with consuming anticipation as he shifts over me.

Looking into my eyes, he falls quiet before he admits in a hushed tone.

"I don't want to hurt you."

11

JARED

J'm torn between my heart and my dick. Dee is a fucking virgin! A virgin! I thought her sexual timidness was an act. What the fuck is wrong with me?

For fuck's sake, Jared. You know what they say about people who assume?

All this time, she has been innocent. Well, in the sexual sense, at least. She's still a seventeen-year-old dancing assassin!

I tried to scare her out of this, telling her it will hurt, but it hasn't deterred her. Her eyes still eat me up like I'm fucking everything to her, and hell, I know what that feels like, because she feels like everything to me.

"Dee. Are you sure you want this?"

There it is. One last chance to back out, and she nods, reaching forward and gripping my hips, digging her nails in.

Fuck.

I claim her lips, wanting to make sure she's as relaxed as possible, and also because kissing her is fucking everything. She kisses me back eagerly, small little whimpers floating from her mouth into mine as I start running my latex covered cock over her sex.

Fuck, today has been the best fucking day ever.

Monday, February 24th. I'll never forget this day.

It's the day she let everyone see how we feel about each other.

It's the day we wrestled and turned each other on, only to finish ourselves off in the bathrooms afterwards.

It's the day she let me get her off behind the school stadium and I practically fucked her panties.

And it's the day she came to me without me asking her to. She showed me her scars. She clearly wanted to speak to me with her voice—something we can work on achieving later—and she wants me to be the one to take her virginity.

I'm never going to be able to let her go!

I push that thought down, focusing on the dancing assassin writhing under me. I want this to feel good for her, but there will be a part that will hurt, and all I can do is try to reduce it.

"I wanna make you come again," I rasp as I break our kiss and look down at her.

With her cheeks flushed, she rolls her hips, chasing the friction from my dick.

"Yes. Do that again."

So she does, and I join her.

Fuck. I might come before I even get inside her.

That would be embarrassing.

As we grind ourselves together, my dick slipping through her folds, I shift, trailing kisses down her neck and chest until I get to her perfect pink straining nipple. One of her sweet little gasps falls from her parted lips as I take it in my mouth, kissing, sucking, flicking my tongue over the tight bud. Her back arches, pushing her nipple in further, and her hands shift to my bare arse, clawing at me with desperation as we writhe together.

"Dee," I pant, turning my focus to her other nipple, "After you come," I suck the bud, wringing another whimper from her, "that's when I'm going to sink my cock inside you."

My words spear her on, and her grinding picks up, telling me she's close.

I'm working on the theory that right after she climaxes will be when she will be the most pliable, if that's even a thing. So that's when I'll sink inside her. If I can hold out, that is. I feel like I'm about to blow.

"Do you wanna come, baby?" I ask, and she nods frantically, her eyes squeezed shut as she bites her lower lip. "Then come for me," I rasp, sliding my hand in between us until I find her sensitive bundle of nerves.

My fingers have barely touched her when she shatters for me, her cries louder than they were the first time tonight, and fuck, I can hear more of her voice.

Her very husky voice.

With vigour, I circle her clit, drawing out her climax, and the moment her cries start to lessen, and she starts to fall lax, I line my cock up to her entrance and I ease inside.

I feel it. The moment my dick meets her resistance, but I push through, hoping like hell that this doesn't hurt her too much, and hating how fucking amazing it feels for me.

Dee tenses under me, her lids flying open and her nails digging into my hips, but I keep going, driving all the way in. A painful cry falls from her lips, so I still as I cup her face.

"Dee. Are you ok?"

Breathing deeply through her nose, her wide chocolate gaze locks with mine and she quickly nods.

"I'm sorry." It's all I can say, but she shakes her head, releasing her claw-like grip from my hip to cup my face, too.

'Kiss me' she mouths, and I relax a little, knowing she's still

109

ok. She still wants this.

I close the distance, taking her lips in mine and melting into the kiss. A moment later, Dee starts moving her hips, and I take the hint and move too.

I go slow at first, knowing it must still hurt. It's fucking hard, though. The way her tight cunt grips my dick like a vise has me dying to thrust harder and faster. I want to completely let go and lose myself in her, yet I don't. Not yet. That will come later. For now, I grit my teeth and hold back, my nostrils flaring as I fight to remain in control.

With each agonisingly pleasurable slow thrust, Dee begins to relax, the pain in her expression softening until it's taken over by need, and her hips start to move more in sync with mine.

Fuck, she's so tight, and so hot, and so fucking good. I take my cues from her for as long as I can, and I know I'm only seconds away from coming, so I shift position, going up on my knees, spreading them, and her wider, and I press my fingers to her swollen clit. Looking down at her, my eyes shift from her face, contorted in pleasure, to where my cock disappears inside her.

"I don't want this to end." I pant, thrusting over and over, my words having a double meaning. I'm not sure if she picks up on it, but she nods, biting her lip again as she matches my thrusts until her eyes roll in the back of her head.

The moment her needy cunt starts clenching around my cock, I'm gone. I soar high, blow hard, and roar loud.

It feels like an out-of-body experience. It's never been like this before. The nameless faces of girls I tried to drown my sorrows in disappear, completely meaningless and irrelevant in comparison to this. To Dee.

A knock sounds on my door, and I only just hear it past the roaring of rushing blood in my ears. Then I hear my dad's voice.

"Uh… Jared? Is everything alright?"

My eyes widen, matching Dee's expression as we both form O's with our mouths, realising that we must have been too loud.

Oh my fucking god, my old man just heard me fucking.

Dee slaps a hand over her mouth as she fights off giggles, and my dick, still buried inside her, shrinks really fucking fast knowing my dad is just on the other side of my bedroom door.

"Yep!" I call. "All good."

I suck in my lips, trying not to laugh, and my dad's voice comes through the timber barrier again.

"Are you sure? I thought I heard you yelling."

A giggle. A real fucking audible giggle bursts past Dee's hand, and I glare at her, unable to hide my own smirk.

"I was watching a scary movie," I call. "I'll tell you about it in the morning."

Dee rolls her eyes at my lie, her hand falling away but her grin still in place.

"Ok. It's late. You should get some sleep." My dad calls, and I nod, even though I can't see him.

"Ok. Night," I call, and I hear my dad mumble good night as he walks away.

"Fuck," I whisper, grinning down at Dee, and she nods in agreement. "Are you ok?" I ask quietly, and again, she nods.

I stare at her for a minute, her dark hair splayed out on my pillow, her big dark eyes bright, her cheeks flushed pink, and her lips puffier than usual.

Reaching out, I run my thumb over her lip. "Stay with me tonight?"

She studies me for a moment as she considers my words before giving me a small nod, and my shoulders relax.

Thank fuck. I want every minute I can have with her before she leaves.

Pushing that depressive thought aside, I slowly ease from her even as I lean down and press my lips to hers.

I take my time kissing her and eventually drag my satisfied arse up, excusing myself to have a quick wash after getting rid of the very full condom hanging from my limp dick.

I return to Dee, who is looking a little awkward, so I wrap her in my bedsheet and lead her out of the room into my dark house, and show her the bathroom and toilet, leaving her to clean up while I grab us a drink.

It's not long before we are back in my room, curled up together in my bed, and I have to admit, I'm really fucking happy right now.

The silence between us is comfortable as I draw circles on her upper arms, loving how relaxed she seems with me now. I have questions I want answers to, though, and since we only have a short time left before she leaves, I hope like hell she doesn't turn to ice on me again when I ask them. I want to keep this version of her, but I really want her to open up more to me, so I break the silence.

"What's your real name?" I ask, and Dee shifts on my chest, her head angling up so she can look at me. "Everyone calls you Dee. But Travis calls you Ell. Is Dee like your middle name or something?"

Dee remains still for a few beats, and I think she isn't going to respond, but then she shakes her head.

"Is Dee a nickname then?"

Her expression morphs into a maybe as she shrugs, confusing me even more. I chuckle.

"Are you ever going to tell me?"

Again she shrugs, but her face looks sincere and sweet so I can't even be mad.

"It would mean a lot to me to know it," I state, offering her a small smile, and she matches it.

"You wanted to speak earlier. You opened your mouth to. Then got mad when you couldn't." I remind her and her smile falls. "I was under the impression that you don't speak because you choose not to. A way for you to control things. But it didn't feel like that. If you wanted to speak to me, you would have. I think." My lips thin as I remember how frustrated she seemed to get with herself, slapping her hands down on the bed when she couldn't get the words out. "Are you scared to talk to me?"

Her breathing increases even as she shrugs and nods, but then shakes her head.

"Why are you scared to talk to me?"

Again, she shrugs, and I frown.

"Does it feel too intimate?"

Her eyes flare a little, and I feel like I've hit the nail on the head, but she shrugs again. Maybe she doesn't know why she can't find the ability to speak out loud to me.

I shift then, rolling to my side so we are face to face. Nose to nose.

"Tonight has been a lot for you, hasn't it?"

When she gives me a slight nod, I continue.

"It was brave of you to come here. To show me your scars." I run my fingers over the raised flesh of one of those scars on her arm. "To trust me enough to give me your virginity." I reach around her and draw her closer, pressing my lips to hers in a brief kiss. "If you ever decide to share your voice with me, I want you to know that I will treasure that sacred moment."

Her eyes glass over then, and she tries to hide it by claiming my lips again. I let her. I don't want to push her. As far as I'm concerned, this thing between us has exploded today, and it's been a lot for both of us.

It's been good. Really fucking good. But a lot.

12

DEE

Feeling safe in someone's arms isn't something I thought I'd ever feel, yet here I am, in Jared's arms, in his bed, after giving him my virginity.

I thought I'd feel different. Like it would be a life-changing moment where I'd finally grow up and be a woman.

I'm still the same person I was before. Just now, I have this needy ache inside me that wants more.

More of Jared. More of his dick. More of his kisses.

Just more.

Which is a problem.

Now, in the morning hours of Tuesday, I do a day count, and calculate that I turn eighteen in a week and a half.

A week and a half!

That's all I have with Jared.

A week and a half.

Fuck. How am I ever going to be able to walk away?

I'd nearly spoken out loud to him last night until I realised I couldn't. I don't know why. It was fear that stopped me, which fucking surprised me. I am in control of my voice, so why wouldn't it just come?

Jared has seen me at my most vulnerable. He hasn't hurt me. He hasn't used me. In fact, he seems to want me as much as I want him. So why the hell can I give him every vulnerable part of myself but my voice?

This is what has kept me awake for a long time after Jared fell asleep, our bodies tangled together in the serenity of his bed.

So many times I wanted to wake him and speak to him with my actual voice. But I just couldn't go through with it. I wanted to tell him my name. Say it out loud instead of writing it in text. I worked myself up to it so many times, and yet I just couldn't bring myself to wake him and say the word.

So, like a coward, while he slept, I tried something else. Something I figure was a small step toward what I wanted. I cleared my throat and spoke the words to him while he slept.

"My name is Elodie."

I'm always surprised by how husky my voice is. I don't remember it being that way when I was little, so I figure it must be because I rarely use it.

I have to use it for my side hustle, and I used it when I called emergency services after the car Jared pushed me out of went over that cliff. And yeah, I whispered a threat to Griffin Marx the other night, but other than that, my voice remains locked tight.

I can hear Jared's parents awake beyond his bedroom door, and I realise that perhaps I should have bailed before they woke. I've been awake for most of the night anyway, so I could have.

The chiming of a phone alarm makes me jump, and Jared shifts under me, groaning and stretching out to turn it off before shifting back to tug me close.

"Good morning Elodie," he mumbles into my hair, and I stiffen.

What did he just say?

His chuckle rumbles in his chest, and he presses his lips to the top of my head.

"Don't freak out. I may have heard you, but it doesn't have to be a bad thing." He strokes my hair back off my forehead before tilting my head up to lock eyes with me. "Elodie is a beautiful name, and fuck, your voice is sexy as fuck."

I roll my eyes and a grin spreads his kissable lips wide.

"I know you didn't mean for me to hear that. So if you want, I can pretend that I didn't hear, and you can tell me your name when you're ready."

I give him a small nod, knowing that I do want that. I want to tell him and share that moment with him. I'm about to open my mouth to say the words, suddenly feeling ready, but he shifts, rolling out of bed and mumbling something about breakfast.

I don't want to think about breakfast, or school, or the fact that Cynthia will be realising now that I didn't come home last night. I don't want to think about any of it. I just want to tell Jared my name. Face to face. No more fucking fear.

I sit up and move out of his bed, grabbing my clothes and dressing as Jared talks about breakfast options. I don't really hear him, my mind too consumed.

Tell him Dee. Say the words. Face to face so he can see my lips move, and I can see how he reacts. Just say the fucking words!

"You coming?" he asks with his hand on his door handle as I finish buttoning my shorts.

I shake my head.

Frowning, Jared takes a step away from his door. "Don't worry about my parents. They will be fine with this."

I shake my head again, stepping back and sitting my arse on his mattress.

"Dee? They are cool. They won't make a big deal out of you being here. I promise." He steps up to the bed, and I reach out and take his hand, tugging him down so he knows I want him to sit too.

"What's going on?" he asks, sitting next to me, and we angle ourselves towards each other.

I open my mouth to speak, and his brows shoot up.

Then I close my mouth and frown.

Just fucking speak, damn it.

"It's ok, Dee. You don't have to. I know I've been pressuring you since your first day at school, but that's because I'm a fucking prick. I probably don't even deserve to hear your beautiful voice."

I clear my throat, and he falls silent, his blue gaze shifting from my eyes to my lips.

He wants this. I want this. Just do it.

"My name is Elodie."

His face.

Holy shit, his face.

His brows shoot high, almost off his forehead, even as his face lights up and his lips shift into the most intoxicating smile.

"Hi Elodie," he whispers, and I can't hide my grin.

I also can't hide how he makes me feel, and I lunge at him, claiming his lips. Jared grips my arse, giving a little squeeze before I find myself straddling his lap and we begin to get lost in each other.

"Jared, hurry up or you'll be late."

I recognise the female voice as Jared's mum, who I met at the hospital. Our lips freeze mid-kiss, and Jared grins and groans at the same time before pulling back from me.

"I'd rather spend the day getting lost with you than face the world."

I grin and nod, because yeah, that sounds good, but I also gesture my head toward his door, because we can't do that. I might be out of here by the end of next week, but Jared has to finish school. Keep going with his life, so he needs to go to school.

Reluctantly, I let Jared lead me out of his bedroom, and we enter the living area to his dad sitting at the table sipping on a coffee and his mum on the phone, her eyes a little wide as she spots us. Or rather. Me.

"Yes, Cynthia. Dee is here."

Jared squeezes my hand, shooting a smile over his shoulder at me as he leads me to the table.

"Good morning, Dee," his dad says, smiling up from his coffee while Jared's mum finishes the phone call.

I give his dad a timid wave and sit where Jared directs as he makes his way to the pantry.

"Dee, Cynthia said she will be over soon with your bag and uniform," Jared's mum states, offering me a strained smile, and I nod and give her a small smile in return.

"What cereal do you like?" Jared asks from the pantry. "Coco Pops, Corn Flakes, or Froot Loops?"

All eyes turn to me for a reaction, so I mouth *'Froot Loops'* and duck my head, not liking the attention.

"Froot Loops it is." Jared nods, gathering up the bowls and milk before returning to the table.

While Jared takes his seat next to me and we work together, silently preparing and starting to eat our breakfast, I keep my eyes cast low, knowing his parents are watching right now.

I know what they are thinking.

Who is this strange girl that doesn't talk?

Why is she in my house?

What does our son see in her?

Jared puts his phone on the table between us, and he scrolls through TikTok with the volume down, showing me the ones of his mate, Simon, which are pretty funny. Meanwhile, his parents eventually start chatting away, and Jared's dad rinses his mug in the sink before he turns on the radio.

I really wish he hadn't done that.

"Police are still asking residents of Timber Valley not to panic. The four new murders over night still aren't considered that of a serial killer."

I stiffen at the news reporter's words, and Jared stills next to me, his spoon halfway to his mouth.

"Oh, my goodness. More murders. What's going on in our sleepy little town?" Jared's mum sounds worried, and I'd like to assure her that unless she's involved in crimes against children, then she'll be ok.

Of course I don't.

"It is a concern," Jared's dad rumbles, frowning.

I can see Jared staring at me out of the corner of my eye, but I keep my focus on eating my Froot Loops, because I know he's going to be pissed that I went on a killing spree without him again.

It's not long before the doorbell rings, Cynthia inviting herself inside to see me, my bag and uniform hanging from her arm. She looks a little annoyed, but she doesn't say anything, just hands me my things and politely tells me to come to her office at lunchtime.

Great.

I dash down the hall to Jared's room to get dressed while Jared's parents are busy seeing her back out, and I start getting changed, trying to ignore Jared's glare as he closes us in.

"Really? Last night? You did that before you came here?"

I shrug, tugging off my cropped t-shirt in the hopes that the sight of my bra might distract him.

It does for like five seconds.

"Why didn't you ask me to drive you?"

I shrug, focusing on getting changed.

"Damn it, Elodie!"

My eyes snap up to his, and he grins.

"That got your fucking attention."

I flip him off.

"Answer my question. Why didn't you ask me to drive you?"

Sighing, I take my phone out and tap out a response. I can see by the expression on Jared's face that he's disappointed I'm not speaking the words aloud, but just because I've shared my voice with him doesn't mean it changes who I am. I'm just not ready to be a vocal person.

Holding my phone up, he reads my words.

'I don't want you involved.'

He chuckles. "It's a bit late for that."

I shake my head, and Jared nods his.

"Yeah, it *is* too late for that. I killed a man, on purpose, Dee. To save you. And I'll fucking do it again if it means you are safe."

Sighing, I tap out another response and show him.

'I've made a new deal with Griffin. You don't have to work for him anymore.'

Jared shrugs. "Doesn't matter. If you're involved, then I'm involved. It's as simple as that. Besides, I know the Marx crew are criminals, but at least they have morals. Some of the things they are working towards are things I can get behind."

I shake my head at him, and he grins, stepping up to me.

"No more jobs without me. Let me help you. Let me spend every last minute we can find together."

His blue eyes dance between mine, and I feel the sincerity in his tone. He just wants more time. Just like I do.

I give in, letting him win this argument, and we come together for a heavy petting session before we drag ourselves apart and finish getting ready for school.

Jared drives us, and we walk in hand in hand, prying eyes watching us as we make our way to our lockers and classes.

I have double Media with Lexi this morning, and I don't even bother with the work, my mind too preoccupied with everything that's happened over the last few days. Especially last night.

She doesn't smile when she sees me. But still sits next to me and works quietly.

That is, until she can't seem to hold in her thoughts anymore.

"Are you still leaving next week?"

Sighing, I consider just walking out of the classroom. I can't be bothered having an argument with the girl Jared used to be head over heels for, but I get the feeling she'd just follow me out and pester me, anyway.

Turning, I give her a nod, and she rolls her eyes.

"You're going to break his heart," she whisper-yells, clearly angry. "Have you even noticed how *into you* he is?"

Maybe I should just tell her. A partial truth, at least.

Sighing, I take out my phone and write my message before showing her.

'If I don't leave with Travis, then he's likely to get killed because of the foster family he's living with. They are bad people, and he deserves a better life.'

As Lexi reads over my words, her glare softens to worry, and her blue eyes dart up to mine.

"It's that serious?" she asks, and I nod before tapping out a response.

'I like it here. I like the Rogans, and even this stuffy school.

Hell, even you seem ok. But it's not safe. Probably not for any of you, but definitely not for Travis. He's stuck in the middle of something bad, and if I can't get him to leave, then he's gonna end up dead.'

"He didn't turn up to community service yesterday." Lexi frowns, shaking her head. "He's rarely a no show. And he usually messages me if he can't make it for some reason. He's ok, right?"

I frown this time. I haven't spoken to him since he came to the Rogans' for dinner on Sunday night. That's only a couple of days. Not even. So surely nothing has happened.

Moving my attention to my phone, I open the Instagram app and the messages.

@hush_tiny_dancer
Hey Trav. Why weren't you at community service yesterday?

I stare at my phone, waiting for a response, but it never comes.

Not while I'm staring at my phone in Media. Not at recess when Jared holds my hand and assures me that my brother is ok, even though he doesn't know. And not in English when I shrug off Jared's attempts at playing Hangman with me again.

By lunch time, I'm beyond worried, and I storm through the school passages to Cynthia's office.

I don't bother telling the secretary that I'm there to see the principal. I just storm past her and shove the office door open.

Cynthia is on the phone, and when she sees me, she sighs and quickly ends the call.

"What is it about my foster children barging in here like they own the place?" she mutters, standing from her desk to round it and stand before me.

I hold my phone up, surprising her, and she reads my words.

'Why didn't Travis turn up to community service yesterday?'

Frowning, Cynthia glances at me past my phone.

"He called in sick. In fact, he must still be unwell because he's not coming in today either."

I turn my gaze back to my phone, putting my words into text before holding it back up.

'Did Travis make the call?'

Frowning again, Cynthia shakes her head. "No. His foster mother did."

My lips thin as my fear spikes.

Travis is an independent guy. He would never get his mum to call for him.

Returning my focus back to my phone, I tap out my words and show Cynthia.

'Can you please call him and check with him and not his mum, that he's ok?'

"Of course," Cynthia nods, picking up on my concern. She moves around her desk, taking out her phone, and taps a few things before pressing it to her ear.

I should have asked Travis for his phone number. I didn't because I wanted to give him the space he needs to make the decision to leave with me. I could have easily found it myself, but I haven't because I wanted to remove the temptation to call him, worried I'd cave and annoy him too much.

"Travis. Hi, it's Cynthia Rogan." She smiles as she talks and then shakes her head. "Oh no, everything is fine. Dee is fine." Her eyes dart to me. "Your mother called in sick for you yesterday and today, so I wanted to make sure everything is ok." She nods as she listens. "Just a stomach bug. Ok. Well, make sure you—"

Cynthia's words get cut off when I snatch the phone from her.

"Travis?"

Nothing but silence meets my ear, and I ignore the gasp that flies from Cynthia as I speak again.

"Travis?"

"Ell?" His voice is a whisper, but I'm so happy to hear it.

"What's going on? Has something happened?" I rush out, but still he doesn't answer my question.

"Shit, Ell. You're talking?"

"Answer me, Travis! Has something happened? We can leave today. We don't have to wait until next week. We can figure it out."

"Calm down. Everything is fine." He reassures me in a hushed tone, but I'm not buying it.

"Then why didn't you turn up?" I ask, avoiding eye contact with Cynthia.

"I can't talk right now," he whispers, and I know everything isn't alright. Someone's there. His foster mum, maybe? Bianca Kerr.

"I have to go, Mrs Rogan. Thanks for checking on me." He speaks louder this time. "I'll stay in bed and get plenty of rest."

Oh no. He really can't talk.

"Shit, Trav. What can I do?" I ask.

"Nothing Mrs Rogan. See you in a few days."

The line goes dead then, and I stare at Cynthia's phone like it scolded me.

"Dee?"

Cynthia's voice reminds me that I'm not alone, and that she just heard me speak.

Shit.

13

JARED

*D*ee has been distracted all day. She's worried about her brother, convinced something is going on. Something involving his foster mum.

It's put a dampener on our time together today, after the epic night we had, and I hate that it's pissing me off. Because that's just selfish. Her brother could very well be in danger.

I sent Trav a couple of vague messages at lunchtime, but he hasn't responded, and I haven't told Dee. Because that's unlike him and it will just cause her more worry.

Deciding to change tactics, I send Trav another message, but this one different, asking for some green apple, which is code for E.

Travis knows me. He knows I'm not into that shit, so hopefully he sees it and knows it means I need to speak with him.

A quick message to Griffin hasn't told me anything either, because as far as he knows, there's been no new developments.

Dee was going to ditch dance after school, but I drove her there anyway and insisted she go inside. If there's one thing

I've learned about Dee and dancing, it's that it can be thera-peutic. Perhaps it's what she needs to help get her out of her head.

Ruby is there with Caleb again, and after the girls move into the studio, Caleb admits to me that Ruby's parents' funeral is tomorrow and she doesn't want to go.

It's such a shitty situation. I feel for them, but I'm fucking glad her parents are no longer here, and hopefully with time Ruby is able to move on.

While Dee is in class, my phone vibrates with a new message, and I'm fucking relieved to see who it's from.

Travis Watson
Green apple ready. Where?

I quickly send him my location and hope like hell he can get here fast. When he informs me he'll be here in five, I excuse myself from Caleb and head out of the studio, back to my car.

Even though he said five minutes, it takes Travis ten to get here, and the moment I see his black eye and a busted lip, I know things aren't ok.

"Dude. What the fuck happened?" I ask as he slips into the passenger seat of my car.

"Nothing. You wanted to see me?"

His tone is clipped and his head darts from side to side, his eyes roaming everywhere like he's worried someone will see him.

"Trav. What's going on?"

He blows out a long breath and turns to face me. "Ell spoke to me today. On the phone."

My brows shoot up. She didn't tell me that part.

"Shit, really?"

He nods. "Yeah. Fucking surprised the crap outta me."

"Did it shock you so much that you walked into a fucking door and gave yourself a black eye?"

Trav smirks. "Funny fucker, aren't you?"

"No. Now talk to me, man. What's going on?"

He shakes his head, looking over his shoulder out the window before turning back to me.

"Bianca found out that Ell is in town."

"Bianca?" I ask and he nods.

"Yeah. My foster mum."

I don't know a lot about Trav's family, but I do know that Griffin said they are bad news, and Dee seems concerned about her brother being with them.

I've been to his house a few times now, and never once have I seen his mum. Or his dad, for that matter. Travis, his older foster brother and sister seem to be there most of the time, and I guess I assumed his parents worked, but fuck, that's a pretty shitty house they live in. If they both worked, wouldn't it be nicer?

Then I remember how they have a basement full of the weed they grow and sell. Maybe that house is just a grow house, and not their real residence?

"So she found out your real sister is here, and what, she gave you a black eye?"

"Something like that," he mumbles, and I frown.

"That doesn't make sense, man. Why would she do that?"

"She thinks I asked Ell to come here. Thinks I've been going behind her back and because she's paranoid as fuck, now she's got it in her head that I'm working for the cops or something. Fucking crazy bitch."

"Are you safe with them?"

My question causes him to stop looking around like someone is about to jump out of thin air, and he shrugs.

"Maybe not as safe as I first thought."

"Fuck," I hiss, leaning back in my seat and shaking my

head. "Don't go back. Come with me. You can stay at mine. You don't need to go back."

Travis shakes his head. "Nah, I can't leave Cassie."

"Your foster sister?"

He nods. "She's beginning to see that things aren't what they seem, and she started asking questions. My older brother, Adam, has her locked in the house. At this stage, I'm all she's got. I'm just trying to figure out a way to get her out. Once I do that, then fuck. I think I will have to run with Ell."

My heart sinks.

No.

I don't want her to leave.

Don't think about it now.

"What about Griffin? He said you could join them instead. Can't you do that? He will protect you."

Travis chuckles. "He says he'll protect me, but he won't. As soon as Ell has her back turned, that fucker will slit my fucking throat."

I shake my head. "No. Griffin isn't like that."

"No offense, Crowley, but what the fuck would you know?"

"I've spent some time with Griffin. He doesn't sound like the monster you're making him out to be."

"Yeah, well, you don't know what he and his brothers are capable of. Or even his cousin. That Devon prick is a fucking psycho."

I have to agree with that. I've met Griffin's cousin, Devon. He's one scary motherfucker.

"Look, I gotta go. But do me a favour. Make sure Ell doesn't come for me. And make sure she leaves, sooner rather than later. She's in real danger if she stays."

Travis leaps out of the car then, and before I can even process his words, he's gone.

What the actual fuck.

This is way more serious than I first thought. I had no idea all of this organised crime was happening under our noses. I knew Trav's foster family dealt drugs, but I didn't think they were like big drug lords or anything.

Maybe they are.

Fuck.

Checking the time, I see that Dee only has ten minutes left of her class, so I open up my phone contacts and call Griffin.

"Crow. I'm busy. Make it quick."

I roll my eyes. He's probably busy fucking his girl.

"Things have escalated in the Kerr household. Cassie is being held against her will in the house by the older one, Adam. And Trav had a run in with someone's fist, maybe the mum's, because she found out that Dee is in town."

"Bianca knows about Dee?" Griffin asks.

"That's what Trav says."

"Fuck. I need to call the Angels. Where's Dee now?"

"She's in her dance class."

"Ok. Do *not* leave her side for anything."

This is a given. I feel fucking antsy not having my eyes on her this very second, but also, the need to be near her, with her, is all-consuming.

"I mean, I won't anyway, but does this mean I'm still working for you? Didn't Dee make a new deal with you?"

Griffin chuckles. "Yeah, sure, there's a new deal on the table, but it's not relevant until she comes through on her end. So until then, stay on her. I don't care what you have to do, but you need to be all over her like a rash."

"I can do that." I smirk, my mind wandering to last night and how I got to feel her silky skin. All of it. Inside and out.

"Good. I'll have one of the guys drop a piece off for you later. You need to carry it everywhere you go," he snaps and I frown.

"I can't take a gun to school," I state and he clucks.

"Keep it in your car when you're on school grounds. Everywhere else, it better be on you. Got it?"

"Yeah, I got it. What do I tell Dee? She's gonna know something is going on. She's already suss about Travis."

"She needs to know that Bianca Kerr knows she's here. As for her brother, tell her that Travis is keeping his distance, so he doesn't lead his crazy arse foster mum to her. Honestly, it's probably what he's doing."

We end the call after that, and my heart fucking races with fear for my girl.

She's a skilled assassin. I have no doubt she could hold her own, but not against a barrel pointed at her head. She's not superhuman.

I push my worries down before I go back into the studio, and then climb the stairs just in time for the last few minutes of class.

I glance through the viewing window to see the girls dancing vigorously, almost like they are angry, arms swinging and punching, legs kicking, and their faces contorted in snarls.

"What are they doing?" I ask Caleb, and he stands from the hard plastic chair he was slouched in.

"Miss Adele has them getting their anger out today. She's a top-notch teacher. This is going to help Rubes with her healing."

I nod and lock onto my little dancing assassin. Her brown hair is tied back in a messy ponytail, her cheeks red, and her face contorted in anger.

I'd never realised until I started watching Dee dance that it could be helpful to her mental health. I thought all dancers did was put on those weird tutu things and twirl around, pointing their toes.

I was so fucking wrong.

14

DEE

*D*ance class was… a lot. I've spent the day worrying about my brother, so much so that I felt like I was on the verge of going on a very public killing spree.

Thankfully, Miss Adele's contemporary class was focused on releasing anger and emotion, and I forced myself to expel the enraged spiralling emotions that have consumed me all damn day.

The class has now cleared out and Caleb leads Ruby away as I'm about to step out through the studio door, but I pull up short because Jared's hulking form steps in my path and my eyes widen in confusion as he stalks towards me, causing me to walk backwards into the studio.

Once inside, Jared closes the door, followed by the viewing curtains, before moving to the front of the room and connecting his phone to the speaker.

"You're not done yet," he rasps, and my brows shoot up as I watch him. "I want you to dance for *me* today."

Now my brows practically shoot off my damn head, which I shake, causing his lips to thin in frustration.

"Come on, Dee. Please dance for me."

I study him for a moment. Even though a small smile breaks on his face, it looks strained. I've been distant today. I know that. Probably not a good way to be after what we shared together last night, so maybe he's looking for a connection with me. Maybe this is his way of gaining my attention.

I can do this right? Dance for him. If I can strip the clothes from my body, bare myself and let him feast on me, then surely I can do this.

Giving in, I offer him a small nod and his shoulders drop in relief before he turns his attention to his phone as he speaks.

"I'm choosing 'Lovely' by Billie Eilish again."

When he glances up, I mouth *'why?'*

He presses play, and the captivating piano intro starts to fill the room as his blue gaze darkens before me.

"Because it's hauntingly beautiful, just like you."

Shit. His words cause my knees to weaken, and I feel myself swoon as I watch him approach. When he reaches me, his hand comes up to cup my cheek before he steps around me, keeping his hand on my hip as he moves.

It's just like last time we were in this studio when he played this music for me.

He asked me to promise that I'll never stop dancing. He said I was born to do it.

I'm not sure about the 'born to do it' part, but I do know that I'll never stop dancing. I think I'd rather die.

Now behind me, he slowly wraps his arms around my middle, and just like last time, my eyes fall to our reflection in the mirror, and he speaks the same words.

"Dance Dee." He starts to sway to the music. "Close your eyes and just let go."

My lids fall shut again, his command impossible to deny, and this time when his arms drop away, I don't cry. This time, I open my eyes, catch his hand in mine, and speak quietly. Out loud.

"Stay right here."

His eyes light up at hearing my voice again, and he nods as I start dancing around him, never losing contact with his body, just like I learnt in class not so long ago.

This time, my dance doesn't convey the pain inside me. This time, it conveys something very close to love. And it's directed at him. At Jared.

My fingers graze over his bare arms, my body pressing close to his, before I turn and weave myself around him.

At some point, I realise he's dancing too. Kind of.

His hips sway, and what we are sharing is more of a dance of love and desire than anything else.

Jared's lips catch mine as our hands tangle into each other's hair and my feet leave the floor as he winds my legs around his waist.

The song ends, and starts again, and our lips stay locked as heat and something else rises up between us. Jared breaks the kiss first, pulling back, and I see that his eyes match mine.

They are glassy with emotion.

He shakes his head, his lips parting like he wants to say something, but then he snaps them shut, and keeps his words to himself.

Shit.

I know what he was going to say, because I want to say it, too. I want to tell him that I don't want to leave. I want to tell him I want to stay. For him. For me. For the Rogans who have put themselves out so much for me.

But Travis.

He's not safe.

We can't stay.

We have to leave.

My heart cracks open then. Pain that I've tried to shield

myself from slices through me, and all I can do is hold on to Jared, take his lips again, and hope like hell that when I have to walk away next week, that it doesn't actually kill me.

"Dee," Jared whispers against my lips, easing back to look at me again when the song starts playing for the third time. "I need to tell you something."

Uh-oh. That doesn't sound good.

Jared must be able to tell by my expression what I'm thinking because he chuckles, walking us over to the speaker and he bends and turns the music off, still holding me, wrapped around his body.

"I saw Trav before."

My brows shoot up, and I push back, wriggling against him until he lets me down.

"He's ok, but he can't contact you right now because his foster mum knows you're in town. He's worried about your safety, so you need to keep your distance for a couple of days."

This isn't good. I don't care for my safety in this situation, only Travis'. His mum is a real piece of work, something that not many people know. I know, though. I've done my research on her. Most people that are close to her stay right by her side, or somehow end up dead. There's no in between. Travis is the one in real danger here. Not me.

"Anyway, I spoke to Griffin, and he told me to stay with you at all times," Jared shrugs, smiling about that, "so it looks like you're stuck with me."

I roll my eyes.

"I know. Tough gig, hey?"

I smirk and slap his shoulder as I pass by, heading out of the room.

The smart thing for Trav's safety would be for me to stay away from him for now. That much I can agree to. The last thing I want to do is make things worse for him, so for now, I will bide my time.

Jared drives me home, coming inside for dinner, reminding me that Cynthia invited him over earlier today. When we enter the house, it's loud with chatter, and I realise Cynthia invited all of Rhys' fellas over for dinner, too.

It's probably not a bad thing. It might help Jared to feel more comfortable with his mates here.

Charlotte is here tonight with her girlfriend at her side, and I take a moment to consider if perhaps it's someone's birthday.

"Do they normally have so many people here for dinner?" Jared asks, and I shrug, because hell if I know.

Rhys is surrounded by her four fellas, and they are all talking to an older guy, probably the same age as Cynthia and Will. Maybe a bit younger.

"Oh hey, Mr Foster. What are you doing here?" Jared asks the man, who turns to us and smiles.

"I'm not a teacher anymore, Jared. Call me Tyler."

Jared scrunches his face up. "That's just weird."

Tyler chuckles, and Rhys giggles, her black lips spreading wide.

I study her for a moment, watching how her eyes roam over her four fellas, and then how her gaze shifts to the older guy, Tyler. The same intense heat that she sends towards her four guys is also directed towards the man, and I catch a very brief look of longing that the man returns Rhys' way.

Holy shit.

Now I understand what I'm looking at.

This man is boyfriend number five. The one they speak in hushed tones about. The older guy.

My gaze darts to Cynthia and Will, who don't seem to be concerned, and then back to Rhys, who is no longer smiling at her fellas, but is glaring at me.

Crap. She knows that I know, and if Jared's reaction to the man is any indication, he has no idea that his best mates are sharing Rhys with this man.

It's not really my business, except for the fact that *he* is a grown arse man, and *she* is still under eighteen. And yeah, she turns eighteen next month, but on paper, this is a huge fucking no no. The people that prey on those underage are who I hunt and kill. This is the kind of stuff I'm trying to stop.

But love is love, and I catch another quick glimpse he shoots her, and shit, he loves her. Like really loves her, and she obviously loves him, too.

But could he have groomed her? Could he be manipulating her?

Another look at her boyfriends and I come to the conclusion that there is no way these guys would allow some older creeper to prey on their girl. So I have to assume she's safe, and she wants whatever it is they have going on.

Not wanting to have a cat fight in front of everyone, because I feel like Rhys is seconds away from pouncing on me, I lift my fingers to my lips and imitate doing up a lock and throwing away the key.

She visibly relaxes, giving me a small nod, and I feel like we've just had a moment of bonding or something.

Needing to get out of my dance clothes, I head into the kids' area in the house and beeline for my bedroom. I can sense Jared on my heels, and the idea of him being in my corner, looking out for, and caring for me, sends a thrill of excitement through my veins.

I shouldn't like the way it feels as much as I do. Not when I'm leaving soon.

Any hope of getting a slither of alone time before dinner with Jared is quickly dashed when the boisterous banter of Rhys' boyfriends follows me and Jared, passing by me as one of them, Simon I think, wraps his arm over Jared's shoulders and hauls him along into the small lounge area.

I'm a little disappointed that they've stolen him away from me, but when I see the way the guys start messing about with Jared, dragging him in for bro hugs and talking about footy, he gives them a genuine smile, something he hasn't done much since I came to town, and my heart melts.

It's great to see him smile.

And it's even greater to see him with his mates.

At least when I leave him in pieces next week, they will be there to pick him up and help him heal.

15

JARED

*B*eing around my mates feels great. I've missed them over the past months, what with them being pussy whipped by Rhys George, and me... well, I've been a fucking head case. Let's just leave it at that.

Simon drags me down onto the couch in the small lounge area that sits in the middle of the kids' bedrooms, and Bossi flops down next to me, grinning as Garrett and Rhys try to connect a phone to the speaker.

We chat for a bit, but then Gaz shooshes us, and we fall silent as a voice comes through the speaker.

"Welcome to another episode of Breaking the Silence. I am Hush, and today I'm following up on the disgusting predators hiding in the regional community of Timber Valley. As with all of my podcasts, the names of victims and some people have been changed to protect their identity, but the known names of the abusers and criminals will remain the same."

I've heard this podcast before. It's all the talk of the town right now, recorded by an anonymous girl who spills the

143

heinous details of people's stories who are unable to speak their truth because it will expose them. She also uses her TikTok account to post information about the podcast stories, which includes images of the perpetrators in the hopes of ruining their reputation and helping the authorities to catch them.

Even though I've heard the podcast before, now is the first time that recognition hits me square in the face. It's the voice. A voice I've only heard a couple of times but is so ingrained in my head and heart that it's like a beacon to me.

Then I recall what she said.

"Welcome to another episode of Breaking the Silence. I am Hush..."

Breaking the Silence?

Hush?

My head whips over my shoulder so fast that Dee, who is still standing in her doorway, isn't able to wipe the look of 'deer in headlights' from her expression in time.

Of course.

Breaking the Silence has a double meaning. Not only is it breaking the silence and divulging the dirty secrets of the scum here in Australia, but when she does this podcast, she is using her voice. It's probably the only time she uses her voice.

Breaking *her* Silence.

Shit. And Hush?

How the fuck didn't I pick up on that sooner?

Dee dashes into her room, quietly closing the door, and I stand, happy that my mates are too enthralled in the podcast to worry about asking where I'm going.

I don't even bother knocking on Dee's door, opening it quietly and slipping inside.

She's standing with her back to me, looking out the

window of her small bedroom, and I have no doubt she can see my reflection as I stand behind her.

"Hush," I whisper. "Not just your assassin name, but your podcast name, too."

She doesn't say anything. Not that I expected her to. She tries to control the narrative by remaining silent. Unfortunately for her, I know her game, and I'm not going to give up just because she feels like ignoring me.

"You're like a modern-day vigilante. Always looking out for other people and making sure they know someone cares. You help them get revenge and closure." I step up closer, gripping Dee's shoulders, and slowly turn her to face me.

Her eyes betray her worry, so I cup her cheek and run my thumb over her lips, hoping she feels how much I care about her.

"You do all of this for other people. No one pays you to do the podcast, do they?" She doesn't respond, but that's ok. I already know that's what's happening here. "But you do it anyway, because you care. You care about getting justice for other people. Mainly younger women and those underage. People who don't have the power to speak out."

This time I bring my other hand up to cup her face, making sure she has nowhere else to look but at me.

"You're amazing."

She shakes her head in my hold and tries to step away, but I latch onto her shoulders, not letting her escape.

"Yes, you are, Elodie."

She stops struggling when I say her real name, almost as if she likes hearing it fall from my lips.

"How many more secrets do you have?"

Her face falls and her breathing quickens, all signs that she sure as shit has more secrets.

"How many?"

Biting her lower lip, Dee raises her hand and lifts her pointer finger.

"One?" I ask, and she nods. "Will you share it with me?"

Her shoulders shrink as she tries to close herself off, but I don't let go of her. I'll never let go of her, even when she leaves. This beautiful creature right here will forever own my soul.

"How about we trade? I'll tell you something. Anything you want, and in return, you tell me your one last secret."

Dee frowns as she considers this before giving me a nod.

Shit.

I don't really have any more secrets to share with her. But maybe there is something she wants to learn about me.

"What do you want to know?" I ask, and she shoots me a small smile, stepping away from my now loose grip before taking a seat on her bed.

I follow, needing to be close to her, touching her every fucking second.

Taking her phone out, Dee puts her words in text and then turns the screen to me.

Tell me what you know about Abbey.'

I frown. "What? You want to know about Abbey?"

She nods.

"But that's not my secret."

She shrugs and shakes her phone, reiterating what she wants.

"So if I tell you about Abbey, you'll tell me your one last secret?"

She nods, so I nod, a little confused, but if that's what she wants, I'll give it to her.

"So me, Abs, Lex and Marcus grew up together. We could hardly be separated back when we were kids. I thought we'd always be friends, but when Lexi's home life imploded, Abbey, who was her best friend at the time, turned on her."

My mind flits back to last year, when all that shit happened to Lex. Abbey was right there with her at first, giving her support. Consumed with worry over Lexi's safety. Then something changed. She started avoiding Lexi's calls. Wouldn't reply to her text messages and emails. It was out of fucking character. That's for sure.

"We couldn't make sense of it at the time. Firstly, it's not in Abbey's nature to be a nasty bitch. She's probably the most innocent of us all. Her family is like super religious, and she's always had a little bit of a goody two-shoes complex about her. But last year she came out of her shell a little more. She was more social. Didn't seem so different from the rest of us."

I remember how Abbey used to have a crush on me. It made me uncomfortable, because even though she's a pretty girl, I just never liked her in *that* way. Lexi, though? Well, that's a different story. One Dee doesn't need to hear.

"When all the shit with Lexi's family started going down, Abbey had already been seeing Daniel Stone. I never liked the prick. Such a fucking know it all, thinks he's better than everyone else kind of guy, but he seemed to treat Abs well and she seemed happy. Until something changed."

I roll my tongue in my mouth as I remember finding out some of the details that had been happening. It fucking pisses me off.

"At first we didn't know what was going on. Abbey sided with Tasha, a girl that doesn't live in Timber Valley anymore, but it turns out that she was secretly seeing Lexi's brother. The one who put me in hospital."

Dee's dark gaze flares with anger, and I forcefully swallow a raging lump in my throat before her dainty hand slips into mine, giving it a squeeze.

Fuck, I adore this chick.

"Anyway," I continue. "Tasha had been blackmailing Abbey, forcing her to take Tasha's side, and it took a while for us to find out what Tasha was holding over Abbey, but when we did find out... well, it's too fucking crazy to believe."

Shaking my head, I think back to those terrifying weeks that Lexi had been fighting to survive against her brother and dad. I'm glad we were able to be there for her, giving her support. Staying with her when she had no one else. Watching her back.

Fuck. I'm even glad that Ayden came into her life.

He fucking saved her. If he hadn't got her out of that house of horrors when he did, then I'm not sure Lexi would be alive today.

Shaking myself out of my thoughts, I return my focus back to Abbey's story.

"So apparently Abbey's parents found her and Daniel fucking. Doesn't sound that bad, right? Probably embarrassing as fuck, and some parental lectures would have to be sat through. But that isn't what happened." I drag my free hand through my hair, still hardly believing what I'm about to say.

"Somehow, Abbey's parents and Daniel's parents came to an agreement that Abbey and Daniel should get married after they graduate University, but only if Abbey sticks to some fucking suffocating rules. And if she doesn't, they will move the wedding date up and see them married sooner. Like as soon as they finish high school, or even before that. Like when Abbey turns eighteen."

I shake my head in disbelief, fucking confused why they are treating their daughter that way.

"They clearly know Abbey and Daniel don't want to get married but are forcing this on them and blackmailing them with compliance. So Abbey isn't allowed to associate with Lexi. She has to keep her grades up and stay out of trouble, and if she doesn't comply, they will marry her off to that prick sooner. It's too fucked up to believe. We don't have arranged marriages in Australia. At least not that I've heard of."

Dee taps out something on her phone and shows me.

'Why is Daniel so mean to Abbey?'

My shoulders drop. "I hate that Daniel is still fucking breathing. He's been hurting her, and there's nothing I can do to help her. Mainly because she asked us to keep out of it." I shake my head in anger. "Daniel turned into a raging psycho after he was forced into the engagement with Abbey. He says she's ruined his life and seems to think that now she is a possession to be used as he wishes. He seems to be holding their marriage over her head as well, making sure she submits or he'll tell her parents that she's not, which will, in turn, move the wedding up sooner."

Dee nods slowly, her eyes dropping to my chest as she thinks over what I've told her.

"Why did you want to know about Abbey?" I ask, and her chocolate gaze returns to mine as she shrugs.

I grin. "Is the vigilante in you going to do something to help her?"

She grins back and shrugs.

"The key to helping her is finding out why her olds have such a strong hold on her. Why the fuck they think it's ok to force the marriage. And what the fuck they get out of it?"

Dee nods in agreement, and I know that even when she leaves this town next week, she will still make it her mission to try to help Abbey.

Even though the thought of Dee leaving makes my gut churn, the idea of her still helping people, potentially in my community, is something I can happily support.

As long as she remains safe.

"Ok, I told you a secret. Granted, it's not *my* secret to tell, but it's what you agreed to."

Dee silently giggles, giving me a nod before her face falls, and she licks her lips.

Shit.

Is she going to speak again?

Her lips part, but then snap shut, so I squeeze her hand, offering my support.

She tries again, licking her lips before parting them, and speaks the words I sure as shit didn't expect.

"I killed Travis' mum."

16

DEE

*T*he moment I drop that bomb of a secret, Cynthia calls us out for dinner, so like the coward I am, I bolt.

I'm a little annoyed that I didn't get changed while Jared told me about Abbey, finding myself so engrossed with the mystery that surrounds her. So while everyone sits at the table in comfort, I'm still in my leotard, which is riding up my arse, and my dance tights are digging into my waist.

My saving grace is that I was able to throw a baggy black t-shirt over the top as I rushed out of my bedroom, so it doesn't look like I'm sitting at the dinner table in a fucking swimsuit, but I do look like I don't have any pants on.

Just great!

Jared is tense sitting next to me as we eat. He hasn't said anything about my revelation, and I just know he's questioning his choices right now.

He knew I killed for coin, but now he knows that I'm a murderer, too. And let me tell you, there is a difference between being a killer and being a murderer.

A killer, or in my case, an assassin, ends lives for the

purpose of completing a job and earning money. A murderer, though, they kill for motive. Revenge. Self-gratification.

So now that Jared knows, I'm sure he must be hating on me. Freaking the hell out, wondering how he got tangled up in the mess that is my life.

I avoid looking at him as we eat. Well, everyone else eats. I pick at my food, my appetite practically non-existent all damn day.

A firm grip on my knee under the table breaks my thoughts, and I realise that my leg was jittery, jigging up and down. I don't look at Jared, but his hand shifts from my now motionless knee to my hand under the table, and links fingers with mine.

Damn.

That simple act. That delicate touch of care breaks down the walls I'd started erecting the moment I fled from my room.

I sneak a glance at Jared, not able to stop the pull he has on me, and his ocean eyes catch mine, before he shoots me a wink.

Jesus. How can a wink mean so much?

What is happening to me?

Wearing a faint smirk, Jared leans in and whispers in my ear. "Why aren't you eating?"

I shrug, drawing my gaze to my very full plate, and he chuckles quietly.

"Here, let me help." He offers, and I frown, wondering what the hell he's talking about.

Leaning closer, he picks up my fork with his free hand, scoops up some mashed potato, and lifts it to my lips.

My eyes widen, locking with his again, and the chatter down this end of the table falls quiet. My cheeks burn red, knowing eyes are on us, but I keep my gaze trained on Jared's, parting my lips and accepting the food.

"Look, Cherry. He likes to feed his girl, too."

My eyes dart up to Simon and Rhys sitting across from us as they watch on, both smiling even as Simon feeds Rhys food. I've noticed that he does that a lot, and the other guys seem ok with it.

I'm not sure why he calls her Cherry. I don't even know if I want to know why he calls her that, to be honest, because when it comes to Rhys, everything is about sex.

Not liking the attention on me, I take the fork from Jared's grip and place it back on the table. A low growl rumbles in Jared's chest, and his eyes turn to slits.

"Dee, if you don't eat, then I'll feed you," he threatens quietly. "You decide."

I shoot him a glare, which just makes him smirk in that sexy way that has my heart fluttering.

Pretending like his words haven't affected me, I roll my eyes, and he mouths the word, 'eat.'

So I do. A little. I play with the peas on my plate more than anything.

The chatter around the table picks up again, so Jared takes advantage of that, leaning back in to whisper against my ear.

"Stop freaking out. Your secret is safe with me."

I dart a glare at him. Does he really think that's my problem? That he will tell someone.

Why the fuck isn't he freaking out about this?

Gripping the side of his shirt, I draw him closer and press my lips to his ear, and slowly draw out my words in a hushed whisper.

"I'm a killer, Jared. A murderer. Why aren't you disgusted by that?"

Jared pulls back and his brows shoot up. "Why would I be?"

My mouth drops open at his words because he fucking should be.

That's when I notice things have fallen quiet again down this end of the table, and I glance around to see Rhys grinning at me while her fellas just stare.

I shoot her a frown and her grin spreads wider as she leans closer across the table.

"You spoke to Jared." She nods quietly. "I mean, I didn't hear it, but you whispered something to him. With. Your. Voice."

Shit.

SHIT!

I shake my head, and she sits back in her seat, crossing her arms over her chest, wearing a smug as fuck grin. "Yeah, you did. I saw."

"You're imagining things, George." Jared jumps in to try and save me, making me want to slap my lips on his in thanks, but I don't take my eyes off Rhys.

"It's sweet that you're trying to cover for her." Rhys giggles, and Simon nods next to her. Shit, did they all see? "What did she whisper?" Rhys asks, directing her question to Jared.

"She said her foster sister is delusional," Jared mocks and his mates chuckle. I'm expecting her to get shitty about them laughing, but she doesn't.

"Was she talking dirty to you?" Rhys asks him, and I roll my eyes at her even though she's giving Jared all the attention.

"She doesn't speak, George. How about you drop it?"

OMG I love this guy.

Wait! What?

"She *didn't* speak, you mean. Because she *does* now. I saw her." Rhys nods, proud as punch at her discovery.

"Rhys, can I have a word, please?" Cynthia's voice

surprises us all, coming from behind me, and Rhys shoots Cynthia a 'really' look over my head before getting up in a huff from the table. They leave the room, and everyone returns to their meals. Everyone except for me.

I don't know what's happening. Everything has changed, and I'm not sure I like it. I'm struggling to maintain my composure, and hell, even Cynthia witnessed me speaking today when I snatched the phone off her to talk to Travis.

I couldn't help it. My worry about him drove my reaction, and I forgot all about her witnessing me talk.

Rhys and my foster mum re-enter the room a minute later, taking their seats. I ignore Rhys for a bit, chasing peas around on my plate with my fork, but when I finally look up, the smug bitch is wearing a shit-eating-grin.

Ugh. I can't take it.

I stand, flipping her off, and storming from the table and out of the room.

In my bedroom, I rip off the t-shirt, the leotard, and tights before rummaging through my pile of clothes for something to wear.

"Damn. My timing is impeccable."

I spin with a gasp at hearing Jared's voice, and he chuckles as I try to cover up my nakedness.

"Now, now, Dee. I've seen you completely naked, splayed out on my bed with your pretty pink pussy on display. Hell, I've even tasted its fucking delectable sweetness." Jared smirks, stepping closer. "So, why are you covering yourself from me?"

I don't know how to answer that. I just am. Maybe it's an automatic response?

Reaching out, Jared grips my wrist and slowly unravels my arm, giving him a full view of my tits.

"There they are. Fucking perfect," he rasps before tugging me flush with him and slamming his lips into mine.

If there's one way to make me forget my worries, it's this right here with this guy.

Like a monkey, I do a little jump, leaping onto Jared and wrapping my legs around his waist. Now that I'm level with his face, he deepens the kiss, walking us over to my bed where he eases me down, pressing me to the mattress in a delicious way.

The fact that I'm completely naked and he's fully clothed is a real turn on. I'm not sure why, but hell, I think it's how vulnerable I feel.

Can vulnerability be sexy?

Hell, if I know!

"Fuck, Dee," Jared rasps as he breaks the kiss, his hand travelling down my bare hip as he stares into my eyes. "I'm not going to stop caring about you because you kill people. Makes me fucked up, I guess, but I don't care. I only care about *you*. Nothing else matters."

Shit.

His words mean so much. I hadn't realised how much I needed to hear him say that, but knowing he isn't repulsed by me, for killing Travis' mum is everything.

"Wanna tell me what happened with Trav's mum?"

I shrug, knowing I should, but not wanting to break up this little party we've started.

"After," I force out, my voice scratchy.

"After what?" he grins, and I blush.

"After you fuck me."

His mouth drops open and his blue eyes flare even as his hardness, covered by his school pants, grinds between my legs.

"Fucking hell, Dee. Your voice is sexy as fuck, and when you talk like that, all dirty," he beams, "nearly makes a grown man arrive to the party too early."

A giggle bubbles up my throat, and Jared chuckles, shaking his head as he stares at me.

"You're everything, Elodie. Fucking everything."

Jared's words spear me on, and I claim his lips again, grinding myself over his bulge. His hands make quick work of getting rid of his clothes before his lips travel over my flesh, exploring my body.

When noise from Rhys and her fellas filters in from under my door, I briefly worry that Rhys might barge in here wanting answers and pestering me about talking again, but as their voices fade like they are closing themselves inside Rhys' room, I relax again, quickly feeling the fire in my veins as it consumes me. The moment Jared flicks his tongue over my needy clit, I reach for my pillow and slam it over my face.

Feeling less timid about what we are doing now, I chase my orgasm quickly, almost scared that someone may interrupt and I might actually die if we have to stop.

Jared must be able to sense my urgent need, and he adds his fingers, two again I think, stretching me as he curls them up.

My climax hits hard and fast, and I bite the pillow, my cries muffled, and I soar.

Coming on Jared's tongue and fingers is my most favourite thing to do, ever!

After the waves start to ease, Jared tugs the pillow away from my face, his grin filling my vision.

"That was hot." He smirks, brushing my hair back off my face. "I could do that all fucking day."

I grin and whisper, "Get inside me."

"So bossy," he chuckles, bending down to pick up his pants before he tugs a condom free.

I quickly forget all about that when he stands, tugs off his shirt and dumps it on the floor, giving me a view of his naked flesh.

Shit.

He's the hottest thing I've ever seen. I wonder if he goes to the gym to maintain those abs? I haven't noticed him going to, or mentioning, the gym since I've been around, but I guess he maintains it somehow. It doesn't matter, I guess, just as long as I get to touch them, and lick them, and travel down them to that V that sends my eyes to his full hard cock.

"Hurry," I rasp quietly, and he grins wickedly before tearing the condom wrapper open with his teeth.

I'm impatient and needy, so I sit up, reaching for his hard length jutting out from him. Jared gasps at my contact as I wrap my hand firmly around his girth before giving it a pump.

"Fuuuck. Your hand feels so good."

Grinning, I lean forward and flick my tongue over the tip. Jared hisses, his eyes wild as he watches from above. I love the way he's looking at me. Lust drunk and wanton. I don't know a lot about sex, but I do know that I want to do things I never knew were even things until now.

Feeling game, I part my lips and press the head of his cock into the heat of my mouth. Jared's hand fists in my hair, and the tug he gives hurts a little, but not in a bad way. It makes me feel powerful. Like I'm able to make him lose control, so consumed by desire that he can't think straight.

It's liberating.

The last time I had Jared's dick in my mouth was the night he drove us to the lookout. He was angry, aggressive, and I can't say I hated it. I was scared of gagging that night, but I'm not so scared anymore, so I take him in deep until I do gag, and squeeze my eyes tight.

"Fuck, Dee. Eyes on me," he rasps, just like that night when he fucked my mouth against his car. I pry my lids open, my eyes locking onto his heated blue gaze while he keeps thrusting. He doesn't let his cock go as deep as I just took it a moment ago, and as I frown around his dick, he shakes his head. "I don't want to hurt you."

I growl around his cock this time, which causes him to smirk, and he shakes his head, slipping his cock free.

"As fucking heavenly it is to have my dick in this hot little mouth," he grazes his thumb over my bottom lip, "I'd rather sink it in here tonight." He leans forward, gliding his fingers up my inner thigh until they come to my slick heat. "Would you like that? For me to slide inside here," he inserts two fingers, and I moan, "and stretch you wide?"

I nod frantically, so he straightens back up, focusing on his cock and rolling the protection on it, before he returns his attention to me.

"I want you to ride me tonight," he suggests, and hell, I'll do whatever the fuck he wants.

Ok so maybe not *anything*, this is still new to me, but riding him sounds fun.

Jared and I shift around, manoeuvring ourselves in place until he is laying back against my mattress and I'm hovering over his cock.

He bites his lip as he stares up at me, palming my tits as I grip his cock and position it at my entrance. Then, I lower myself down.

I tense up as the stretch bites a bit, and Jared shifts his hands to my hips.

"Easy, Dee. Just take it slow. Don't hurt yourself."

Jared has changed so much since the accident. He's so much more attentive. Caring.

I guess I have changed, too. I've never been so open with another person before.

It's like we finally accepted that we can't fight this thing between us, and our souls have morphed together. I never thought I'd trust Jared like this. Not after he was such an annoying arsehole in the beginning, but I do trust him. And that's big for me.

I let my body adjust to Jared's size before I start moving, practically salivating from the feel of him hitting so deep. It's intoxicating. Jared uses his grip on my hips to help me get a rhythm going, and before I know it, our bodies are working together, building an intense pleasure so deep inside me that I never knew existed.

The sounds of the bustling house beyond my bedroom door fall away as we lose ourselves, and the only reason I know I'm being vocal when I start convulsing around his cock is because he slaps his hand over my mouth until I'm spent.

17

JARED

Fucking Elodie Porter is my favourite thing to do. Nothing will ever top it.

Ever.

After our session in her bed, we go for a walk, needing to get away from the noises coming from Rhys' room.

Thank Christ the twins were watching a cartoon in the theatre room before they went to bed. Poor things would be scarred for life hearing that shit.

I take Dee to Firelane Park, which was the park I picked her up as the 'package' the first night I'd worked for Griffin.

Dee knows why we are here. To talk about Travis' mum and Dee's claim that she killed her.

We sit on the landing at the top of the slide, and Dee takes out her phone and writes out a message before showing me.

There's a lot to say. Too much to say out loud, so I'll do it this way.'

I nod in understanding, knowing that Dee can still choose if and when she wants to speak, and I wait patiently as she puts her words into text, handing her phone to me when she's done.

'Long story short, Trav's mum was an abusive bitch, and my dad was a loyal, decent man. He took what she dished out until what she dished out was too much.

She was beating him that day. Used a frying pan and wouldn't stop. Biggest rage I'd seen her in. She was beating him because he didn't cook Travis dinner but got him takeaway instead. Dad only did that because Trav begged for the fast food and Dad gave in. I'll never remind Travis of that, though. I never want him to feel guilty or blame himself for what happened.

Anyway, his mum came home, found Travis and me eating the burgers and fries and she lost it at my dad. When Travis begged for her to stop, she turned and told him to shut the fuck up, and that she was coming for him next. I knew she meant it. She always did when she said that to us.

I ran and got a knife from the bench block. Stabbed her in the arm in the hopes it would get her off my dad. It worked. She got off him but started coming for me, so I ran, grabbing Trav by the arm on my way past, racing for the front door.

I wasn't fast enough. She grabbed him by his hair and threw him against the wall. It must have knocked him out for a bit because he fell still and quiet, and at first I thought she'd killed him, but I didn't have time to find out when she started towards him with the frying pan raised. I got in front of her with the knife and stabbed her in the belly.

When she leaped away from me, I lost my hold on the knife which was sticking out of her gut. Then she went crazy. She dropped the frypan, pulled the knife from her flesh and lunged for me, slicing it at me. I was able to mostly protect myself by keeping my arms up.'

"Your arms?" I whisper, turning to look at Dee, and she nods, pulling up her sleeve to run her fingers over the scars.

My heart is racing with pain and anger as I try to picture

a little innocent version of Dee, trying to save her brother's life. Her life.

My gaze drops back to the screen to keep reading, but first, I take Dee's hand and link my fingers with hers, not wanting her to ever feel as alone as she must have felt on that awful day.

'When I stabbed her, I must have hit something important because she stopped attacking and tumbled to the floor, groaning. Then, all I could see was the knife on the floor, waiting to be picked up, and all I knew in that moment was that I needed to kill her so she couldn't hurt Travis or my dad again.

So, I picked up the knife. I remember it was slippery in my hand, because of all the blood coming from my arms, but I gripped it tight and straddled her, and when she slowly blinked her eyes open, I struck, stabbing her chest over and over.

I was told later that she had forty-three stab wounds.'

Fuck. Forty-three stab wounds is a lot.

'Travis must have come to during my rage, and when he opened his eyes, all he saw was me killing his mum.

We were separated after that. The police never let us near each other until about a week later. I'll never forget that day. I tried to talk to Travis. Explain what happened, but he told me to stop talking. He said he never wanted to hear my voice again.

So I gave him that. I stopped talking, and then they sent me to a psychiatric facility, and Travis went into the foster system.'

I feel like fucking crying. I hate that they went through that brutality, and were then separated. All those years, Travis never knew what really happened.

"Dee. I'm so sorry," I mumble, biting back my emotions as I pass her phone back before pulling her onto my lap. "Does Travis still not know what happened?"

Shrugging, Dee shifts back and taps out her response on her phone before passing it back to me.

'He knows more, but he apparently repressed the memories.

He's only just started to remember how his mum really treated him. He'll need time, and then maybe one day, if he wants to know my version of that day, I will tell him.'

"Christ. I don't know what to say," I admit, and she shrugs, leaning in close.

"It is what it is. Can't change the past. But I can change Travis' future, which is why I'm here. To try to get him out of this place and into a better life." She takes a moment to clear her throat, her voice still so husky when she talks.

She seems to be thinking of her next words, and my heart races in anticipation of hearing her voice again. I fucking love hearing her speak. I'm so fucking honoured that she shares this part of herself with me now.

"The jobs I do for the Angels and Griffin have allowed me to grow a nest egg in offshore accounts. The Angels helped me set them up. The Australian government would be all over me if they saw the money I make, especially because of my age. When I'm eighteen, it'll be easier for me to be independent without having to avoid the authorities, which is why I've waited until now to come for Travis."

I hate the thought of her leaving, but I get it. She's trying to protect her brother, and there's something noble in that.

"So you do those jobs to get the money? Is that the only reason?" I ask, and she shrugs.

"That and I enjoy getting revenge for someone else who can't manage it." She looks down to her lap at her fidgeting fingers. "I like killing, though. Sometimes too much."

Damn.

I should be freaking out, right?

I should probably be counting the days until she leaves, knowing she's a lethal weapon, but fuck, I'm not. I can't. I don't think there's anything she can do to make me stop wanting her.

We chat for a while there in the dark. I don't think she

realises how much she's using her voice, and I don't mention it, because I'm scared she will lock it away again if I make a big deal about it.

It's nearly ten by the time we wander back to Dee's house. I have a feeling her foster parents are gonna insist I go home, but I'm not leaving Dee. They don't know why, of course. I'm sure they just think I'm a horny teenager. And yeah, I am, but I'd be here regardless of mine and Dee's sexual status.

"Hush." A voice calls quietly from behind us as we're about to turn up the path to Dee's house, and I still, while Dee spins on her heel, ready to pounce.

"Stand down. It's just us." I turn to see the two Angel sisters stalking out of the shadows from across the street.

I want to relax at the sight of them, but I don't know them, or if we can truly trust them.

Dee doesn't attempt to communicate with them other than shooting them a warning glare, and the taller one, Amanda, I think her name is, smirks.

"If looks could kill."

"What do you want?" I ask for Dee, and Amanda takes a moment to eye me, her expression neutral but fucking scary, before she shifts her gaze back to Dee.

"We've just come from visiting Griffin, a little concerned with the sudden spike in the murders in this area. He advised me that you have a new arrangement."

Dee nods.

"Care to fill us in?" the other blonde, Bec, asks.

Dee turns her eyes to her phone, preparing her response before holding it up for the Angel sisters to read.

When they frown, Dee turns her screen to me so I can see too.

You tell me.'

Sighing, Amanda speaks. "Griffin tells us you broke into his house and held him at knifepoint."

My eyes widen and I glance at Dee, who is smirking before she puts her words into text and holds up the phone for the three of us to read.

'I was ambushed at the farmhouse last week. He and his crew were the only ones that knew I'd be there, so there's a big chance he has a mole in his ranks. Jared and I could have died. I won't risk his life, so I made a new deal.'

"Your birthday is next Thursday. You really think you can kill everyone on that list, plus take out the enemies in Griffin's way from claiming full control of Timber Valley in that short time?" Bec asks, and Dee nods, while my jaw practically hits the pavement.

"You shouldn't have done that." Amanda blows out a frustrated breath. "We don't want you dealing with the Kerr gang."

Dee shrugs, tapping out a new response and holding it up. *'My brother is mixed up with those people. He'd be safer if they were dead.'*

"How about we have a word with Griffin? Get him to take the Kerr gang off the table and you just focus on the Carnal Unicorn list. That's still thirteen more kills in just over a week. That's still a lot to ask." Bec offers and Dee shrugs, casting her eyes back down to her phone.

'After tonight, it will only be ten on the Carnal list.'

"What?" I snap. "You're going out tonight?"

Dee nods.

"Who's driving you?" I ask, stepping closer to her, hating that the Angel sisters are watching us.

Dee smiles and points at me.

Frowning, I shoot a worried glance at the Angels before returning my attention back to my girl and speak through clenched teeth. "I thought you didn't want me involved."

Dee leans forward and whispers in my ear. "I don't, but I don't want to be away from you either."

I fucking grin like I've won the lottery, forgetting for a split second there that we aren't alone. I worry about what the Angels will make of Dee whispering to me, but they don't even look shocked. Just annoyed that they had to have this conversation in the first place.

"Fine." Amanda throws her arms up. "Finish off the Carnal list, but please reconsider going after the Kerrs. Griffin's enemies aren't your problem. We can make sure he still upholds his end just for the Carnal list."

Dee eyes the Angels curiously, narrowing her eyes at them.

She's suspicious of their intentions, and she's not afraid to let them know.

This little pocket rocket has more balls than anyone I've ever met.

Even though the Angels seem concerned about her going after the Kerrs, I feel like the Kerrs are the ones that should be concerned. I have a feeling they've never come across someone like Hush before, and they'll be wishing they never had.

18

DEE

I'm still walking on cloud nine after last night. Once the Angels left, and I dealt with Cynthia and Will, who wanted to talk about me and Jared, and me talking on the phone to Travis, I was able to sneak Jared in through my window where we quietly fooled around for a couple of hours before we snuck out and he drove us to Redfield.

I'd already arranged a new car with Griffin, so it was parked where he said it would be, and we swapped cars, driving to my three marks for the night.

They were all straightforward and boring, but because Jared was there, it was exhilarating to kill while he spied on me. I'd actually demanded that he stay outside to keep watch, but I felt his eyes on me, peering through a window or door, his heated gaze taking everything in as I ended each life.

And I liked it.

Those feelings should probably worry me, but I can't find it in me to care how serial killer they seem right now.

Nor could I care when I spotted Jared's lust drunk eyes after each kill, and how hard he was.

Afterwards, we didn't make it far on the way back to Fox

Pines once we swapped back from Griffin's car to Jared's. He had to pull over when I couldn't keep my hands off him, and I fucked him right there in the front seat of his car on the side of the road.

I can't get enough of this guy.

Jared slept in my bed when we got back just after four in the morning. We were both exhausted, yet it hasn't seemed to take the pep out of our step.

Today is the school swim carnival. If it weren't for my good mood, care of Jared and his tongue, fingers and dick, I would have ditched this event. I hate swimming carnivals. Mostly because I don't like to swim since I can't do it very well. But also because I'm not typically a person to do what the masses are doing.

I'm on the yellow team with Jared, Rhys, Simon, and Abbey. It's the first time I've seen Abbey get a breather outside of class from her psycho boyfriend and his mates. He's on one of the other teams, and because she's hiding up the back of the tent, out of sight from most people, I decide to take a chance and join her while Jared cheers on Simon in a race.

Abbey frowns at me as I sit next to her, and I note that even though it's hot, she hasn't taken her blazer off, or attempted to blend in by wearing yellow. Much like me.

As far as most people are concerned, I don't speak, unless your name is Jared, and maybe Travis, or I'm recording a podcast that no one but Jared knows is me. So having a conversation using my phone is normal, and it allows me to say or ask things that no one will know about unless they read over our shoulders. Which they can't, given our position in the tent.

Taking out my phone, I use my notes app to communicate with Abbey.

'Hi.'

I angle it towards her and watch as she reads it and frowns, so I tap out a new note.

'I was hoping we can have a conversation, and since I don't talk out loud, and I'm pretty sure you don't want certain people hearing or knowing you're talking to people, I thought we could do it this way.'

I tilt it her way and she huffs, shaking her head and redirecting her gaze back out to the front of the tent.

I keep trying, and put more words into text before angling it her way. She ignores me, keeping her gaze trained forward, so I elbow her arm, and she shoots me a death glare.

"What do you want?" she hisses and I nod my head towards my phone, so she drops her gaze and reads my message.

'I'm going to be upfront because I'll be leaving Fox Pines soon, and I can't go without trying to help you. I know you are being mistreated by your boyfriend. What I don't understand is why you put up with it.'

Obviously I know more after Jared shared some details with me, but I need to see what she says about it.

"Mind your own business," Abbey hisses between clenched teeth, and I swear she could be a ventriloquist with that skill. I can't even see her lips move.

I shake my phone with the new message and even though her head is facing forward, her eyes drop to my screen.

'Is he holding something over you? Can you go to your parents?'

"I already told you to mind your own business," she hisses a little louder this time, but I press on.

'As you can see, I'm not good at following basic instructions.'

When I jiggle my phone again, Abbey darts her gaze down and smirks.

Finally. A small win.

It's not lost on me how similar this is to how me and

Jared were in the beginning. Me refusing to communicate, him doing everything he could think of to get my reaction.

'Is there anyone you can talk to?'

I shake the phone again and Abbey frowns as she reads it, shaking her head.

'Anywhere you can go?'

Again, she shakes her head.

'Have you heard of Angel Org?'

Abbey shakes her head, but frowns a little more, her head staying in my direction this time.

'I'll leave you their card. They can help you disappear.'

Abbey scoffs. "I doubt it."

I frown at that. She's in a very negative place. Probably feels unbelievably trapped, so I tap out my response and show her my screen.

'Why do you say that?'

She looks like she is rolling her tongue in her mouth, trying to keep her emotions in check. Then she speaks in a whisper.

"So many of them are in on it. They might seem like the nicest people, but it's like they live two lives. Good and evil. And they are the evilest. This Angel Org group is probably a part of it, and if they aren't, you can be assured someone in their ranks is."

What is she talking about? Her message is cryptic, so I form my response and angle my screen to her.

'What? I don't understand.'

"Never mind." She shakes her head. "Best you keep away from me. That's best for everyone involved."

I'm about to offer her a response, but she stands and walks off.

Shit.

Damn it. I was hoping she would elaborate. It's clear that this is more than overprotective parents, though. She mentioned that Angel Org could be in on it, or someone in their ranks could be. Is this another Carnal Unicorn type of thing?

I glance around and spot her school bag right next to where she was sitting, so I do the only thing I can think of, and I slip the Angel Org card inside, and hope that her parents or boyfriend aren't the ones to find it. Hopefully, if she gets desperate enough, she will reach out to them, regardless.

I move back towards the front of the tent to pretend like I'm taking part in the swimming carnival activities, exhaustion starting to creep in from my lack of sleep lately.

It's late morning when my phone vibrates with a notification, and I take it out to see an Instagram message from Travis.

@trav_theman
I need to see you. Come out the front of the swim complex. Alone.

My brows shoot up at his message.

He's here?

I don't think, just stand quickly, my eyes darting around for Jared. He's back by the poolside, egging on another mate in a race. Travis wants to see me alone though, so with my eyes on Jared, I quickly sneak off, heading to the female toilets where I can exit on the other side without anyone seeing me.

I manage to make it through the front gate of the complex without getting caught, and I quickly search for Travis. Only he's not there.

An old yellow mustang is parked at the curb, and a larger woman in her late forties or early fifties is propped against the bonnet, sucking on a cigarette like her life depends on it.

Shit.

Bianca Kerr.

I did my research. I know what the woman who was meant to provide my brother with a safe home looks like.

"And here she is. Miss Elodie Porter in the flesh. Travis' big bad sister." She laughs to herself, her voice scratchy from the cancer sticks she clearly frequents.

I take a step closer, lifting my chin in confidence, and again she laughs.

"You got some balls on you, girl. Coming here thinking you can steal my boy away."

My brows shoot up at that. How does she know I'm here to take Travis away?

"Adam said you aren't much of a talker. Mute or something, he called ya." She scoffs, tossing her smoke butt to the road and leaves it to burn out as she steps closer to me. "Adam spotted you harassing my son while he did community service at that uptight school. Seems you're not very good at taking a hint, love." She's so close now, I can smell the stale cigarette stench wafting from her clothes and skin. "He's not interested in you. He's never going to leave with you, so you should just do everyone a favour and leave us alone."

If she thinks I'm going to balk at her words or the way she puffs out her chest trying to make herself bigger, she has another thing coming. I won't show her any weakness. She needs to know, right fucking now, that she's not dealing with a quitter, so I shake my head and snarl at her.

She looks surprised for a moment before she starts cackling. And cackling. And cackling.

Why don't I have Thana with me? I could kill Bianca Kerr right here and now. That would take care of a lot of problems.

"I see you're a stubborn one. What's it gonna take to get you to leave, girl?"

I shake my head and her eyes narrow.

"Fine, looks like I'll just tell you the truth, then. The truth the Angels and the police have been keeping from you all these years."

My eyes widen.

The Angels? How does she know the Angels?

"I have to say, they did a good job of keeping you hidden. The psychiatric hospital was a nice touch. Made it impossible to get to you."

What?

"Then the witness protection. Hell, they must have paid a helluva lot of money to make sure you were hidden. But then you ran away." She cackles again, and I shake my head in disbelief.

Witness protection?

What?

"The kicker was where you ended up. No one could find you for a long time, meanwhile a cold-blooded killer had you in training, teaching you skills no child should learn." Bianca reaches out to touch my face, but I flinch away and take a step back. She sighs, tilting her head to me, and I study her face, the wrinkles cutting deep around her lips and eyes like she needs a good drink of water. She's all dried up like an old prune.

"I'm sure those Angel sisters had no idea what to do with a teenage killing machine, other than to put you to work. Which is exactly what they did. Didn't they?"

How does she know this?

"There's a number of reasons why they've been protecting you, Elodie, but the biggest thing they've been trying to protect you from," she grins wide, flashing her yellow teeth. "Is me."

Lightning fast, her hand whips out and wraps around my throat, her grip crushing.

I gasp, but don't panic, because that will only cause more complications, and I need to be as clear-headed as possible.

"If you know so much about me," I rasp, and her eyes widen at hearing my voice, "Then you know I have the ability to kill you before you take your next breath."

She cackles again. "Sure, if you had a weapon on you. Which you don't."

"How do you know?" I choke out, and she grins wider.

"Because if you did, I'd already be dead."

19

JARED

*M*y eyes dart around the practically empty tent in search of my little pocket rocket, only they come up empty. Shit. Where's my girl?

I spin around, finding Hastings and Rhys up close and personal, and I hurry to their side.

"You guys seen Dee?"

Rhys and Simon turn to me as if they are coming out of a trance, and shake their heads.

"Nah, I haven't seen her in a while. She was talking to Abbey before, though." Rhys offers and I frown.

Abbey?

Another quick glance around, and I find Abbey sitting to the side of the group, her head buried in a book. I'm not meant to be talking to her, but since Dee isn't with her, I don't really give a fuck about the consequences of me interacting with her.

"Hey, Abs," I call, stumbling over someone's towel left in a heap on the grass. When I reach Abbey, she glances up from her book. "Do you know where Dee is?"

Abbey frowns at me like I'm disrupting her sleep, giving

her head a jerking shake before dismissing me completely and returning her gaze to her book.

The urge to call her a bitch is on the tip of my tongue, but my urgency to find Dee is greater, and with panic, I spin around, trying to find her.

"Dee!" I call, gaining attention from those close by. "Dee!"

"Hey, man. I'm sure she's here somewhere." Simon grips my shoulder in an offer of comfort, but I shove his grip off, pushing past him.

"Dee!"

Fuck.

Something is wrong!

Dee wouldn't just go off on her own without telling someone. Not when she knows she's not safe.

Fuck!

FUCK!

"Hey calm down, Crowley. She can't have gone far." Shaun offers, rushing up to my side.

I push past him too, continuing to call for my girl. I gain so much attention that the teachers try to intervene, but I ignore them, starting to run as I realise Dee isn't here.

I check the pools, and then the toilets, not even bothering to apologise to the girl that comes out of the toilet stall with a squeak when she sees me in there searching.

It's no use though. Dee is nowhere to be found.

The moment I step through the gates to the front of the swimming complex, I freeze.

There she is, my girl, being choked by a woman three times my fucking size.

"Hey! Get the fuck off her!" I explode, my fists balling as I charge forward.

The woman's eyes dart over Dee's shoulder, and as I hear my mates charge out the gates to my side, the woman releases Dee.

She curls her lip, her eyes falling to Dee's face in a monstrous glare.

"I said, get the fuck away from her!" I hiss, storming closer, and the lady starts backing up.

That's when I hear it.

Dee's voice.

"You better sleep with your eyes open, Bianca, because I'm coming for you."

Suddenly manic screaming leaps from Rhys as she comes charging past, towards the oversized woman with her face contorted in fury and her fingers raised like claws. She's hell bent on making this woman back away from her foster sister, regardless of the danger she could be putting herself in. And it works.

The woman balks, nearly tripping as she stumbles backwards, thrown off guard by the unusual behaviour, quickly scrambling to the yellow mustang, getting inside as hastily as a woman her size can, before she burns rubber and speeds off.

"Jesus, Kitten. Don't run head first into danger like that. You could have been hurt." Bossi scolds, and Rhys turns back, not looking worried about anything else but Dee.

Ignoring them, I rush forward, crowding Dee in, my eyes travelling over her face and neck, which is red from the grip that ugly arse woman had on her.

"Dee. Tell me you're ok."

Her chocolate eyes are hard with fury, but she nods.

"I'll be even better when I drain that bitch of every last drop of blood in her body."

"I knew it!" Rhys cries, pushing me to the side as she grips Dee's shoulders. "You *are* talking. Who the fuck was that bitch?" Rhys demands, giving Dee a little shake, but Dee clamps her lips shut. "Oh, come on. Give me something. If you're not going to tell me about who I just chased away, at least say something to me." Rhys wags her brows. "Say, I want to kiss Rhys."

I shoulder her out of the way. "Fuck off George, she's mine. You have your own clan of lovers."

"I think we should be focusing on what Dee just said." Simon interjects, coming around to face Dee. "You gonna drain that bitch of every drop of blood? Are you a vampire?"

Dee cracks a smile. Jesus, I love seeing her smile.

"Who was that lady?" Shaun asks and Dee shakes her head, no longer willing to talk.

I think back on what Dee said to her when the lady released her neck. Dee called her Bianca.

"Shit, was that Travis' foster mum? Bianca Kerr?" I ask, and when Dee nods, my heart sinks. She really is in danger. What if I hadn't come out when I did?

"We need to call the Angels and Griffin," I state and Dee shakes her head, anger flaring across her face before she turns and storms back into the swimming complex.

"Dee knows the Angels?" Rhys asks, not an ounce of playfulness left on her face.

"Uhhh." I rake my hand through my hair, not sure what I should and shouldn't be saying. "You'll have to ask Dee."

I dash off after Dee and hear Rhys huff behind me before I hear Simon and Shaun tend to her. I don't have time to answer her questions. Right now, I need to make sure my girl is ok, because Bianca Kerr coming at her like that is fucking bad. Really fucking bad.

I follow Dee back to the yellow team tent, and watch as she gathers up her bag, so I do the same with my things.

Looks like we are outta here. Thank fuck.

Spending the day at a swimming carnival when I only have days left with Dee isn't how I want to spend my time. I know she's been insisting on attending school for my sake. I'm pretty sure she has it in her head that attending is what's best for me for when she leaves, but school is pointless at this stage.

Nothing matters but her.

Nothing.

We hurry out of the complex, ignoring the teachers and dodging her foster mum, before climbing into my car and driving to my house. Since Dee's foster dad works from home, going there when we are meant to be at the swimming carnival isn't an option.

Dee remains quiet during the drive, and I leave her to stay in her silent mode as I focus on getting her to safety. Her silence isn't unfamiliar, but the expression she's wearing is unsettling me.

I wait until I have her back in my bedroom before I ask her anything, and I sit on my bed as she paces in silence.

"Talk to me. What happened? Why did you go out there and talk to that woman?"

She shakes her head, not speaking, but continues pacing. Then she stops as if she's thought or remembered something, and she takes out her phone.

I guess she's gonna use her notes app to speak to me. The idea of that disappoints me a little. Now that I've heard her voice, I want to hear it all the time, but I also understand that she needs to do things in her way. She will use her voice when she can.

Dee hands me her phone, and for a moment, I'm confused. It's not showing the notes app and any of her thoughts. It's showing a message thread. An Instagram message thread between @hush_tiny_dancer and @trav_theman.

"Are these messages between you and Travis?" I glance up at her and she stops pacing to look at me and nods. Then she steps forward and points to the ones from today, so I read the one Travis sent.

@trav_theman
I need to see you. Come out the front of the swim complex. Alone.

My brows shoot up, and I glance back at Dee.

"So you got this message, and you went out there? Thinking it was him?"

She nods.

"But it was his foster mum?"

She nods.

"Was Travis there at all?"

She shakes her head and starts pacing again.

"So that was the one and only Bianca Kerr, and she used Travis' phone, or his account at least, to lure you out there?"

She nods again and then shakes her head before coming to a stop and frowning. Then she turns back to me, her face a mask of pain as she parts her lips to speak.

"Do you think Travis was in on it?"

I fly up off the mattress and tug her to my chest, wrapping my arms around her.

"No. No, I don't. He'd never do that to you. I know things have been strained between you, but he'd never hand you over to his foster mum. Never."

Nodding against my chest, Dee relaxes in my embrace, slowly slipping her arms around me and returning the hug.

"She said some things... I'm so confused." Dee's voice is so quiet. Almost like she's scared someone will hear her admission.

I pull back and tilt her chin up to me. "What did she say?"

She opens her mouth to speak, but then snaps it shut again and shakes her head before burying her head in my chest again.

Shit.

I walk backwards with Dee still in my arms, and when the backs of my legs hit my mattress, I ease down, taking Dee with me. I settle us against my pillows, and she snuggles into my side, holding me tight like she's scared I'll disappear.

Shit. I'll never disappear on her... but she will on me. That day is drawing closer and closer and I just wish time would stand the fuck still for once.

I just want it to stop and give me an eternity of holding Dee in my arms.

Is that so much to ask?

20

DEE

*G*riffin and the Angels look rightfully confused as I enter the private bar upstairs at the Red Room, with Jared on my tail. I'd sent them a message asking them to meet me, and I also asked Griffin to bring his woman. I'm not sure why I asked her to come, only that I feel like she is a decent person, and I could use her support.

I smirk when I see how Griffin stands in front of her as if he's trying to shield her from my wrath.

Idiot.

I don't have any qualms with him or her, but he doesn't know that yet.

The Angels, however? Well, they have a lot of fucking explaining to do, unless Bianca Kerr was lying to try to turn me against them.

It's possible. Maybe she thought I'd react first before asking questions, killing the Angels and eliminating one of the Kerrs' problems.

The Angels, who are chatting, fall silent as they see me, dressed in all black, with Thana strapped to my lower back. They know this look. This is Hush's kill outfit, and they realise then that they aren't meeting with Dee, they are meeting with Hush.

"Hush. We were surprised to be summoned without any explanation. If it were anyone else, we wouldn't have dropped everything by such a demand," Amanda states, her eyes trailing me as I come to stand at the opposite end of the table as Griffin.

"Why is that?" I ask, and both the Angel sisters' brows shoot high.

"You're talking?" Bec asks, her gaze darting between me, Jared—who is now to my right—and up to the other end of the table, to Griffin and his woman, Aggie. "I didn't know you were talking to people now."

I shrug. "Answer my question. Why would you drop everything for me?"

Both Angels frown, briefly glancing at each other before shaking their heads like they are confused.

Sighing, I clear my throat, my raspy voice not used to being used this much, and I stop beating around the bush.

"Sit." I demand, and even though everyone but Jared frowns at me, they all sit while I remain standing. "I had a run in with Bianca Kerr earlier today."

"What!" The Angels shoot out of their seats in shock, but all Griffin does is raise a brow.

He's interested in what I have to say, but the Angels are panicked.

Interesting.

I gesture for them to sit again, staying silent until they take the hint and lower back to their seats.

"Are you ok? What did she do?" Amanda asks, and it's Jared who answers.

"She tried to fucking choke her!"

Again, the Angels fly out of their seats, and I huff, my

shoulders dropping as I tip my head back to stare at the ceiling while the Angels start hurling questions at me.

I need to have a chat with Jared about keeping his mouth shut.

"Enough!" The deep boom is loud, and the table rattles from the force of Griffin's fist, and my eyes lock on Aggie, who starts whispering in his ear.

He gives her a nod while Bec and Amanda calm down, getting comfortable in their seats again as Griffin stands.

"Why don't we all remain quiet and let Hush finish speaking?"

The Angels turn their gazes back to me and I give Griffin a nod of thanks before continuing.

"Bianca seemed to know a lot about me. My past. And the two of you." I deadpan and their eyes widen.

"Maybe we should talk about this in private," Amanda suggests, but I shake my head.

"Nope. I'd prefer to discuss this right here with everyone in the room, and since I'm not sure if I can trust the two of you right now," I shoot the Angels a glare, "I've asked Griffin and Aggie to be here because, funnily enough, they are the only people aside from Jared and my current foster family that I trust."

Is it wise to trust one of the Marx men? Maybe not all Marx men. But this one, yes. I do trust Griffin, and I need him on my side if I'm going to make it to my eighteenth birthday alive.

"Look, Hush. I'm not sure what Bianca told you, but I'm sure she was just trying to put a wedge between us. Doing that would make us both weaker," Bec states and I nod.

"That's true, it would, which is why you aren't already dead."

The room turns eerily still at my words. The expressions

on Bec's and Amanda's faces are lethal, yet they remain in their seats.

"Explain to me why *you* were the ones that hid me in a psychiatric facility after I killed my step-mum? Explain to me why *you* then had me moved from that facility and into what I thought was foster care, but was actually witness protection?"

The Angels' faces lose their murderous glare and morph into worry.

"Explain to me why it was the both of you that found me when I ran away from my witness protection family and took me from that man? The only man who *never* tried to touch me or *hit* me or *lock me in closets.*"

Amanda opens her mouth to say something, but then snaps it shut, clearly thinking better of it, so I continue.

"Tell me why you've been keeping me hidden from Bianca Kerr? Why it's always been the two of you doing this? Looking out for me? I don't even remember you being around after I killed Catherine, but you must have been if you were the ones to put me in that facility." I place my hands on the table in front of me and glare at the Angels. "Who are you to me?"

The Angel sisters turn to each other, not saying anything, but their eyes seem to communicate with each other.

"It's in your best interest to be honest," Griffin states, his voice broking no argument, and I relax a little. This is why I wanted him here. I needed someone in my corner to make sure I don't get lied to. To make sure the truth comes out today.

As if in agreement, both Angels nod at each other before slowly turning their gazes to me.

It's Bec who speaks this time.

"Catherine, Travis' mum, the lady you killed… was Bianca Kerr's sister."

My brows shoot high, and I ease myself into the chair behind me, Jared's warm palm coming to rest on my thigh under the table, letting me know he's here. He supports me.

"Because of marriage, Catherine and Bianca have different surnames, but before they married, they were Catherine and Bianca Weaver." Bec explains, "Because of this, being a close blood relative to Travis, when Catherine died, Bianca was able to do a deal to have Travis put in her care. She tried to claim you, too, but we couldn't let her take you, and we knew you weren't safe from her with us since we were still small potatoes in the underworld back then and the only thing going for us was money, so we used that money and arranged for you to vanish. We knew that Bianca's only desire to get her hands on you was to kill you for what you did to her sister."

"But why?" I ask quietly, my head spinning from this revelation. "Who am I to *you*?"

Amanda clears her throat, sitting taller in her chair before she speaks.

"Your dad, Joey," she says before snapping her mouth shut, taking a moment to compose herself as her eyes turn glassy. "Your dad was our brother. Our half-brother."

My brows shoot high.

What did she just say?

"We are your aunties, Elodie."

21

JARED

*W*hat the actual fuck?! The Angel sisters, who seem to hold some sort of powerful authority over most of the organised crime in Australia, are Dee's aunties?

No fucking way!

"You're kidding, right?" I hiss, shooting the two blondes a fucking death glare. "You're trying to tell me that you are Dee's aunties?"

They nod and I scoff.

"No way. I don't fucking believe you."

Dee shoots me a questioning look, her eyes glazed with unshed tears, and I quickly lean forward and press my lips to her forehead before standing.

"Whether you believe us or not is not our concern, Jared. Our only interest is, Hush."

I laugh, but there's no humour in it.

"Yes, Hush. You call her a name that isn't even her real name."

"Amanda said her real name a minute ago," Bec adds and I snarl.

"If you are really her aunties, then why the fuck would you want your niece to be a killer? It makes no fucking sense. No one would want that for a child!"

The sisters exchange another look and nod in understanding.

"It was too late by the time we got to Elodie after she fled from witness protection. It took us two years to find her," Bec darts her concerned gaze to Dee. "Lesley had trained you day and night. Conditioned you. When we managed to get you away from him and into our care, you were very unhinged. You were a killer. It's all you knew. It's the only language you spoke. Violence. Kill." Bec shakes her head as she remembers. "We had to keep you locked up in the beginning. We had to sedate you just so you wouldn't kill us when we came to take you back."

Amanda reaches out and takes her sister's hand, giving it a squeeze before turning her eyes to Dee.

"One day, something changed in you. You seemed calmer. More communicative, even though you wouldn't talk. At first we couldn't figure out what caused the big shift in your behaviour, but slowly as the days went on, you started to get more aggressive again."

Bec nods. "It took us a while to figure out what was happening because you would fluctuate between a lethal weapon bursting to kill. And a calm, sweet girl who liked to read and draw." She shakes her head, her expression surprised. "It turns out you'd been spying on us, watching the work we were doing, trying to build an organisation aimed at eliminating the predators in this country. You helped yourself to our intel and slipped out of the house in the middle of the night and did the job for us. You killed the people on our lists, came back, and were calm for a number of days, sometimes satisfied for a couple of weeks, until you did it again."

Amanda smiles. "We were so shocked when we realised what had been happening, and then it just all made sense. You'd been conditioned to be a killer, and even though it went against everything we believed in, we knew that the best thing for you was to give you the outlet you needed." Amanda turns a hard glare at me. "That's how two aunties can stand back and let our beautiful little niece be a killer. And as long as she was in our fold, we could control how many kills and jobs she took."

Fucking hell, as fucked up as all of that sounds, it kinda makes sense.

Jesus fucking Christ.

I can't believe this is what happened to my little pocket rocket.

"It's by far extremely bad parenting," Bec nods, "but we didn't know how else to help her, and there was no way we were going to give up on her."

Nodding, I retake my seat next to Dee, replacing my hand on her thigh, and notice her trembling slightly. This is a lot for her to take in. Hell, it's a lot for *me* to take in.

Dee clears her throat, and we all turn our attention to her, knowing she is getting ready to speak.

"So Travis has been with his auntie all of this time?" she states and glances at Bec and Amanda. "Has he been safe with Bianca? I know that house hasn't been a good one to grow up in, but can you be sure she didn't direct her anger about her sister's death towards Travis?"

"We can't be one hundred percent sure. We do know that Bianca drummed it into Travis' head that you killed his mum because you were unhinged and not because you were trying to protect him. But over the years we've kept watch on the family, and nothing has indicated he's been in any real danger. Until now."

Dee stiffens. "What do you mean, *until now?*"

Griffin clears his throat this time, and our gazes shift to the other end of the table where he's lounging back in his chair, one hand wrapped around a glass with a lick of amber fluid, and the other linked tightly with his woman's.

"Travis is a bit roughed up. Bianca is back in the house, which is weird. She hasn't stayed there in three years. Our sources say the kids live in that dump, maintaining their grow house while the parents live in luxury out by Redfield Lake."

At Griffin's words, Aggie stiffens next to him, and shoots him a glare. I'm not sure what that's about, but if I have to guess, I'd say they must live near the Kerr leaders.

Dee stands abruptly. "I need to get Travis out of that house."

Griffin shakes his head. "Travis won't leave because Cassie, his foster sister, is being held captive there now. She was asking too many questions, and Bianca got suspicious of her. It seems that having Cassie locked up helps them to keep Travis obedient by using Cassie's safety against him."

"How do you know this? Have you spoken to my brother?" Dee asks, and Griffin shakes his head, his eyes darting to me.

Fuck.

I told Dee that Trav came to see me, but I didn't tell her about the stuff with Cassie and that Trav looked roughed up.

Slowly, eerily so, Dee turns her head until her death glare causes me to shrink back.

"You forget to tell me something?" she hisses, and I raise my hands in surrender.

"Travis didn't want me to tell you everything because he knew you'd try to get him out and he knows it's not safe for you or for Cassie. Which he's right about. That crazy bitch has got it out for you, Dee. You can't go to Travis, and he needs to stay away from you. It's the only way to keep you both safe."

I know she knows I'm right, but a look of betrayal flicks across her face, anyway.

Shit.

I take a step towards her and she shifts away, turning her back on me as she starts to slowly pace.

Her head must be swimming with everything she's learned tonight.

"Dee. Travis won't leave without his foster sister," I state. "And he does want to leave. I know that much. He can see what his foster parents are really like, but if he leaves now, I'm pretty sure they will hurt Cassie. Or even kill her. That's why he's being compliant. Obeying them. He's just trying to keep everyone alive."

She spins abruptly and stalks towards me. And fuck, the urge to step back and run for my life is strong, but I stay in place. Right now Dee is more Hush than anything, but I care about every version she is, so I'm not going to back down.

"You should have told me!" she hisses, baring her teeth as she jabs a pointed finger to my chest.

"And what would you have done?" I ask and she growls before turning on her heel.

"Jared is right, Hush," Griffin adds. "You need to be smart about this. If you still want to leave this town with your brother alive, you can't react on fear. You have to be strategic about this."

Dee stares at Griffin for a few long moments and then, as if she's just snapped out of a trance, she directs her wrath to her aunties.

"Is that everything? Have you told me everything I need to know?"

Amanda slowly shakes her head. "You should probably know that even though the police reports say that Catherine went off the rails at Joey for feeding Travis fast food, the real reason is that your dad was a police informant, and Catherine found out he was feeding the cops information about the Kerr family business. The business Catherine worked in."

Shit. Is that why Bianca thinks Trav is working with the cops? Is she paranoid, thinking Travis is like his dad?

Dee nods, appearing to take that bit of information well, and fuck, I know better. Inside, behind those big fucking walls, she's going to be freaking out. How could she not? I just want to wrap her in my arms, knowing that her already fractured heart must be hurting more than ever.

22

DEE

My head is a mess. My heart hurts. And I'm so angry right now, I'm afraid I might accidentally kill someone I'm not meant to. To top it off, even though I'm pissed at Jared for keeping stuff about my brother from me, instead of wanting to hurt him, I want to fuck him. Which is confusing as hell.

Our meeting disbursed not long ago, the Angels leaving when I dismissed them, not able to force another word from me. And Griffin and Aggie left not long after, leaving me pacing with Jared's eyes on me until I couldn't take anymore of his silence.

Making our way back through the Red Room, I stop in the passage, glancing down each end. One way goes out into the club where the girls dance on poles and men drool over them, and the other leads to the private rooms.

"What's wrong?" Jared asks from behind me, standing so close that I can feel the warmth of his body at my back.

I glance back over my shoulder at him, biting my lip as I stare at his, looking totally kissable.

"Dee? Why are you looking at me like that?"

I grin, turning back the way we came, and head to Griffin's office.

"Dee?" Jared calls, catching up to me. "What are you doing?"

I don't answer him, of course. Where's the fun in that?

Pushing Griffin's door open, I ignore his startled expression as I walk in on him and Aggie having a private moment together.

"Uh-hi?" Griffin mutters as I storm to his desk and push him aside, causing him to stumble into his woman.

"Dee. What are you doing?" Jared asks again, and yet again, I don't answer him.

Opening Griffin's top drawer, I find what I'm looking for, grab it before shutting the drawer.

"Hey!" Griffin snaps, grabbing my wrist before I can get away. "What are you doing with that?"

I glance up to see Jared's confused expression before shooting Griffin a raised 'really' brow and it takes him a moment to switch on to what's happening.

"Oh." He releases my wrist quickly, like I've just burned him, and his eyes dart to Jared. "Was this your idea?"

Jared huffs, throwing his hands up. "I have no fucking clue what is happening right now."

Griffin chuckles, turning his gaze back to me as I head to his office door. "Well... ahhh. Have fun with that."

Aggie giggles as Griffin wraps his hand around her waist and draws her close, and I hear Jared cursing behind me as he follows me out, closing Griffin's office door behind him.

"For fuck's sake, Dee. What's going on?" Jared hisses, but I keep walking, turning the corner in the passage and heading toward the private rooms.

When I stop in front of room eight, I use the key I stole from Griffin's drawer and unlock the private room, pushing the door open and go in.

"Uhhhh. What are we doing in here?" Jared asks, hovering in the doorway, and I snicker quietly, unstrapping Thana and placing her on the small table at the side.

With Jared still standing in the open door, I turn to him, making sure he's watching as I grab the hem of my top and tug it over my head.

That's when he clues in on what I'm doing, and he grins, shaking his head and stepping into the room, shutting and locking the door behind him.

"Here?" he asks. "Really?"

I nod, working my pants down and revelling in the way his blue gaze darkens as he watches.

"Fuck it." He chuckles, and grabs his t-shirt at the back, pulling it off in one swift move before stalking closer.

I suck in my lips as I stifle my smile, not wanting him to see. He thinks he's about to get lucky. He thinks it's that easy.

Not tonight.

As he nears, I back up, my back hitting the wall as he goes to cage me in, but at the last second, I duck under his arm, gripping his hips, and spin him to face me before I shove him hard against the wall.

A small gasp escapes him, and that faint noise excites me more than it probably should. If Jared has a problem with a female being dominant over him, he doesn't show it. Instead, his eyes flare wide with excitement, and he grins while licking his lips as I step into his space. I stand on my tiptoes, reaching up to his height even as he leans down, meeting me, and our lips clash in a heated kiss.

Jared's hands slide around my back, tugging me closer, and I spend a couple of minutes enjoying the brush of his tongue and the nibble of his lips until I know he's good and worked up.

I can feel his hardness pressing between us, tempting me so much that my panties feel instantly damp. I think I'm addicted to his dick. But also his tongue. And lips. And fingers.

Hell, I'm just addicted to everything Jared Crowley.

Easing our lips apart, I slide down his body, keeping my eyes on his as I lower to my knees and start working on his pants until they are open enough for me to access what I want. As soon as his cock springs free, I take it in my hand. It's size too thick for my fingers to meet, and I give it a pump, wringing a hiss from Jared's lips.

"You hungry, Deranged?" he asks, and I smirk up at him, nodding before flicking my tongue over his tip and using my free hand to tap the inside of his ankles, silently telling him to widen his stance.

"You wanna suck me?" he asks this time, and again I nod, this time parting my lips and sinking his tip inside my mouth.

His eyes roll back in his head, and that's when I act, dropping my hold on his dick. Reaching down to the cuffs attached to a spreader bar chained to the wall by his feet, I quickly clamp them shut around his unsuspecting ankles.

His reaction time is slow because he is so lust drunk, so by the time he realises what's happening, I have his feet secured.

"What the fuck!" Jared yelps in shock, and I smirk, using his distraction to tug down the wrist cuff chained to the wall on his right side, grabbing his wrist and securing it too.

"Hey!" he growls low, his voice curious. "What are you doing?"

I pull the chain tight, and his cuffed wrist jerks up taut before I secure the chain in place so he can't move it.

"Dee!" he says in warning, but I just flash him a smile. "I'm happy to play, but a little fucking warning wouldn't go astray."

I shrug, taking his other wrist and noticing how he easily

lets me secure the second wrist cuff before pulling it tight as well.

"You gonna say anything?" he asks, not really looking angry, but not looking all that comfortable.

"Like what?" I rasp, my voice extra scratchy. "Does it annoy you that I kept my plans to do this to myself?"

His brows shoot high before his eyes narrow.

"This is payback?" he asks. "For keeping the Travis stuff from you."

I shrug. "Maybe. Or maybe I just want to leave you here alone and tied up, not knowing what I'm doing or if I'm safe."

His eyes darken and his lip twitches. "Don't you dare fucking leave me here. You going off on your own is *not* the same as me keeping information from you about Travis."

I don't respond.

"Come on, Dee. You know, I was just trying to keep you safe."

I nod slowly, because yes, even though I'm pissed, I do know that.

"You still need to be punished," I announce, and he slowly nods.

"How? You gonna torture me with sex? Edge me until I snap?"

I shrug. "Maybe."

He chuckles. "Do you even know how to do that?"

I tilt my head as I slowly pace in front of him, palming my tits as I move. "I'm sure I can figure it out."

Slowly, a grin spreads his kissable lips wide.

"Come on then. Do your worst."

Shit.

How exactly do I do this?

I didn't really think this through.

Again, Jared chuckles, obviously recognising my waning confidence.

"Wrap those pretty lips around me again, Dee. You can start by torturing me with your mouth."

Good idea.

So that's what I do, falling to my knees again, gripping his hard dick and taking him into my mouth.

I watch up through the fan of my lashes as he tries to fight his arousal, but eventually, he gives in, his lids falling shut while I work him over with my lips and tongue until he's so worked up that he starts thrusting his dick deeper into my mouth.

I love this part. When he can't hold back from thrusting. It makes me feel powerful and ignites me from the inside out.

But I'm not here to make it easy for him. So that's when I pull back, letting his thick length pop free.

His eyes shoot open, a look of pain crossing his expression, but I know he's not in any *real* pain, just mind blowing need.

"Fuck," Jared hisses, his hips jutting forward in search of my mouth. "I need more."

Biting my lip, I shake my head, slowly shifting back, his blue gaze nearly black from his pupils being nearly blown.

He's high right now.

High on me.

And fuck if that isn't a powerful feeling.

My panties are soaked through, so I sit on the padded bench in the centre of the room and face Jared, his chest rising and falling and his thick cock looks almost angry as he takes me in.

Slowly, I part my legs, wondering if he can see how wet I am, and when his nostrils flare, I know he can.

"Fuck, Dee. I wanna taste your sweet cunt so bad."

I smirk at him and travel my hand down my front to the aching spot between my legs and give a gentle rub.

"Yes," he rasps. "Take your panties off so I can see you."

I consider denying him, but hell, I'm only human and the ache between my legs is almost painful, so I stand and slowly tug the thin scrap of fabric down.

I try to move seductively as I do this, having no idea if I actually look sexy, or like an awkward baby calf learning to walk for the first time. I have to assume that I don't look too ridiculous, given Jared's heated expression and the way his breathing increases.

Once my panties are on the floor, I turn and sit back down, holding my breath as I part my thighs again and bare myself.

"Fuuuck, Elodie." Jared growls, "I wanna touch you. Taste you."

Biting my lower lip, I slip my fingers to my sex and slide them through my folds. Jared moans, and as I bring them back through, I hold them up before slipping them into my mouth, tasting myself.

Who the hell am I right now? Not that I hate how confident I am, but hell, this is what Jared Crowley does to me.

"Fuck. Dee. Untie me." He pants, but I shake my head. "You've made your point. Let me free so I can worship you."

Again, I shake my head, returning my fingers to my pussy and start circling my clit.

"Fuck, this is torture. Please Dee. I'll do anything. I swear. Anything. Just release me."

I'm tempted to give in, because honestly, I don't enjoy torturing him like this. I hold strong though, ignoring his plea, and concentrate on building my arousal.

I close my eyes for a minute, letting go and enjoying the sensations as I apply pressure to my most sensitive spot. When I open my eyes again, Jared's face is screwed up in painful agony as his hips thrust back and forth, his dick finding nothing but thin air.

Rising from the bench, I stalk towards him, and he looks at me hopefully.

"Are you going to release me now?"

I shake my head, bending down to where Jared's jeans have pooled further down his legs, finding the back pocket, and pulling out his wallet.

He stays silent as he watches me, his eyes darting from my face to his wallet as I slip the condom I know he keeps there free.

"How did you know that was there?" he asks, and I grin.

"I saw you put it in before we left earlier."

He sighs, his cock jerking as I tear the top of the foil wrapper open, and pull out the condom.

"You gonna put that on for me?" He almost sounds like he's begging now, so I put him out of his misery and nod before palming his dick and pressing the latex to his tip.

Once it's rolled on, I give him a couple of light tugs, and he sinks his teeth so deep into his lower lip that I fear he's going to draw blood.

"Dee," Jared whispers, desperate for my hand to return as soon as I remove it.

I stand back and study him for a moment, wondering what the best course of action is here, then I leap at him, wrapping my arms and legs around him like I'm a spider monkey.

Air flies from both our chests, but we think little of it as our lips collide, and I press my heat to his hard cock which is now trapped between us, and I moan into his mouth.

Breaking the kiss, I glance up, eyeing the bar above his head before hoisting myself up a little higher, using his body as leverage until I grip the bar and lower down so we are at eye level.

"You want me to fuck you?" I whisper, and he groans.

"So fucking bad."

Releasing one hand from the bar, I shift back a little, wrapping my hand around his shaft and line him up to my entrance. Then I re-grip the bar and slowly press my pelvis forward, taking him inside me.

"Fuuuck, Elodie. Your pussy is heaven."

My heart soars when he uses my real name. It somehow means more to me than ever before, and I grin, claiming his lips as our bodies quickly sync up, coming together in a wanton craze.

Over and over we thrust, and over and over our cries fill the crimson space of room eight as we turn frenzied.

I grind my clit over his pubic bone as we thrust, loving the texture of his hair covering that area, and I quickly feel myself spiral.

"Fuck. Yes." Jared pants before he bites my neck lightly, and just like that, I start convulsing around him.

The roar that flies from him is loud and animalistic. The sound calling to me in a primal way before an ache settles in my chest.

I think I love him.

I think I've actually fallen in love with a guy I have to leave next week.

How fucking cruel is that?

23

JARED

*I*t's business as usual for Dee after we leave the Red Room, her lethal demeanour falling easily into place as we take one of Griffin's cars and cross more names off that damn list she has. Eight names, to be exact.

Eight fucking names.

Eight fucking kills.

I don't know how she does it. It's almost like she detaches herself from what's going on, which I guess is a good thing. If she enjoyed it too much, I'd probably be concerned.

On the way to the first kill of the night, we'd argued because I wanted to come inside each location with her, but she refused again saying I would be a distraction and she didn't want to worry about me while she was trying to take a life. Then she also pointed out that she needs eyes outside in case there's another ambush from who we assume are Carnal Unicorn members trying to protect their secrets.

I couldn't really argue with that, so as she went into each building, I waited in the darkness of the shadows outside, keeping watch.

Did I obey that rule completely?

No, I fucking did not.

Why? Because I'm a nosey bastard, and also I can't help but enjoy watching her kill.

It's weird to think that way, I know, but I do. I really fucking do.

It's almost like watching her dance. There's an air of captivation to it. The way she moves almost like she is gliding, the precision in the way she wields that fucking Crocodile Dundee blade. It's truly a sight.

So yeah. I stayed outside, but I still watched the few times I could, through a door or a window. And yeah, my cock was hard all fucking night.

After victim number eight, we drove the car back to the location Griffin had left it in, Dee changing from her kill clothes—that's what she calls them—to her regular clothes.

Her kill clothes get shoved in a plastic bag and left in the car for Griffin to dispose of. Something that makes me fucking uncomfortable.

Who's to say he actually gets rid of them? He could be keeping them to use against Dee later on. But when I bring this up to her, she shakes her head and dismisses it, trusting the criminal who blackmailed her, us, into doing his dirty work for him.

By the time we leave Redfield, where all tonight's kills happened, and get back to the Rogan residence in Fox Pines, it's nearly 5am.

Dee quietly takes a shower while I slide into her bed and wait, and when she joins me ten minutes later, we both lie in the silence, wrapped in each other's arms.

"Where did you get the knife from?" I ask her, not able to sleep.

"Thana," she says, and I frown.

"You got the knife from Thana? What or who is that?"

She giggles. "The knife is Thana. That's what I call her. And the Angels gave her to me."

"Hold up. You have a name for your knife?"

She nods against my chest. "Thana means death. I thought it suitable since she sends so many to their deaths."

I chuckle. "Dee, you do know that *you* are the one that does that."

I feel her shrug. "Not without Thana."

We fall silent for a few moments, and I know she's stewing over everything that happened tonight. Especially the stuff with the Angels. Her fucking aunties.

"Talk to me." I urge, and she sighs and shakes her head. "Dee, I know you're a solitary person. I know you like to hold your secrets close to your heart, but you don't have to. Not when you have me. Let me carry them with you."

She squeezes me then, and a sob escapes her, telling me that she's crying.

Shit.

I didn't want to make her cry, but then I guess everything she learned is a lot to unpack.

"So you had no idea you were related to the Angel sisters?" I ask, and she sniffs, shaking her head against my chest again. "Do you think they are telling the truth?"

This time she nods against my chest, but she still doesn't speak.

"It means they are Travis' aunties, too. Don't you think it's weird they haven't been more concerned about him?"

Again, she nods against my chest.

"Does…" I trail off, not sure if I should ask this question, but when Dee pops her head up, her tear-filled eyes connecting with mine, I can't *not* ask. "Does this change anything with you leaving?"

Her face falls momentarily, and she shrugs.

"Because you know, I'd really like you to stay. For good."

There, I put it out there. I told her how I feel.

Her face softens, and a small smile tugs at the corners of her lips, but she tries to hide it.

Fuck. Does she like the sound of that? Of staying?

I don't find out though, because she rests her head back on my chest, giving me a squeeze before she falls asleep.

Fuck, I want her to stay so bad it hurts.

I don't want to say that to her, though. I don't want to make her feel like she has to stay, or feel bad because she has to leave. I just want her to want to stay and decide to do it.

I try to imagine what life would be like with Dee forever by my side, and a grin tugs at my lips.

She would frustrate the crap outta me. I know that much. But it won't matter, because that's part of what we have together. The push and the pull. The taunting and teasing. The silence and the loud moments.

I've changed so much since the car wreck. The anger I'd been feeling only a matter of weeks ago seems to have disappeared. For some reason, which probably has everything to do with Dee, I feel more at peace.

I glance down at her in my arms, her head tilted up to me while she sleeps on my chest. She looks so innocent right now. So sweet, like she couldn't hurt a fly.

I know better, of course, but it doesn't change the fact that underneath the armour she wears, she's nothing more than a girl wanting to build a life.

The question is, will that life be with me?

24

DEE

a hand shaking my shoulder stirs me awake, my lips blinking open to see Cynthia staring down at me.

"Dee. You're going to be late for school."

Her hard eyes dart over my shoulder to where I can feel the heat of Jared's body snuggled up to mine.

Oops.

I reach over to the bedside table and grab my phone, opening the notes app and typing out my response.

'Sorry. I didn't get much sleep. Can I have a few more hours and come in later?'

Turning my phone to Cynthia, her eyes move over my words and her lips thin.

"I think the reason why you didn't get much sleep is the real problem here, Dee. I've been lenient so far, but you can't keep sneaking out, or sneaking him in. And you need to go to sleep at a reasonable hour."

I nod, not wanting to argue, but I make no move to get out of bed.

Sighing, Cynthia straightens. "Fine. Come in later. But

this isn't to happen again. The rules around here are about to change."

I give her a nod, and she spins on her heel, stomping out of my bedroom, and closing the door behind her.

"I think you made her mad," Jared rasps against the back of my neck, and my lids flutter shut as I grin, quickly falling back to sleep.

When I wake again, I can sense Jared awake, so I pry my lids apart to see that I'm facing him this time, and he's staring at me.

"Good morning." He grins, and I'm helpless to hold back my smile. "We should probably get to school so your foster mum doesn't skin me alive."

I snicker at that, and Jared leans forward, pressing his warm lips to my forehead.

Is this what happiness feels like?

To feel cherished and important? If I stay and don't leave when I turn eighteen at the end of next week, will Jared continue to feel this way about me? Will it always be this... addictive?

I really want to find out. More than anything.

Well, maybe not more than anything.

Travis' safety is at the top of my list, but hell, staying and being like this with Jared is a very close second.

"Shower," I rasp, my voice huskier than normal from just waking, and I gesture my head to Jared.

With a big smile, he nods in agreement. "Yeah, I need a wash. How about you use the bathroom first, and then I'll shower?"

I nod, needing to pee and splash water on my face.

I go through the mundane tasks of getting ready, and as Jared passes me in the doorway of the bathroom, he cages me in, one arm on the door frame above my head, while the other cups my nape. And then he kisses me.

It's the kind of kiss that turns my legs into jelly, and my insides to molten lava, and if I didn't know that William was here in the house somewhere working, I'd be getting naked by now.

Jared pulls back before I do, dragging my lower lip through his teeth before easing away from me.

"You'd better go before I fuck you so hard your foster dad will hear."

I roll my eyes at him and walk away, but his hand meets my arse in a loud slap before I even make it a step.

His chuckles fade as he closes himself in the bathroom, and with a blush stained expression, I head out to the main living area to wait.

"Oh, hey kiddo," Will says when I enter, his face lighting up with a warm smile.

I offer him an awkward wave, going to the fridge and grabbing a juice box.

"Where's your fella?" he asks from where he's sitting at the kitchen bench, some paperwork spread out on the counter as he eats a sandwich.

Using my phone, I tap out my response and show him.

'Shower.'

Will nods, taking a sip of his coffee.

"So, it's your birthday on Friday. Are you still planning on leaving?"

My brows shoot up at his forward question.

Ok, so it's not necessarily forward, but everyone else but Jared has been dancing around it, which kinda suited me fine.

I offer him a shrug and he nods as he watches me jab the straw into the juice box and take a long sip.

"You know, Cynthia and I would really love for you to stay. When we asked you to stay with us, we didn't mean just

223

for a while until you age out. We are offering you a family for life."

Shit.

Heat pricks the backs of my eyes at his words, and I suck harder on the straw, nearly choking on the juice.

I want to say yes. I want to stay here and build a life. A real one with family and friends and, and, and... love.

But can I really do that? Maybe if Griffin is successful in cleaning out the scum like the Kerrs, Travis could stay too and be safe. He already has friendships he's made. Hell, I think he may even have a girlfriend if the thing between him and Tillie is serious.

We could both stay. Be close to each other and rebuild our relationship too.

Will is still watching me, but I don't respond. I don't know if I can, or should, so I keep my lips sealed shut and finish my juice box.

Jared joins us in the kitchen a few minutes later, freshly showered, his blonde hair still damp.

Ooohhh, sexy.

"Hello, Jared." William straightens in his chair, his demeanour changing before my eyes.

"Hey Mr Rogan." Jared offers him a smile, but it's not returned.

"Now that you are both here, let me go over a few rules."

My gaze darts to Jared's before we both glance at William.

"I realise we can't have one set of rules for Rhys and another set for you, Dee. So this relationship the two of you have," he gestures between me and Jared, "isn't a problem with us. However, there will be no more sneaking in and out. You use the front door. I don't care what time of day it is. Just no more sneaking. Ok?"

Again, Jared and I glance at each other and when I turn my gaze back to Will, I nod my head in understanding.

"Also, stop staying up all damn night. Today is the last time we allow you to take time off school because you stay up all night. Next time you hardly sleep, you suck it up and go to school, anyway. Understand?" he asks firmly, and both Jared and I nod.

"Ok good. Well, get to school before the Principal calls and gives you both detention."

Slowly, Will smirks, and my shoulders relax.

I've never had rules that I obeyed before. My lack of respect for any foster parents I've had in the past made it easy to ignore their bullshit. But Cynthia and Will? They are different. I *do* respect them. A helluva-lot.

I imagine if I did stay, I'd happily obey their rules. It would be easy to, really. They are pretty cruisy with relationships, and more than anything, I know their rules come from caring and not trying to control.

As I move to Jared's side, he takes my hand, and we make our way out of the room.

I turn back, glancing at Will, and notice he's still smiling at us.

Hell. Could I stay?

Could I finally have a home and be happy?

25

JARED

*W*illiam Rogan is a decent person. I heard what he said to my girl before I entered the room. He told Dee that they wanted her to stay, and I could tell by his tone that he really meant it.

And fuck, I stood there waiting for her to say ok. To agree and tell him that she wanted to stay… But she didn't.

She is a woman of very few words, though, so hopefully the week she has left before she turns eighteen is enough time to convince her to stay.

Fuck, I want her to stay more than I want to breathe.

I drive back to my place and run in to get changed into my uniform before driving us to school. I don't want to go today, but right now, I don't want to push our luck with the Rogans, so I grin and bear it.

We've already missed the first three periods of the day, making it just in time to get to English class with Miss Dice.

I hardly hear what she is droning on about at the front of the classroom as we take our seats up in the back corner, Dee taking the seat closest to the window today.

Even though my eyes are cast forward like the rest of the

sheep in the class, my mind is on last night and that cheap room with red walls at the Red Room where Dee punished me for keeping things from her.

If you ask me, it was fucking worth it.

Jesus, I don't think she realises how fucking hot she is. Fuck, when she bared herself to me, I wanted to break the damn restraints and dive into her tight, hot cunt.

Fuck it. Now I'm hard.

I eye Dee from the corner of my eye, noting that she appears to be listening to Miss Dice. Slowly, I inch my hand under the table until I find the smooth flesh of her knee and drag my hand back, pulling her tartan skirt with it.

My touch makes her squirm, but she doesn't push me away. In fact, her legs widen a little more, giving me better access, and fuck, my dick jerks in my jocks.

Leaning closer, I slide my hand higher and whisper. "Touch yourself. Right here in class."

She stiffens at my words, and I bite back a smile as I try to appear like a well-behaved student.

Shifting my hand from her leg, I reach up, gripping her wrist sitting on top of the table, and drag it underneath, pushing it between her legs.

Her gasp is faint as she tugs her wrist free, quickly glancing around to see if anyone is watching what's happening in the back corner of the room. No one notices though, all busy focusing on whatever the hell Miss Dice is telling them.

"Fine. I'll touch you then," I whisper, returning my hand between her legs, and I resume my journey up her thigh, getting impossibly close to her heavenly pussy.

"Tell me to stop, Dee." I whisper, glancing at her flushed face, but she keeps her eyes trained on the front of the class, pretending to ignore me.

Little minx.

She likes dubious acts. She likes not being able to give a verbal yes or no. It fucking turns her on. And fuck, it turns me on, too.

Sucking my lower lip between my teeth, I face forward again while continuing my slow path until I find the damp heat of her panties.

Fuuuck.

Another gasp flies from her lips, this one more audible than the last, and I'm tempted to throw her over my shoulder and storm out so I can wring orgasm after orgasm from her.

Oh, man. That would be perfect.

When Dee's hand comes to rest over mine under the table, my brows shoot up and I glance at her to see her lids closed as her chest rises and falls quickly.

Damn. She's close to moaning out loud, and while I love hearing that, I don't want any other fucker to hear, so I slowly pull my hand away, and her eyes dart open.

"Sorry, Dee. Not here."

She glares at me, rage written across her expression, and I can't help it. I throw my head back and laugh.

"What's so funny, Jared?" Miss Dice calls from the front, and I shoot Dee a wink when her eyes widen, before turning my attention to our teacher.

"Nothing, Miss. Sorry."

"Get to work then," she calls, and I glance around to see what the other students are doing before my eyes go to the board.

Thank God she wrote the lesson plan on the board.

"I don't wanna do this work." I lean in and rasp in her ear. "I wanna take you somewhere private and see how many times I can make you come."

Biting back a smirk, Dee opens her workbook to the back page and writes a response.

'Please stop talking about making me come. I don't think I can handle it.'

I grin at her words. "Are you horny, Dee?" I whisper and she writes her response.

'Extremely.'

"Fuck. Me too. I'm so hard right now," I admit quietly, and her nostrils flare before she writes.

'Stop.'

"You are already so wet. Imagine what it would be like to feel my tongue glide over your pussy lips."

Dee whimpers, pointing to her previous response.

'Stop.'

"I can't." I admit, "You've turned me into an animal. Besides, you know the rules. I'll only stop if you say the words out loud."

She rolls her eyes at me, and I grin again before studying her face. She looks away, obviously uncomfortable at the intimacy of it while we are in the middle of English class.

Should I remind her that she was about to let me get her off?

Maybe not.

"Why are you shying away from me?" I whisper and Dee frowns, shaking her head.

"Is it because I have a hypnotising cock?"

A snicker falls from her lips before she can stop it, and I beam.

"I can't believe it was only days ago that I was an angry arsehole tormenting you with the promise of said hypnotising cock. How did you turn me from being a crazed, angry arsehole to, well… a happy arsehole?"

Dee shrugs and writes her response before showing me the page.

'Magic pussy?'

I throw my head back, laughing too loudly, once again gaining the attention of Miss Dice.

"Do I have to separate you two?" Miss Dice huffs and I stifle my rumbling laughter as I glance at her, shaking my head.

"No Miss. Sorry."

I glance at Dee, who is blushing but grinning broadly, while scribbling over her words, not wanting anyone to read her part of our conversation.

Fuck, I love this playful side of her. I imagine it would be like this a lot more if she were to stay and all of her worries vanished.

I really fucking want that for her. And if I'm being honest, I really want that for me, too.

26

DEE

*T*ravis didn't show up for community service again after school, so while Jared is chatting with Lexi, he lets me slide his phone from his pocket, and watches me at a distance as I bring up Travis' number and hit call.

I'm working off the theory that if Bianca thinks it's someone else calling, then she won't answer it, if she's nearby, but if she does answer it, I will just hang up.

It rings a few times before the call connects, and relief washes over me when I hear Travis' voice.

"Hey, Crowley. What's up?"

"Trav," I rasp, turning my back to Jared and Lexi, realising that Lexi can see me talking on the phone. "It's me. Can you talk?"

"Yeah, I'm doing good, buddy. You after some stuff?"

Shit. He can't talk. Someone must be nearby. There's background noise. Voices. A TV maybe.

"I just need to know if you're ok," I say quietly, and he chuckles.

"Yeah, man. I can get that for you. Cash upfront as usual."

The background noise fades, and a moment later, I hear the click of a door closing.

"Ell. Hey sorry. Now's not a great time."

"Shit, Trav. Did you know about Bianca coming to the swimming carnival and luring me out?"

"What?!" he snaps. "What the fuck are you talking about?"

My heart starts to calm as his reaction confirms he didn't know about his foster mum and her attempt to choke me.

"I got a message from your Instagram account, asking me to meet you outside the pool when we had the swimming carnival yesterday. It was her, Trav. She was leaning against a yellow mustang. She told me some stuff, and threatened me, and then fucking tried to choke me."

"What!"

"Shhh," I urge. "Calm down or they will know something is up."

"You're being serious right now?" he asks quieter.

"Yes. Jared scared her away… or well, maybe it was Rhys who did that, but either way, she vanished pretty quickly when my friends came out."

My friends? Is that what they are?

"I'm gonna fucking kill her," he hisses. "She stepped over the line with Cassie, and now you. She's fucking crazy."

He's right, that bitch is as crazy as they come, but he needs to be careful, because crazy will get him killed.

"Trav, I need you to come to me. We can run, or at least hide, until the Kerrs are wiped off the earth. There's so much about our past that I've only just learned, and I know Bianca will kill me the first moment she can, and I wouldn't put it past her to use you to do it. You're not safe with her, or any of them. I'm sorry about Cassie, I really am, but it's better if you just come to me, and we can ask Griffin to help get Cassie out of there later on."

"What have you learned about our past?" he asks, and I

roll my eyes, even though he can't see me. Of course, he latches on to that part of the information and not the pressing issue of him needing to escape the Kerrs' clutches.

"Long story short, the Angels are our aunties. They are... were dad's half-sisters. And the reason why Bianca is so adamant about killing me is because she was your mum's sister. She's *your* auntie, Trav. She's not going to stop hunting me until she gets revenge for Catherine's death."

"Fucking hell," he rasps. "She's been my auntie all this fucking time and hasn't said anything?"

"Yes," I state and he curses again.

"Fuck. Ok, Ell. I'll meet you at sunrise tomorrow. Outside the Rogans'?"

A lump forms in my throat, and tears prick my eyes as he says the words I've been waiting so long to hear. Clearing my throat, I answer. "Yes. Ok. Sunrise tomorrow morning."

We quickly say our goodbyes and hang up, and I turn to see Jared standing right behind me.

"Sunrise tomorrow? That's when you're leaving?"

The tears that I'd been fighting pop free, burning trails down my cheeks as I take in the broken look on his face.

Technically, we could stay and get Griffin to help hide us, but then we'd owe him, and this stupid cycle of favours will never end.

Slowly, as I peer up through blurry eyes, I nod.

Jared is silent for a moment, sucking in a breath as he drags his eyes from mine to look out over the school oval behind me. He's biting the inside of his cheek, a deep frown tugging his brows closer and his nostrils flare.

Oh fuck.

This is harder than I thought.

"I'm sorry," I whisper on a sob, and his blue gaze, filled with his own tears, darts back to mine before he reaches out and tugs me to his chest.

He holds me so tight, pressing his lips to the top of my head and lingering there for long moments.

This is it. Our last night together. I wanted another week, but after the revelations of yesterday, I was stupid to let myself think that I could have more. I need to keep my brother safe, and the only way to do that is by running far away from here.

Jared and I stand on the fringe of the oval for a long time, both of us together, yet dealing with turmoil in our own heads.

When we pull apart, Jared cups my face, using his thumbs to wipe away my tears.

"What do you want to do on your last night in Fox Pines?"

I sniff a few times, batting away the last of my tears. "I want to kill the last people on the list."

Jared frowns. "Why bother? You're leaving anyway. It's not your problem anymore."

I shrug. "I'm angry, so I need to kill someone. And also, if I finish the list, when I'm gone, Griffin can't hold anything over you or your family."

He shakes his head. "Nah, fuck that, Dee. I can handle Griffin myself."

"Fine, but I still need to kill someone."

He grins. "My little dancing assassin." He strokes my cheek, and my brows shoot up.

"Shit. Dancing. I completely forgot that I have dance class today," I rasp, my brows shooting up.

How the hell did I forget about that?

"You'll dance again soon, Dee. When you and Trav find a place to settle down, promise me you'll find a new dance studio."

Shit. Here I am, leaving him high and dry to deal with the chaos that's yet to hit the Timber Valley region, and Jared is concerned about me dancing again.

"I promise." I nod.

We stare at each other for a few more long beats, but then Jared breaks our eye lock, tugging me to his side before we slowly make our way through the school to his car.

He drives me up to the lookout, and when I realise where we are, I shoot Cynthia and Will a text saying I won't be home for dinner and will be out late, but promise I'll come through the front door. They reply a few minutes later with a thanks for letting them know.

Shit. I'll miss them, too.

I was never meant to get comfortable here. I was never meant to like my foster family, or the snobby catholic school, or make any friends, and certainly not find a boyfriend. Yet here I am with all of those things. Things I've never had before, finally feeling like I might belong. Only I can't. I have to leave.

When we pull up, we sit in silence for a few minutes, and it's the first time I hate the quiet. I just want to scream.

I turn and look at Jared, his eyes cast out the windscreen, his hands still gripping the steering wheel, his knuckles white with tension.

"I need you," I whisper, and his eyes dart to mine.

"Fuck. I need you, too," he growls, reaching across the space as I move toward him.

He lifts me easily onto his lap while he shifts the seat back, and I straddle him, feeling the press of his erection as I get comfy. Our lips collide next, our hands frantically gripping at each other's clothes like we need to get closer, and I have the overwhelming need to climb under his skin.

What a weird thought, but it's how I feel. I can't seem to get enough, and as we start shedding the top halves of our clothes, our pelvis' start grinding together, building friction.

By the time our top halves are naked, we are both panting with insatiable desire, and I rise up a little, working to get

Jared's pants open as he grasps onto my panties and tears the crotch, leaving the fabric clinging to my hips as my sex becomes exposed.

There are no words exchanged. No dirty talk required. Just us, our bodies, and this need that I fear will never be sated.

Jared grips his cock, lining it up, and I sink down on him, both of us moaning as we come together in the most intimate way. I'm well aware that he's not wearing a condom, and I don't fucking care. I need this. Skin on skin. No barriers between us. I'll worry about birth control later. Maybe Rhys can help with that?

Our bodies work together, picking up a good rhythm and we stare into each other's eyes, not willing to break the connection. I don't realise I'm crying until Jared reaches up and swipes away my tears before pressing his forehead to mine as I ride his lap.

"I need you to know something," he whispers. "I need you to know that my heart will always belong to you. No matter how long we are apart, or if we never see each other again. It's yours, Elodie. Everything I am belongs to you."

A loud sob jumps out of my throat before I press my lips to his, kissing him with the taste of my tears as we clutch onto each other and let ourselves go.

I climax first, my cries loud in the confined space of his car, and Jared's grunt follows until we are a limp mess tangled together on the seat of his car.

I want to tell him I love him, but I can't bring myself to do it. There's no point telling him that. Not now that I'm leaving in a matter of hours. So I keep the words in and hope that when I walk away, I won't die from a broken heart.

27

JARED

*W*hen Dee said she wanted to kill someone tonight, she wasn't kidding. She had a particular name on the list she'd been leaving until last, knowing that all the deaths before him would send fear through him as he waited his turn.

Technically, there are two people left, but she is determined to take out Police Sergeant Tommy Wanders first, wanting to make sure the job is done before she leaves.

Police Sergeant Tommy Wanders was the poor fool she called out on the podcast I started listening to when I recognised her voice. He was the reason Terence Hill and the Feast Nights at Vixen's Lodge managed to fly under the radar for so long, and as we drove in one of Griffin's cars to the Sergeant's house, Dee explained that Tommy was the one who pulled the strings to make sure Rhys was put in a room alone with her predator of a father when she went to visit him in prison.

I don't fucking know how Dee knows all of this information, but shit, it's impressive that she's able to find out things that even the cops can't seem to get their hands on.

Unfortunately for Tommy Wanders, his time on this earth has come to an end, and soon he won't be able to prey on and exploit any more minors.

"You sure I can't come in?" I ask Dee for the hundredth time as I pull the car up outside a house a few doors down from the target.

She shakes her head, her eyes focused out the windscreen as she mentally slides her persona from Dee to Hush.

"I need you outside. Watch the street. Same deal as last night," she says quietly with a level of calm that's almost eerie.

"Fine," I sigh, shutting off the engine.

I guess I should be glad she's talking to me now. After the emotions of the afternoon, Dee reverted back to using her notes app to communicate. I hated that she did that, knowing we were mere hours away from having to say goodbye to each other. I wanted to hear her voice every chance I could get, but I understand why she retreated back to her old ways.

She's struggling to deal with her emotions.

Something I'm all too familiar with.

We wait a few minutes, watching the street and houses around us. It's late. Nearly midnight. A lot of people tend to stay up late, but it seems that the houses in this part of Redfield are all early to bed given their dark and quiet houses.

Cracking the car door open, Dee slides out silently, and I follow, although I'm not as fucking quiet. If she were staying in Fox Pines longer, I'd get her to teach me how she moves like a ghost.

Pain pierces my heart at the reminder that this is our last night together, and I swallow the lump that forms in my throat, knowing now is too dangerous to be falling apart.

I follow Dee, or should I say Hush, up the street, pulling the balaclava down to cover my identity at the same time she does before we silently run across the front lawn of the police sergeant's house.

There are cameras here, her intel correct as I spot one above the front door. She reaches up, spraying something over the lens, and then drops to one knee as she pulls out a small light, flicking it on to the door lock, before inserting some sort of tool that I realise is for picking locks.

She works quickly, the lock clicking open only seconds later, and she stands, putting the tools into her pocket before unsheathing her blade.

Thana.

Turning back to me, Hush holds her hand up, reminding me to stay out here, and when I nod, she disappears inside, closing the door behind her.

I hate this part. Waiting outside while she puts her life on the line to slaughter a bad guy. I feel unusually anxious, so I start to pace before wondering if there's a window I can peek through.

The windows at the front of the house are all dark, thick drapes blocking me out, so I peer down the side of the house, noticing a light on towards the back. A quick check over my shoulder tells me all is quiet out here, so I creep down the side of the house, being careful to step on the pavers and not the stones as I go, to avoid someone hearing me.

When I get to the window with the warm yellow glow illuminating out into the night, I press myself up against the bricks of the house and slowly peer past them, into the house.

It looks quiet. I can't see anyone, but I think I can hear something.

A thud sounds, and I wait, wondering if that was Tommy's body falling to the floor. Then I hear a crash before Dee's small frame flies backwards into the room, slamming to the hard tiled floor.

FUCK!

I don't hesitate a second, bolting back towards the front of the house, not caring if someone can hear me. Stones crunching under my feet as I rush around the corner. By the time I make it to the front door, my heart is just about leaping from my throat, and I tug out the gun from the back of my pants, silencer already attached, and I flick off the safety.

With my gloved hand, I open the front door, gun raised as I enter, and the deep voice of a man floats to me from the other end of the long passage.

"You fucking little cunt! You think you can kill me? I'll fuck you up the arse so hard you'll wish you were never born!"

I move slowly, trying to remain silent, hoping the element of surprise is on my side.

I hear a slap, some grunts and even Dee cry out before something crashes, and I use the noise to move faster, finally getting to the end of the passage.

There's broken glass, furniture upended, and blood, but I ignore all of that as my eyes land on the large naked man smeared with blood, holding Dee's wrists in one of his big hands, as he tries to pull her pants down.

I see fucking red!

No longer caring if he can hear me, I crunch over the glass, and the moment he startles, his head turning to me, I point and shoot.

The guy stiffens, his head jerking back as a crimson circle forms on his forehead.

Dee pushes him off her, scrambling up quickly, and rushes to me.

"Is that your blood?" I ask, looking over her frantically, and she shakes her head, glancing over her shoulder as she pants from exhaustion.

"It's his. Thana didn't get much of a chance to do her thing before he attacked."

"Fuck, Dee," I whisper, pulling her to my chest.

She's not shaking like I thought she would be, and that's how I know it's still Hush here with me.

"I have to call Griffin," she states, pulling back and I hand her my phone.

While she speaks to Griffin, making arrangements for what I assume is a clean up given her DNA is probably everywhere in here now, I look around the house finding a room with four computer monitors, and on each screen is a different explicit scene playing out.

It takes a moment for me to realise that two of the monitors are displaying men with... children.

"Fuck," I grunt, spinning away, my chest rising and falling rapidly.

Dee steps into the room flicking the light on, and that's when I notice the blood on the floor and chair.

"He was sitting here jerking off," she states, her tone quiet but deadly. "These screens aren't recordings. They are live, happening right now, somewhere in the world."

"What?" I snap, turning to face the room, but avoid looking at the screens.

She nods. "I told Griffin. He's on his way with his crew and a hacker that should be able to at least get a general location... Maybe."

"I can't..." I shake my head, feeling sick to my stomach, and Dee takes my hand, and I notice she has now taken off her balaclava.

"This is why I do what I do. I know it's not my fight, but those kids," she points to the monitors, "they can't fight for themselves. So, I do it for them."

I nod, understanding now, more than ever, why this fight

she's fighting, along with the help of the Angels and the Marx family, is so fucking important.

"You could have been killed. Or he could have raped you," I state, my voice a little pitchier than usual.

"Yeah, I could have." She shrugs like it's no big deal.

"Fuck," I hiss and drag her to my chest again.

We wait about twenty minutes before Griffin and his crew turn up. While they get to work doing whatever it is they do, Dee cleans up in the bathroom, removing the clothes and putting them in another bag before handing them to Griffin.

"What do you do with them?" I ask Griffin, pointing to the bag.

He looks from me, down to the bag, and back up to me. "Burn them." He shrugs like it's no big deal.

"How do we know for certain you do that? Maybe you're keeping them to blackmail Dee with later on."

Griffin chuckles and Dee's brows shoot up.

"You've seen the scum we are dealing with, kid. If it weren't for Hush, we wouldn't have eliminated half the sick fuckers we've come across. There's no way I'd ever leave evidence that could lead back to her."

I narrow my eyes. "If you ever try to fuck her over again, I'll kill you myself," I snap, and Griffin smirks.

"I don't fucking doubt that. Seems you're a pretty accurate shot. We could really use you on our team."

In a heartbeat, Dee AKA Hush, has Thana pressed to Griffin's throat. He stills, his eyes wide and his men all freeze, their hands hovering near whatever weapons they are carrying. Dee doesn't speak. She doesn't have to. Griffin knows.

"Ok. Ok. I won't mention it to him again," Griffin agrees and I smirk as Dee backs off, returning to my side.

Griffin's men relax and get back to their tasks, and Dee

links her fingers with mine, giving them a squeeze as she gestures her head to the front door.

Time to leave.

"What. No goodbye?" Griffin asks, and Dee rolls her eyes. "Come on. I'd like to think I'm more than the prick that blackmailed you."

Dee stares at him for a minute before stepping forward and giving him a one-armed hug while still holding my hand.

"Look after him."

I hear the words she rasps quietly in his ear, and Griffin's eyes dart up to mine as he nods.

"Of course, kid. I'm kinda fond of the bossy arsehole."

I chuckle at his statement, and Dee grins, turning her back on the local leader of the Marx crew or whatever they call themselves, and we leave the house.

The drive back to Fox Pines is slow, because for some reason I have it in my head that if I take longer, time will slow down and I can have Dee to myself for a little longer.

Every time I think of her leaving, I push the thought aside, not wanting to let myself feel that pain yet. Because fuck, I'll have plenty of time to feel it once she's gone.

That's when I know I'll die on the inside once and for all.

28

DEE

*I*t's a little after 2am when Jared pulls up outside my house. When he shuts off the engine, we sit in silence for a beat before I make the first move and get out of the car. Jared follows, and we link fingers again, slowly walking up the front path of the Rogans', knowing this is the last time we will be doing this together.

Shit.

Don't think about it.

When we reach the door, I go to grab the handle but notice it's damaged.

I still, my heart wanting to leap with fear, but my training kicks in, keeping me calm so I can hear properly.

"Dee—"

I hold up my hand, quickly shushing Jared's words, and that's when I hear it. A deep voice and a whimper.

I turn to him, gripping his hoodie and tugging him down to me to whisper in his ear.

"The house has been broken into. Someone is inside, and I think they are hurting my foster parents."

Jared stiffens, standing tall and puffing his chest out in an instant.

I creep away from the front door, tugging Jared with me, and we move to the front window outside Cynthia and Will's bedroom.

Leaning over the small garden bed, we hear a slap, another whimper, and then a gruff voice.

"Either you tell me which one is her bedroom, or we wake up all of the kids. Don't make this fucking harder than it needs to be."

Eyes wide, Jared and I stare at each other, and he leans down to my ear to whisper.

"That's Adam. Trav's foster brother."

Shit.

That's what I was worried about.

"Contact Griffin," I whisper close to his ear. "I'm going in through the back."

I dart off, but his big hand wraps around my wrist, stopping me short. His face is furious when I turn back, and he shakes his head.

"You're not going in alone," he whisper-yells. "You were already nearly killed tonight. I'm not sitting out here twiddling my fucking thumbs while you're in there in danger."

Normally, I'd roll my eyes, but this time, I lurch forward, wrapping my arms around his neck, and kiss him. He returns the kiss, almost dominating me, showing me that the alpha in him is lurking close to the surface, the one I met before this softer version of Jared came out.

Shit, I think I love both versions.

Breaking the kiss, I give him a nod, and we move together to the side gate. While I silently unlatch it, he shoots Griffin a text, and then we sneak through the backyard together.

Happy that I left my window open earlier, we slip in

through there, and I draw Thana from my back holster as I approach my bedroom door.

A quick glance back shows Jared has the same gun raised that he had earlier, and I frown, wondering why he didn't leave it in Griffin's car when we swapped them out on the way back here.

Cracking my door open, I listen to make sure I can't hear anyone near, and when I know it's clear, I swing it wide and move out into the central living area that the kids' bedrooms surround. Rhys' bedroom door is shut, as is the twins' door, but Charlotte's is open, which likely means she's not home. Probably at her girlfriend's again.

The door to the main living area is also closed, so I approach it and listen, and I can faintly hear noise coming from the front of the house.

"What's the plan?" Jared whispers, and I dart my gaze around before answering.

"We get the twins, Rhys and whichever guys she has with her out of the house, and then we go kill us some uninvited guests."

Jared smirks. "You're so fucking hot right now."

I grin, shaking my head before gesturing to Rhys' room.

"You go wake Rhys and your mates up. I'll get the twins and bring them to Rhys' room. Make sure they have their dicks covered before the twins get there."

Smirking, Jared nods before taking off in the direction of Rhys' room.

I watch him silently open the door and slip in, and then I do the same, slipping into the twins' shared space.

Their beds are side by side, close enough that they can reach out and touch if they want to.

I rush forward, flicking on their bedside lamp, thankful that the glow is dim, before shaking their shoulders until they rouse.

Slowly, two sets of dark brown eyes blink open, and they both start to squint, which is when I realise they can't see me properly. They need their glasses.

I hand each of them their glasses from the shared bedside table, and they slide them on, half sitting up, their little faces creased in confusion.

"Dee?" Connor asks, so I nod.

"I need you both to listen very carefully," I whisper, and both sets of eyes widen.

"You can talk?" Archie asks, and I press my finger to my lips.

"Shhh. This is an emergency, so I need you to listen. Ok?"

They nod quickly, shifting to the edges of their bed.

"Don't panic. I need you to stay calm, because calm is the way to stay safe. Understand?"

They nod again.

"Ok. There are some bad men in the house talking to your mum and dad. I need to get you to Rhys' room, where she will sneak you out of the house, to somewhere safe. Ok?"

Their little lips quiver as fear kicks in, but they nod.

"Ok. Let's go. Hold hands, and no matter what happens, you run as quietly as you can to Rhys' room, and you stay quiet until she says you can make a noise, ok?"

They rush their nods, holding each other's hands before Archie grabs mine.

Shit.

It's so little and trembling in fear. They are only nine years old. Too young to be this scared.

My heart pangs at the reminder that Travis was the same age when I killed his mum.

Shit.

None of this would be happening if it weren't for me, which is just another reason why I need to leave with Travis. Everyone will be safer if we are gone.

I open their door again, peering out. The only person in sight is Jared, standing in Rhys' open doorway waiting for us.

I tug on their hands, and we rush out, Archie dropping my hand as they dash silently to Rhys' room, and a moment later I join them, Jared closing us all in.

"What I want to know is why the hell you have a gun?" Rhys snaps at Jared, and when she takes me in, her mouth drops open. "And why the fuck do you have a big knife?"

"Now's not the time," I snap, and Rhys' eyes widen.

"I forgot you're talking now. Sexy AF, by the way."

"Jesus, George. Now really isn't the fucking time," Jared snaps and Rhys rolls her eyes like Jared is being dramatic.

"Come on," Shaun whisper-yells from Rhys' open window. "Let's go."

The twins grab Rhys' hands, tugging her to the window, and they climb out with Shaun's assistance into the backyard.

"Go to the park a few blocks over and hide in the shadows. Don't come out unless it's me, Jared, or Griffin Marx."

"Or the Angels," Jared adds, and I look back at him with a frown.

"Griffin is on his way." He holds up his phone. "With your aunties."

"Wait, what? The Angel sisters are your aunties?" Rhys asks, but I ignore it.

"Go!" I hiss, and without another word, they rush off into the darkness.

I relax a little, knowing they will be safe, and turn my focus back to the people who aren't.

Cynthia and Will.

"Game plan?" Jared asks as we dash through the kids' living zone, and I shrug.

"Kill them if the Rogans aren't going to be collateral," I state, and he nods.

At the door dividing us from the rest of the house, I take a deep breath, summoning more calm, and then I ease it open.

A quick glance shows no one down at this end of the house, so we move out, heading towards the front.

The voices get louder the closer we get to Cynthia and Will's bedroom, and when I hear a male cry out in anguish and a woman scream like an animal, I throw the door open wide, blade raised.

My eyes dart over the scene, a little confused at first.

Adam Kerr is leaning against the wall, laughing hysterically. A man I don't know, but who is clearly on the Kerrs' payroll, is lying on the floor clutching his junk as blood pools on the carpet below him. Cynthia is on her knees on the floor near the man, arms tied behind her back and her lips and teeth stained with blood. And William is what I am hoping is unconscious and not dead on the floor behind Cynthia with his hands tied behind his back.

"Oh, good." Adam laughs. "You've come to watch the show." He slaps his knee, still laughing. "Funniest fucking thing I've seen in ages."

"Fuck you, Adam! She bit my dick!" The man on the floor hisses, and hell, I'd laugh too under different circumstances.

Go Cin!

"Now kid," Adam turns serious, his eyes flicking over my shoulder to where Jared is standing, gun raised. "I'd think twice before doing anything rash. We are only having a bit of fun." Adam turns his eyes to Cynthia. "Isn't that right, Principal Rogan?"

"Come closer." Cynthia hisses through her blood-soaked teeth. "I dare you."

Again, Adam starts laughing hysterically.

"It's time for you to leave," I tell Adam, and he immediately stops laughing and glares at me.

"Good idea. You're coming with us."

My brows shoot up, but it's Jared that responds.

"Like fuck she is."

"Oh, she is." Adam narrows his eyes at Jared. "Bianca is waiting for her with Travis, who doesn't seem to be doing so well tonight."

"What do you mean?" I ask, and Adam smirks.

I wanna smack that smirk right off his smug face!

"He's gone a few rounds with my fists. He was out cold when I left."

There's no stopping how my heart rate picks up as anger engulfs me. Any sense of calm I had has vanished and a low growl escapes me.

Adam laughs again. "Oh, this is going to be fun."

"Shoot him," I snap at Jared, but before he can respond, a loud clunk sounds, and Jared tumbles forward, face first, into the carpet.

"Took your fucking time, Reggie," Adam hisses, shooting a glare at the man that just knocked Jared out.

I cringe at the thought of another hard hit to Jared's head.

"I was taking a fucking dump. I told you that having curry for dinner was going to come back and fucking haunt me," Reggie snaps and Adam rolls his eyes.

Ignoring both of them, I lurch at Reggie, swinging Thana, her sharp edge nicking Reggie's arm, and he jumps out of reach.

"Fucking crazy bitch!" he yells, but it's the whimper behind me that pulls me up short.

Glancing over my shoulder, I see Adam standing next to Cynthia with the barrel of his gun pressed to her temple.

"Uh-uh, savage girl. If you want your foster mummy to live, then you need to drop that fucking sword of a knife, and come quietly with us."

My eyes dart to Cynthia's and even though there are tears streaming from her eyes, she shoots me a glare and gives her head the slightest shake.

Shit.

She's willing to die.

For me.

I drop Thana without another thought, and Cynthia whimpers.

"No. Dee. No."

"I have to," I whisper. "I'm sorry I brought this into your house. Thank you for being the most welcoming and caring family I've ever had."

"Fucking boo hoo," Adam snaps, shoving Cynthia away from him before stalking to me, but addressing Reggie. "Tie up the boyfriend. We don't want him waking and following us."

When Adam is in front of me, he sneers, flashing his teeth as he looks me up and down. "It's gonna be fun taking you for a ride on my dick."

"Stay the fuck away from her," Jared slurs as he starts to rouse, but it's too late. Reggie has already bound Jared's wrists behind his back, and he drags him across the room to where Will is still unconscious.

Shit.

I really hope he's just unconscious and not something more.

Adam makes quick work of zip tying my wrists together behind my back, and Jared watches in confusion as he tries to piece together what happened while he was out cold.

"Reggie, pick up Munro and let's get the fuck outta here," Adam demands, and Reggie moves to the dick bleeding guy curled into a ball, and helps him stand, crumpled over.

"Stop!" Jared yells, as Adam starts hauling me by my bound wrists to the door, and as he drags me over the threshold, with tears in my eyes, I say my last words to Jared.

"I'm sorry. I love you."

JARED

uck!
FUCK!

She's gone. She's actually gone. They fucking took her!

I leap up from the floor awkwardly, stumbling and face planting the carpet, my body uncoordinated from my hands being bound behind my back, and perhaps too, from being knocked out once a-fucking-gain!

"Jared," Cynthia cries, moving over to me on her knees. "You need to calm down."

"No!" I roar. "NO!"

"What's happening?" William mumbles as he comes to, and a sob escapes his wife.

"They took Dee." She starts crying, and I use my forehead to push myself back up off the carpet to my knees.

"I need to get her!" I grunt, trying to stand again. "They are going to kill her. Fuck, that prick will probably rape her first!"

I'm losing my fucking mind. I can't breathe. Shit. I can't breathe.

"Jared, listen to my voice," Cynthia snaps, and I try, but it's hard to focus on anything. They are going to fucking defile my girl. "Jared. You can't help her unless you calm down. Listen to my voice. Can you hear it?"

"Yes," I hiss even as my lungs constrict.

"Look at me," she insists, and I glance over my shoulder to see my school principal's tear-soaked cheeks and glassy eyes. "You can do this. You can breathe. Just try to calm your heart. Try to suck air in."

Nodding, I latch onto her voice and try. And fuck, it works.

"Good. Again." Cynthia insists, so I do it again and again. "That's it."

A loud crash rattles the windows as the front door slams open against the wall, and I freeze until I see Griffin Marx step inside with his gun raised. His men come in after him, and one look at me and he lowers his gun.

"Where's Hush?" he snaps, and Cynthia snaps back.

"Who is Hush, and who the hell are you?"

Shit.

"Crow! Answer me!" Griffin ignores Cynthia, his eyes trained on me.

"They took her," I rasp, feeling my throat start to close over again.

"They're gone?" he asks and I nod.

Griffin directs his men to do a sweep of the house before he steps into the room and proceeds to cut us free.

"Excuse me, but you need to tell me who the hell you are, and what the fuck is going on!" Cynthia cries, and I hang my head as I sit on the end of her bed.

"Cyn." Will tries to wrap her in his arms, but she shoves him away, determination written across her face as she waits for answers.

"Mrs Rogan, this is Griffin Marx. He's uh... an acquaintance of Dee's." I offer, and her eyes narrow.

"What sort of acquaintance?"

"The sort that will help get Dee back." The new voice that floats to us from the door belongs to Amanda Angel, and I glance at Cynthia to see her brows shoot up.

"Amanda?"

"Jared, perhaps you can go with Griffin and fill him in with what happened," Bec suggests, stepping into the room next to her sister. "Amanda and I will tell Cynthia and William the truth."

"Well, someone better start telling the fucking truth around here!" Cynthia snaps, and I stand from the bed as Bec and Amanda comfort the Rogans, and I head to the living area with Griffin.

"We have to go, man," I snap. "Adam Kerr took her. He said he was going to rape her before she dies. We have to go."

Griffin nods, barking orders to his men to do a drive-by of the Kerr house before I tell him that Rhys and the others are hiding at the park up the road.

The house quickly gets overrun with Marx crew, and the Angels take the Rogans up to the park to get the others, while I stare at the gun on the counter that I had earlier.

I want to pick it up, drive across town to that shitty fucking house, and shoot every motherfucker in sight.

But I know I can't. I'm not trained to be that fucking skilled, and I know going in guns blazing might end up in Dee's death prematurely.

Fuck.

FUCK!

Why didn't I pull the trigger when we first entered the room?

Why did I fucking hesitate?

Now she's gone, and I may never see her again, and I never got to tell her that I love her back.

30

DEE

The car trip takes about twenty-five minutes. How do I know that? I counted. There's not much else to do in the boot of a car with only darkness surrounding you. So if I'm correct, we are pulling up somewhere near Redfield. Perhaps Redfield Lake?

It's entirely possible we went in the other direction, but I don't think the Kerrs would go east. No, I have a feeling we have just stopped at the house Griffin said the Kerrs own on the lake.

The boot flies open, and I snap my teeth at the hands coming towards me, but it's not enough to deter them, and their rough grip hurts as I'm pulled out of the trunk and slung over a shoulder.

Adam's shoulder.

I glance around, taking in as much as I can, but unfortunately, we are in a big garage, so I can't see anything outside, but the yellow mustang is enough. I am definitely at Bianca Kerr's lake house.

We enter a passage, and a door opens before we descend a staircase.

Shit. A basement.

Houses in Australia don't typically have basements, but the Kerr houses do. It's where they grow their weed, or make their drugs, or, in this case, hold their captives.

"Hey! Hey!" Adam laughs before slapping my arse hard. "Look what I found."

"Fuck you, Adam! Let her go!"

Shit.

Travis.

I dart my head around trying to see him, but it's not until Adam flings me off his shoulder and I slam back onto a table that my eyes connect with Travis' as the wind flies from my lungs.

I ignore the fact that I can't breathe for a few long moments, and keep my eyes trained on my little brother, assessing him for injuries.

He's pretty banged up, one eye swollen shut, his lip split and dry blood staining his chin. There's a cut in one of his eyebrows too, and his right hand is wrapped in what I assume is the t-shirt that he's no longer wearing, blood staining the fabric. His pale skin is painted in purple and yellow bruising, and there's even a fucking burn mark on his chest.

I'm going to kill Adam Kerr if it's the last thing I do.

"Ell. Are you ok?" he asks from where he's tied to a chair at the edge of the room, and I give him a nod, even as Adam starts cackling like a crazy person.

"She's gonna be alright when I fuck that innocence from her."

"Don't go near her!" Travis roars, and I flinch.

I've never heard him sound so animalistic.

"Oh, but I have to." Adam snickers, moving closer to me to run his fingers up over the curve of my hips.

His first mistake was not tying me down.

The moment he's close enough, I rear up and headbutt him, causing him to stagger back as blood starts pissing from his nose.

"You fucking cunt!" His fist is like a brick, slamming into the side of my face with such force that I see stars.

I guess *my* mistake was not headbutting him hard enough, because now he's securing me to the damn table.

Crap.

In my temporarily dazed state, I can hear Travis yelling. Screaming. Cursing. And a minute later, I know why.

As I shake the haze from my vision, I see, and feel, a very naked Adam Kerr start to cut my clothes from my body.

Well, fuck. This isn't good.

I struggle, my arms biting with pain, with the way they are being squashed under my back, my wrists still bound behind me. My feet are tied in place, spread apart on the tabletop, and a rope is weaved between my arms and my back, securing my top half in place.

"What a pleasant surprise. Such a curvy little thing for a shortie." Adam grins, his eyes travelling over my nearly naked form, and I silently pray he leaves my bra and panties in place.

"Stay away from her!" Travis yells again, going crazy in his chair, shuffling it back and forth.

"Save your fucking breath, Trav. I thought you'd learned from the way I fucked Cassie in front of you earlier that you'd know there's no way I'm stopping."

"You didn't fuck her!" Travis bellows. "YOU RAPED HER!"

The anguish in Trav's tone is making me start to panic. I think about the beautiful moments Jared and I have spent together, and know that I'd rather die than have the act of sex tainted. Why do men like Adam Kerr have to use their dicks as weapons?

Suddenly, my view of Travis disappears as Adam's hard cock fills my line of sight, and I quickly squeeze my eyes shut.

"Come on. I know you want it. All girls want it." He cackles, and I hear the vile slapping sounds of him jerking off close to my ear.

"No! Stop!" Travis yells, and a moment later, a crash causes Adam to abandon his wanking session and turn away from me.

"What the fuck are you trying to do?" Adam snarls at Travis, and I now see part of Travis' form, toppled sideways on the floor, still bound to the chair.

Adam starts laughing hysterically, turning his back on Trav and returning his focus to me. "You two are fucking nut jobs."

"There's a nut job in this room, and it isn't me or Travis," I hiss, which only angers Adam, and he leaps up on the table over me, standing while resuming his wank session.

"You think you're real fucking clever, don't you?" He jerks faster, biting his lip as his face contorts into pleasured pain.

I squeeze my eyes shut, not wanting to see the moment he shoots cum on me, but the roar of Travis startles my eyes open, as he charges for the table we are on, his arms still bound to the chair, but the bottom half is broken away, giving him use of his legs.

I thank whatever god there is that he must have broken the chair when he toppled it over, and I watch as Adam leaps off the table towards his foster brother before they clash in a thud.

I'm terrified that Travis is going to get himself killed, and I start screaming for help. Over and over.

I never thought I'd be so happy to see Bianca Kerr in my life, but her entrance into the room, and deep bellow, directed at Adam to stop works, before she ambles down the staircase with a skinny man trailing behind her.

As the room falls silent, I'm left wondering if I've just traded one devil for another, or if they are about to band together to make my life a living hell.

31

JARED

Griffin has me locked in the Rogan house with the family and my mates. He thinks he's doing me a fucking favour, trying to protect me, but I'm about ready to start killing people if they don't let me out of here very fucking soon.

Everything is taking too much time. Time Dee doesn't fucking have!

I never realised how many men Griffin had on his payroll until today, a hoard of them pulling up in blacked out SUVs, climbing out to cover the Rogans' front lawn that is still new and trying to grow. They surrounded Griffin as he spoke to them, and minutes later, the twenty or so men got back in the SUVs and sped away.

Meanwhile, I had to watch from the front window of the room William uses as an office, trying to fucking read lips.

I bet Dee could have read their lips.

Shit.

Dee.

"How did you get messed up in all of this?" William asks

from behind me as I pace, waiting for Griffin to come back inside the house to give me a fucking update.

I shrug. "I was in the wrong place at the wrong time," I snap, but then shake my head, raking my hand through my hair. "That's not true." I glance up at William, who's looking a little worse for wear. "The moment I met Dee, my whole world changed. Even if I hadn't been at that place that night, I would have still ended up involved somehow since I couldn't seem to leave Dee alone."

"What place on what night?" William asks, confused, and I sigh.

Can I tell him?

The Angels have filled him and Cynthia in on everything relating to Dee, even the jobs she does as Hush. They even have an idea of what Griffin does.

Why they're trusting them with such sensitive information has me stumped, but the Rogans don't seem to be freaking out about it as much as I thought they would. Maybe because of the stuff that happened to Rhys?

Shit, I don't fucking know.

"I was with Travis one night," I admit to Will, "and a drug deal turned bad. Dee showed up, and then Griffin and his cousin were called in to help, and well... here we are." I skirt over the finer details of the night. Like Pike getting stabbed with a screwdriver and bleeding out and dying.

Slowly, William nods.

"Do you love Dee?" he asks, surprising me, and I nod quickly.

"More than anything."

He smiles. "You've helped change her. I know it's because of you that she's started speaking."

I shrug. I can't really tell him that I tried to force her to speak numerous times by using sex. William seems like a nice man and a pretty chill dude, but I don't for a minute doubt he'd throw punches if I said that to him.

"She just needed a home where she felt safe," I say instead. "I'm not the only reason she feels comfortable enough to talk."

William smiles again, but his eyes shift over my shoulder out the window with a frown, and I spin to see one of the blacked out SUVs pulling back up. Two men get out, speaking quickly to Griffin, and the next moment, Griffin throws punches into thin air before throwing his head back and roaring in rage.

Fuck. No.

Dee!

My heart races as I watch Griffin suck in some deep breaths, dropping his chin to his chest and putting his hands on his hips while he thinks. Then he barks some more orders, pointing stern fingers at his men before they nod and return to the car.

The moment Griffin darts his head in our direction, I straighten, ready to fight this motherfucker if he doesn't fucking fill us in on what has happened.

He speaks to some of his other men who are guarding the house and then he storms up the path and comes inside.

"What the fuck happened?" I snap, and Griffin huffs.

"My men went to the Kerr house in Mercy Court. It was empty, trashed, and they found a lot of blood."

An audible gasp flies from William, but Griffin holds his hands up.

"Hang on, let me finish. We don't believe it's Dee's blood. We know Adam Kerr had been keeping Cassie, Travis' foster sister, captive. The blood looks old, so we think it's hers. The problem is, we don't know where they are. The Kerrs have a lot of places they could be hiding out. An obvious one is the lake house, which we thought may be too obvious, but I don't think Bianca Kerr is trying to hide. So our next best bet is that they have relocated their operation to the lake. My men are going to run surveillance on it now."

"Surveillance? Fuck that! Just go the fuck in there and get my girl!"

Griffin glares at me. "Stop thinking with your fucking heart, Crow. That shit will get Dee and everyone else killed. She's a smart and skilled girl. She can handle herself for a while. We need to know what we are walking into, so suck it up for a bit longer. Once we have more intel, we will go in and make sure the Kerrs never fucking breathe again."

I want to believe Griffin, that Dee has the skill to handle this situation, but then I keep thinking of Adam's words.

Sure, Dee can handle a fight, but rape?

Fuck. I can't even bear to think of what he could be doing to her right now.

32

DEE

*P*ain explodes across my cheek as Bianca Kerr proves that she is definitely here to make my life a living hell. Something wet and warm runs down my face, over my jawline and down my neck as I slowly turn my gaze back to the large woman. One glance at the rocks on her fingers tells me that the wet sensation on my face is most definitely blood, caused by those chunky rings she's wearing, piercing my flesh.

"You little cow! Say something!" she hisses, and I just smirk.

Yep. I've returned to keeping silent, and it's infuriating her.

I'm hoping it gives me more time. She wants answers. Details about what happened the day her sister killed my dad, and in turn, I killed her sister.

The moment I spill those details, I'm dead, so now she's dealing with the quiet version of me.

The silent Hush.

"Bianca! Please, stop!" Travis cries out from across the

room, where he has now been bound to a large concrete post. There's no way he's escaping that.

"You disappoint me, Travis." Bianca sneers. "After everything I've done for you. Everything I've taught you. Here you are defending the girl that killed *your* mum." Stepping away from where I'm now bound by my wrists to an overhead beam hanging like a sack, Bianca ambles towards my brother. "She stabbed her, Travis. Remember? Not just once or twice, but forty-three times. Forty-three times, Travis!"

"She deserved it," Travis hisses with venom lacing his tone, and Bianca gasps before closing the distance and back handing him.

"Take that back!" she screams, sounding more and more unhinged.

"Let me fuck her voice outta her." Adam snickers from the side of the room where he's been sitting casually, puffing on a smoke, looking bored. "I'll get her talking again."

Bianca straightens from where she's glaring down into Travis' face, his body slumped, but struggling against the bonds that keep him bound to the post.

"Not yet," Bianca snaps. "But Cassie looks like she wants some more."

My eyes widen as I take in Travis' foster sister, naked and curled in a ball in the far back corner of the basement. Her whimpers increase when Adam stands from the chair and my eyes dart to Travis' to gauge his reaction.

Pain. Pure torturous pain contorts his expression, and he starts shaking his head.

"No! Leave her alone! Don't fucking touch her!"

Adam cackles like a fucking psycho, dropping the butt of his cigarette on the concrete floor and stubbing it out with his bare fucking foot, before swaggering like he's just walked into a damn party, towards Cassie.

"What's it going to be, girl?" Bianca turns back to me and

snarls. "Are you gonna talk or are you gonna let Cassie suffer for your silence?"

Cassie screams as Adam drags her across the basement floor, his hand fisted in her hair as she flails about.

"Time for round eleven." He chuckles, pulling her to stand before shoving her face first onto the thick timber bench I was tied to earlier. "Or is it round twelve? I can't remember. Can you, Trav?"

"You fucking sick cunt! I'm going to kill you!" Travis roars, and shit, my eyes prick with heat, knowing what's about to happen.

"Fine!" I scream, startling Bianca, which just makes Adam cackle louder as he slaps Cassie's bare arse, now bent over, facing the room. "What do you want to know?!"

"Finally, she speaks!" Bianca sing songs, before she starts hacking over and over, sounding like a damn warthog.

Douglas Kerr, Bianca's stick thin husband, darts out of the shadows from behind me, rushing a glass of water to his hefty wife. He holds it up to her lips, doting on her like she's a queen, and all he gets in return for his efforts is a shove as she snatches the glass and takes care of herself.

Douglas Kerr clearly wears the skirt in this relationship.

Cassie's whimper drags my gaze from Bianca to see Adam standing behind her, cock in hand as he guides it between her legs and thrusts forward hard.

Travis roars again, tears streaming down his face as my own fall, and Bianca starts clapping. Like watching her foster son raping her foster daughter is good fucking viewing.

"STOP!" I scream. "I'll talk. I'll tell you anything! Just stop!"

Bianca throws her head back, laughing as she points at me and then Travis.

"Look at these two, Dougy. Look how pathetic they are."

"Fuck you, bitch!" I sneer, which just makes her laugh even more.

"Don't worry. Cassie is a whore. She's used to being fucked like this." Adam grunts as he slams into her over and over so hard that Cassie's screams are warranted. "You, however." He chuckles, taking a moment to pull his cock free and fist it, giving it a jerk as he grabs a bottle of oil and pours it over his dick. "You're not used to being fucked like this, are you?" He licks his lips, tossing the oil aside and wanking his cock faster. "It's going to be fun breaking you."

"Stay the fuck away from her!" Travis yells again, but it falls on deaf ears as Adam approaches me.

"Have you even taken a cock before El-o-die?" He draws out my name before licking his lips, his eyes dropping to my bra, and then to my panties. "I bet you're real fucking tight." Stepping flush with me, his vile breath nearly makes me gag, and his heated bare skin presses against my front as he stabs his hard dick against my panty clad sex. "I bet I can make you bleed."

Travis is absolutely losing his mind. The words flying from him are animalistic and incoherent, but I can't focus on anything else but this crude arsehole in front of me, trying to scare me with his dick.

I can't help it. I smirk and then say something I probably shouldn't.

"The only one who will be bleeding is you, when I cut off your puny dick."

33

JARED

*M*y knee won't stop jigging as we speed through the outskirts of Fox Pines, with Redfield Lake our destination.

"Calm the fuck down!" Griffin hisses as he steers the car, overtaking slow motherfuckers on the highway.

"How about you drive faster?" I retort, and Griffin snarls.

"If I drive any fucking faster, we will end up wrapped around a tree, and then who the fuck will save her? Huh?" he snaps, and I grit my teeth, balling my fists in my lap, itching to swing them at anything that stands between me and Dee. Fucking anything!

"Don't make me regret bringing you, Crow. I'll kick your arse out on the side of the road, right fucking now, if you don't fucking calm down!"

My lip curls as I shoot Griffin a death glare, and the fucker smirks.

"Look, I know you care about her. Hell, we all do. But you gotta get your head straight, man. Don't be the reason she gets killed."

My face falls at Griffin's words, and I know he's right. I know I need to listen to reason. Dee's life depends on it.

That's if she's still alive.

FUCK!

34

DEE

I cringe as Adam drags his tongue up the column of my neck, trying to turn my head away when he draws it over my chin and towards my mouth. His hands are all over me now, and I know I should've kept my mouth shut, because it's only made him pay me more attention. But at least his attention is no longer on Cassie.

Fuck.

I hate scum like this fucker. How did Travis ever survive growing up in that household? Did they do stuff like this all the time? What has Travis had to endure?

"Tell me what I want to know, girl, and I'll get him to back off." Bianca sneers from over Adam's shoulder as she watches on.

"What exactly do you want to know?" I snap, and she grins.

"I want to know why you stabbed my sister so many times?" She snarls, her glare hard, her voice cracking with emotion.

"I needed to make sure she was dead." I shrug, while

Adam steps back from me, looking over his shoulder at his foster mum.

"She would have been dead after the first few stabs. Why did you slaughter her like that?"

"She killed my dad, so I killed her. It's not rocket science, Bianca." I roll my eyes, and I don't even see the backhand coming when Adam's hand cracks across my face.

"Don't be a smart bitch!" he growls, getting too close as he starts pumping his cock again.

"Your dad was nothing but a snitch!" Bianca screams, and again, I shrug.

"And your sister was nothing but a psycho bitch on crack!"

SLAP!

That one shook my brain a little, my vision turning dark briefly, and my hearing waning. As I shake it off, I can hear Travis' yelling, pleading for them to leave me alone.

I don't really mind that they have their focus on me, though. It means they aren't laying a hand on him or Cassie, and I need it to stay that way until I can figure out how to get us out of this.

"Can I fuck her now?" Adam sneers, directing his question to his foster mum, but baring his yellow teeth at me.

"Yes," Bianca snaps, and my eyes widen.

Shit.

She knows how much this will kill Travis. Why is she torturing him, too? He's her nephew, for fuck's sake.

Grinning wide, Adam presses close to my dangling body, his hand roughly grabbing between my legs as he tries to push his fingers inside me despite the fact that my panties are in the way.

It hurts, his fingers harsh in their pursuit, and my sex dry as a bone, but he persists, pressing himself up close, his hard cock rubbing against the bare skin of my abdomen.

"STOP!" Travis screams while Bianca laughs, and her creepy husband grins wide watching on.

"Let's fuck." Adam cackles, finally drawing his fingers from between my legs, turning his head back over his shoulder. "Doug, grab me the oil. I need to be really fucking slick to sink into this tight bitch."

I glance around quickly, trying to figure out how to stop this. It's a bit fucking hard when both my hands are strung up, but I still have my legs. I could kick him in the nuts, I suppose, but then what? I risk another punch to the face and blacking out completely. Then I'll likely wake up to him raping me.

Shit.

SHIT!

Real panic grips my heart like a closing fist as I watch Adam slather his dick with more oil while his parents watch on. This is really going to happen. He's really going to rape me.

But at least it's not Cassie again.

I keep reminding myself of that, my eyes darting around the room to find her slumped on the floor, her skin covered in dirt and blood and face so badly beaten that I'm sure it will leave permanent damage. Cassie may have been whoring herself out before all of this happened, but she doesn't deserve this. No one does.

She'd been a sex worker for the Kerrs, something they drummed into her head from a young age, no doubt. They groomed her into that role, and now they treat her like trash.

I wonder what she would be doing with her life now, if she never went into the Kerrs' care. I wonder if she would have found happiness.

"Fuck, I'm so ready to break your hymen." Adam grins, shifting closer again, and I roll my eyes, feigning boredom.

"Too late. That ship sailed years ago." I lie, and hell, it's worth the fist in my hair, reefing my head back, just for the look of disappointment on Adam's face at my words.

"How about your arse?" he snaps, spittle hitting my nose. "How many have fucked you there?"

I start laughing. "So many. It's practically prolapsing."

Jesus fucking Christ. I can't let him go there.

Growling with fury, he shoves his hard dick between my thighs, fucking the narrow space there.

The urge to lift my legs apart to stop him from touching me that way is strong, but that will give him easier access to my sex, and I need to avoid that for as long as possible.

He grips my hips tight as he starts thrusting, and the moment he hooks his fingers in my panties to pull them down, a large explosion rattles the basement from somewhere above, before the unmistakable sound of gunfire starts.

Finally.

While Adam freezes, his eyes going wide in panic, I hoist my legs up, wrapping them around his waist tight and locking my ankles behind his back, taking him off guard. His eyes go wide in surprise, but I don't give him a chance to say or do anything about it before I sink my teeth into his neck, right over the jugular.

I'm not sure why there is such a big craze about vampires, because blood does *not* taste good. At all! But what is good is the heated gush that fills my mouth, pouring down my chin and chest. It's fucking epic knowing I have his life source spilling free.

Clamping my teeth together so tightly that I tear a chunk of his flesh away, I try not to gag on its texture as I spit it free.

His roar is loud as he struggles against my hold, pressing his hand to his neck, but I keep my legs locked tight, my ears picking up more gunfire somewhere above us. As Adam flails, I latch onto the other side of his neck, doing the same thing, mashing my teeth closer together while he tries to punch me in the head.

He lands a few blows, but I keep my teeth deep in his flesh until they finally meet and I tear more flesh from him.

His struggles are getting weaker, his concern focused on the amount of blood he's losing rather than fighting me off, and while I spit as much of his flesh and blood from my mouth as I can, my eyes catch Bianca and Douglas fleeing up the stairs with guns raised.

Suddenly, Adam stiffens, his back arching as a gasp flies from his lips, and I peer over his shoulder to see a leg of the chair Travis broke earlier, protruding from his back.

"Set her free!" Travis calls, and the battered face of Cassie comes into view, her shaky hands darting from where she just staked Adam, to look up at me.

As Adam's body starts to fall limp, I unhook my ankles and let him flop to the floor with a thud.

A loud crash from above shakes Cassie out of her daze, and she moves as quickly as she can, reaching up and unfastening the leather cuffs restraining me to the beam overhead.

As soon as I land back on the floor, I give my wrists a rub and shake my hands around, trying to get the blood flowing again as I gesture my head to Travis.

"Can you get him free?" I ask Cassie, and she nods before stumbling to him.

I jump around a few times, trying to get my body back in fighting form, needing to pump the blood everywhere.

"What's the plan?" Travis asks as Cassie sets to work on freeing him.

"Simple. Kill Bianca." I shrug, looking around the basement for a weapon before glancing back at Travis. "What's at the top of the basement?"

He just stares at me and shrugs. "Your guess is as good as mine. This is the first time I've ever been here."

Shit. The Kerrs really did keep this part of their life a secret from everyone. They lived in this fancy lake house while their foster kids lived in a dump. Why didn't they bring their foster kids here? Why didn't they share their wealth with them?

Because they are cruel fuckers that need to die.

While they lived it up off the money their foster kids made them, their kids slummed it in a shitty house, in a shitty neighbourhood, peddling their shitty drugs.

"Right. Well, you two should stay here until I come back for you," I state, moving towards the staircase.

The moment Travis is free, he leaps up off the concrete floor towards me.

"No, Ell. Stop. You're not going up there alone. We don't even know who's shooting."

I grin at my brother. "I do. It's Griffin Marx and his crew. They aren't a threat to me, but they might be to you until Griffin knows you're no longer supporting the Kerr business."

"Supporting it? We never had a choice." Cassie cries, her puffy split lip trembling.

"I know that, but I need to make sure Griffin knows that, too," I state. "Now stay here. I'll come back for you."

As I move past Travis and Cassie toward the stairs, he grabs my upper arm, stopping me.

"No. It's too dangerous for you, Ell."

I smile. "Maybe for Ell, or even Dee. But it's not too dangerous for Hush." I peel his fingers from my arm before giving his hand a squeeze. "Hush has a job to do, and she won't stop until it's done."

"Who's Hush?" Cassie asks, but Travis doesn't answer her, his brown eyes locked with mine.

"Fine, but we're coming. I'm not staying down here for one minute longer."

I get it. I don't want to either, so I nod. "Stay behind me and don't engage in any fights. And if we get separated, find Griffin and tell him you're no longer associated with the Kerr gang."

Both Travis and Cassie nod, and I don't waste another second, beelining for the staircase and taking two at a time.

The door is ajar at the top of the stairs, and I peek through to see the kitchen off to the right, although I can't see what's off to the left.

Bianca's gritty chain smoking voice floats to me from beyond the kitchen, and I latch onto it, making it my focus.

She must die.

Taking a deep breath, I push the basement door open and step out into the short passage. A glance behind me shows the laundry room, so I continue forward into the kitchen, my eyes assessing everything as I move, even honing in on the large knife block on the kitchen bench.

Bingo.

I dart quickly into the space, grabbing three knives and passing Travis and Cassie one each as they creep into the room, huddled together.

It's more for Cassie's sake than anything. Her frail body trembling with fear as Travis tries to keep her moving, and I notice she's now wearing a t-shirt. Maybe they snagged one from the laundry?

"Put the gun down!"

I know that voice. It's Griffin's, and I've never been happier to hear it.

There's a mirror on the wall giving me a view around the corner, and I see Bianca in a standoff with Griffin and his men. Why they don't just shoot the bitch, I don't know, and I don't fucking want to wait.

Sucking in a deep calming breath, I round the corner, stepping over Douglas Kerr's dead body, narrowly avoiding the blood pooling from his chest, as I come into view of Griffin and his men.

Griffin's eyes snag on me immediately, and I see his shoulders relax a fraction.

Naw, was he worried about me?

I also see his men's eyes land on me, travelling the length of my body, which is when I remember I'm in only a bra and panties.

I mean, it could be worse.

"You really think I'm that stupid?" Bianca sneers. "The moment I put the gun down, I'm a dead woman."

My vision morphs into a red haze as I hear that woman's vile voice and I raise the knife, getting a feel for its weight in my grip.

"Hold your fire," Griffin says quietly to his men, and they give him a nod, their eyes either on me or Bianca.

I take that moment to make my presence known.

"You're a dead woman, regardless."

My voice stiffens Bianca's spine, and the moment she whips around, I rush at her, leaping onto her wide frame and slamming the knife into her upper chest.

The gun tumbles from her hand as she tries to gasp, her eyes wide with panic as she realises she's about to die.

With my legs wrapped around her as much as they can, I keep stabbing, and stabbing until Bianca stumbles backwards and falls hard to the floor.

I go with her, not releasing my legs' grip on her sides, and continue to plunge the knife into her, counting each one out loud.

"Seven! Eight! Nine!" I hiss, snarling each number with venom as I keep going.

I ignore the pain that slices through my side, and the

warm gush I feel run down my hip and leg, focusing on counting out my stabs with a clear number in mind.

"Twenty-seven! Twenty-Eight! Twenty-Nine!" I scream, hacking away at her now lifeless body.

There's yelling coming from somewhere nearby. Another gunshot. But I don't stop, my eyes on Bianca's mangled chest, now nothing but blood and torn flesh with the hint of bone, as I continue to scream out each time I sink the blade into her.

My body slowly starts to tire, my onslaught slowing as I count the final numbers.

"Forty-one. Forty-two. Forty-three."

I still. My hand trembling from exhaustion as I slowly release my grip on the knife as my hearing starts to come back to me.

It's silent.

Eerily silent.

Darting my eyes up from the bloodied corpse under me, I see so many faces I don't know staring back. Some with disgust. Some with shock. A couple wearing smirks.

"Dee." My name falls from lips I long to kiss again, and I glance to my side to see Jared and Griffin standing over me and the now dead, Bianca Kerr.

"Jared," I whisper, my body swaying where I'm straddling Bianca, a wave of numbness rushing over my body.

I glance down then, to my side. There's so much blood, and it's not all Bianca's. It's mine, and it's coming from a huge shard of thick glass protruding from the side of my abdomen.

"Oh," I slur. "That can't be good."

Then.

Everything goes black.

35

JARED

*T*he last twenty-four hours have been a nightmare. Each time Dee wakes, it's like she's possessed by an animal, screaming and writhing about on the hospital bed. After the first time, when she clawed at the nurse's arms and face, they restrained her to the bed and sedated her. Now when she wakes, she can't harm anyone or herself, but the screaming and writhing are still there.

The part of the hospital we're in isn't a normal ward. It's secluded and heavily guarded by Marx crew, a new development Griffin explained when Dee first arrived in the facility.

I don't know how he does it. How he's able to arrange such things and have authorities turn a blind eye, but now, this section of the hospital is Marx property, and only select staff will work here, taking care of Marx people.

Griffin ordered Travis and Cassie to be brought here too, something I'm sure Dee will be happy about if she'd just wake up and not scream the place down. Each time she rouses and screams, Travis hobbles out of his bed across the hall and comes to Dee's bedside, and each time the nurses sedate Dee, he has some choice words for them before Griffin's men drag him back across the hall to his and Cassie's room.

"Has she woken again?" Bec asks, coming to Dee's bedside to take her hand, her blue eyes oozing concern as she stares down at her niece.

I shake my head. "Not yet. It shouldn't be long until the sedation wears off again, though."

Bec nods. "She went like this after she killed Travis' mum, which is why it was so easy for us to get her into the psychiatric facility. The only time she was ok was when she got to see Travis about a week after it all happened. But he wasn't happy to see her and said something to her that upset her. It was after that when she stopped talking. The only sound she made then was screaming. She was also a little like this when we took her from the man that trained her to be a killer. It's like she goes to such a dark place that she struggles to find her way back."

I turn to the Angel, her normally well-groomed blonde hair looking a mess as wisps stick out from her ponytail.

"She'll come back to us, though, right?" I ask, and she nods.

"I believe so."

"We will be here waiting for as long as it takes." Amanda's voice comes from behind me, and I see her leaning against the door frame, watching us.

I hope they hang around for Dee's sake. I think now that she knows the Angel sisters are actually her aunties, she'd like to get to know them.

Hell, since the Kerrs are dead, she doesn't have to leave now. The few Kerr gang members left are slowly getting picked off by the Marx crew, which means Dee can stay and make a life here. Make a life with me.

A thrill rushes over me at the thought of keeping her.

Claiming her as mine once and for all and knowing that we have all the time in the world.

Fuck, I want that.

I can't help it. As soon as Bec releases Dee's hand, I take it, shifting closer to the bed to get in a good position since her hands are secured in cuffs on each side of her hips.

I stay by her side like that for a long time, the Angels retreating back out into the hall eventually, their voices hushed as they talk with Cynthia and Will.

My eyes feel heavy with sleep when Dee's fingers squeeze mine.

My gaze darts to hers, and my heart starts to race as her eyes move rapidly under her closed lids before she starts breathing heavily.

Shit.

No.

Not again.

Suddenly her lids fly open, her dark brown pupils almost black staring straight at the ceiling as the first scream rips from her lungs.

"Dee." I try to say calmly, hoping she can hear me. "Deranged. It's ok. Shhhhh."

Commotion sounds behind me as the room fills with the people who care for her. Cynthia rushes to the other side of the bed, taking Dee's free hand as she starts thrashing. Scream after scream echoes in the small space while a nurse rushes in with a syringe before injecting its contents into the cannula attached to Dee's hand.

It doesn't take long to work. Dee's screams and thrashing slowly falling away as the drugs take her back under.

I hate it. I really fucking hate it.

"Can't you just leave her for a bit?" Travis snarls at the nurse, having rushed over to check on his sister again. "Just let her go and see if she eventually calms down. She can't hurt anyone. You already have her chained to the bed like she's a madwoman."

"We're giving her less and less of the sedative," the nurse explains. "Our main priority is to keep her calm so she can heal. She's likely to pop her stitches at this rate."

Travis curses under his breath as the nurse leaves again and one look at his expression shows he's scared. Really fucking scared.

Just as scared as me that our girl will never come back to us.

36

DEE

*M*y lids flutter open, a warm glow lighting my way out of oblivion. My eyes feel like sandpaper as I blink, which seems to match my throat as I try to swallow, silently begging for saliva to build.

As my surroundings become clearer, I realise I'm in a hospital bed in a small room, the mattress hard and plastic-y at my back. My body feels heavy. Exhausted. Like I'm being weighed down by a mountain of rocks, and attempting to turn my head to get a better look around is a real struggle.

Eventually, I manage to move enough that I can see a head of blond hair resting on the bed down near my hand. As feeling starts to waken my body more, I can sense that there is a hand in mine, underneath the resting head.

Jared.

I try to squeeze my fingers, but at first, nothing happens. When I try again, the signal from my brain to my digits registers, and they curl tighter around Jared's hand.

He doesn't move. Not at first. So I part my dry lips to try to speak, but I can't seem to make my voice box work. I frown, I think. It's really hard to tell, with how drowsy I feel, and I know I need to wake myself up more, so I suck in slow deep breaths, taking in more and more oxygen, in the hopes it will wake me more.

When I feel my head getting clearer, I try to speak again, but all that comes out is a hushed croak.

What the hell happened to me?

Giving up on my voice, something I know I don't need to get by, I focus back on my hand and give Jared's hand another squeeze.

The mess of blond hair jerks up, and Jared's blue, shocked gaze meets mine.

"Dee?" he whispers like he's not sure it's me.

Do I look different?

Fuck. I need to find a mirror.

Parting my lips again, I waste a breath on a voice that doesn't want to come, so I offer him a half smile and try to nod.

I think I nod. If I do, it's not much of one. My head still feeling woozy.

"Shit, Dee. You're awake," he rasps in surprise, so I offer him another small smile and attempt another nod.

His face lights up like it's Christmas morning, his eyes turning glassy, like he's about to cry.

"And you're you," he whispers again, and I frown.

What?

I'm me?

Well, yes, I'm me. I never haven't been me. Have I?

Now I'm confused as all hell.

Loosening my hold of his hand, I try to reach up to his face, but my wrist won't move.

My gaze darts down to the bed, and that's when I see it. My wrists are in straps, secured to the bed.

My heart kicks into overdrive as I try to lift both wrists, realising they are both definitely tied down.

Some sort of weird fucking whimper escapes me as I shake my head, panic gripping me by the throat, my wide eyes darting to Jared.

"Shhh." He stands, looking over his shoulder before glancing back at me. "It's ok. Calm down."

Doesn't he know that when you tell a chick to calm down, they do the fucking opposite?!

I jerk in the bed, a strangled cry ripping from my throat as my ankles don't move either, telling me they are strapped down too.

No. NO!

Instantly I'm taken back to my past, my body strapped on a mattress, my hands and feet cold, my body trembling from the chill in the dark room with no blanket in sight.

Not again. I don't want to go back there.

A scream launches from me as I start thrashing on the bed, my vision flicking between present and past.

My past is dark and cold and so lonely. I don't want to go back.

Shaking my head and blinking rapidly, the present fills my vision. Warm light and air reach me, and I stop screaming but still try to tug my limbs free of the restraints.

"No!" I hear Jared yell, his broad shoulders filling the doorway as he blocks someone from entering. "She's ok. She woke up fine. It's the restraints that's set her off this time. They need to come off."

"It's too dangerous to remove the restraints," a female voice snaps, but Jared doesn't budge.

"You're not putting any more fucking drugs into her!"

"I don't take orders from you," the lady hisses, and Jared shifts in the doorway like he's trying to block her, as if she keeps trying to get past him.

"If you so much as try to step foot in this room, I will fucking end you." Jared's tone is lethal, and my thrashing stops as my body responds in a way it probably shouldn't in this situation.

My chest rises and falls rapidly as I try to calm myself enough to talk. I'm not sure why I'm restrained to the bed, but I *do* know I need to show I don't need to be. I remember that much from my time in the psychiatric facility after I killed Catherine.

"P-please," I rasp, my voice scratchy and painful. My voice isn't loud, but Jared must hear me, his blue gaze darting over his shoulder to lock with mine.

Then he shifts a little, keeping his hand secured tightly to the door frame, and the lady, a nurse, looks in past him.

"Please," I rasp again, a little louder this time.

That's all I say. She understands what I'm asking for, and with an angered sigh, she nods and looks back up at Jared.

"Fine. I'll come in and remove the restraints."

"Nope." He shakes his head. "I will remove the restraints. No one else comes into this room until Griffin gets back. If you try, it will be the last thing you do."

Rolling her tongue in her mouth, the nurse glares at Jared, but then nods and storms off, giving me a view of Travis, who must have been standing behind her in the passage.

His brown gaze is wide with happiness as he sees me, and I return his smile until I notice the crutch he's leaning on, and the moon boot on his foot.

"I'm ok, Ell." He reassures me from the hallway, and I wonder why he's not coming inside until his gaze turns to Jared. "You gonna end me if I try to come in there?"

Jared nods. "Yes. You know what Griffin said."

"Yeah, well. She's awake now, so tell the arsehole to come in and we can have that fucking chat he's been bugging me about."

Jared nods and Travis glances back in at me.

"I'll come and see you later. Ok?"

I nod, a little confused about why he can't come in here, but since he doesn't seem too concerned about it, I won't worry over it.

Travis turns and hobbles back into the room across the passage, and Jared shifts back into my room and closes the door before turning back to face me.

"You really ok?" he asks, and again I frown.

"What happened? Why am I restrained?" My voice is still husky and scratchy, but it seems to be working better now.

Closing the distance between us, Jared reaches for my wrist and starts unbuckling the restraint.

"Bianca managed to stab you with a massive fucking shard of glass. You passed out from blood loss." Jared stills his hands for a moment, squeezing his eyes shut before shaking himself out of his memory. "You had to have a blood transfusion and surgery, but they patched you up." As my wrist slips free of the strap, Jared's eyes meet mine. "But when you woke up, you..."

I frown as he drops his gaze and slowly rounds the bed to work on the strap at my other wrist.

"What happened when I woke up?" I ask, and he avoids my eyes as he works on the strap.

"You weren't yourself."

His words are quiet, and my heart sinks, understanding exactly what he's talking about.

"Did I..." When his blue gaze darts up, I swallow the lump in my throat and continue. "Did I hurt anyone?"

Jared doesn't say anything, and that alone tells me everything I need to know.

"Shit," I whisper. "Who? How many? What did I do?"

Freeing my other wrist, Jared avoids my eyes again, and he steps to the end of the bed, tugging the sheet out of its neat hospital corners, and folds it back to reveal my restrained ankles.

"Jared?" I ask again, and he sighs.

"Just a nurse. You clawed her pretty good. She's got some deep scratches that are still healing."

"Oh," I whisper, heat pricking the backs of my eyes as shame sweeps over me.

I may enjoy hacking into my victims, but I don't like hurting innocent people.

"Hey," Jared croons, his big hand wrapping around my foot and rubbing it. "It's ok, Dee. No one blames you. It's not your fault."

He's right, I know. I wasn't in the right headspace when I did it, obviously, but still, I did it regardless.

Slowly pushing myself to sit upright, I feel Jared's eyes on me as I shuffle down the bed a little, trying to get to my ankles so I can free them faster.

"Stay there, Dee. I'll do it," he offers, but I ignore him, still shuffling down the bed.

That is, until I feel something weird under the blankets, between my legs, and I still, eyes going wide.

"What?" Jared asks, freeing one ankle. "What's wrong?"

"Uhhh…" I glance down at my lap, unsure what to say, and Jared's chuckle meets my ears.

"You wondering what's between your legs?"

My eyes dart up to meet his amused expression, and I nod.

"You have a catheter in. Better that than you pissing the bed." He grins and starts working on the last restraint.

"How long have I been here? What day is it?" It must have been a while if I needed a catheter.

Finally freeing my second ankle, Jared gives the skin there a rub as he meets my eyes.

"It's Tuesday. You've been here for four days."

My mouth drops open at his words. "What?"

He chuckles, and rounds the bed, coming to my side and reaching out to cup my cheek.

"Four of the longest days of my life," he admits, his expression morphing from amused to worried. "I've never felt more helpless in my life. When they took you..." His words trail off, and he looks down at the bed as he struggles with his emotions.

I reach for his hand, needing his touch, and the moment he glances up, we both shift, colliding together in an embrace that has me wanting to crawl under his skin.

"Fuck, Dee," he whispers into my hair. "I was so scared I was going to lose you."

I squeeze him tighter, and a moment later he pulls back, pressing his forehead to mine as he stares into my eyes.

"The nurses checked. Said that he... That there were no signs of..." He shakes his head against mine, struggling to speak, and I consider what he said.

"Are you talking about Adam?" I ask, and Jared nods, pulling back to capture my soul in his intense gaze. "He didn't make good on his threat, if that's what you're meaning?"

I see Jared's shoulders visibly relax as he comprehends my words.

"He didn't get a chance to, because I ripped his throat out with my teeth."

Well, technically, it wasn't his throat, but it was close enough.

To anyone else, my words would make them cringe. Maybe even take a step back.

Not Jared Crowley, though. Nope. He fucking grins.

"That's my girl."

The smile that spreads my lips wide is big enough that my teeth show, and Jared's face lights up.

"Fuck, I love seeing you smile like that. It's the most beautiful thing I've ever seen."

Heat blossoms over my cheeks and rushes to my chest as his eyes dart to my lips.

I want to kiss him. I really do, but if I've been laid up in this bed for four days, then I need to brush my teeth.

The moment Jared leans forward, I slap my hand over his mouth, taking him by surprise. His blue gaze darts to mine, brows high on his forehead in question.

"Teeth," I whisper. "I need to brush them. And have a shower. And..." My eyes drop to the sheets covering my lower half. "Get this stupid tube out of my hoo-ha."

Jared's laugh is loud in the small space, throwing his head back and clutching his middle.

"Hoo-ha?" he chuckles, trying to compose himself.

"Yes," I grumble, shooting him a glare that lacks menace.

Blowing air past his lips, he works harder, trying to calm his laughter before gripping each side of my head. "I'll arrange for the catheter to be removed from your hoo-ha, while you call Griffin." He presses his warm lips to my forehead before tugging his phone free and handing it to me. "He'll be happy to hear your voice."

As Jared steps away to get the nurse's help, I give Griffin a call, surprised when he's actually happy to hear my voice, and then proceed to question him about Travis, and why he's not allowed in my room. Apparently, each time I woke in a psychotic state, it sent Travis into a fit of rage to the point that it got so bad last night they were considering sedating and restraining him, too. So Griffin demanded he stay in his room, and advised him that Jared will look out for me until I woke up, at which time, they would have a discussion about where Travis' loyalties lie.

My heart sinks at that, not knowing how Travis will respond to that question, especially after Griffin confirms that the Kerr family has been eliminated, along with all but one of their gang, who Griffin reassures will be dead by the end of the day.

Which leaves me with one question.

Will Travis want to leave with me, or stay?

I guess technically, now that the Kerrs have been wiped from existence, we could stay here in Fox Pines. Something I'd very much like. I could stay with the Rogans... Shit. The Rogans.

I didn't ask Griffin about them. How the hell could I be so selfish? The last I saw of Cynthia and Will, they were in their bedroom. Will was knocked out cold on the floor. And Cynthia looked a little battered, her cheeks stained with tears as she watched Adam take me away.

My lips part to ask Jared about them when the door slowly opens, and the nurse that was in the doorway arguing with Jared earlier slips in with a trolley, her wary eyes flicking to Jared.

"Uh. You'll need to step out while I do this." She orders Jared, who shakes his head and crosses his arms over his chest.

"Nope. Just like when you inserted it, I'm not leaving."

She rolls her eyes at him. "She was unconscious then. Now she's awake and alert and can look after herself."

"I already made myself clear earlier. I'm not leaving. Now do your job."

He turns and faces me, pushing his chair closer to the bed. He takes a seat, his eyes on me, his back to the nurse as he takes my hand in his, and offers me a warm smile.

Shit. He really is staying for this.

"I won't look." He winks, pressing his head to the side of mine.

He's sweet, in a possessive kind of way.

I should probably hate it, yet I don't. For some reason, it

draws me closer to him. I like how protective he is of me. I like feeling like I belong to him, and he to me.

I like it a lot.

The nurse does a few things and slips on some gloves before peeling back the sheets.

"Ok, honey. I need you to part your legs for me."

I tense, but nod and do as she asks, feeling extremely exposed to a stranger right now. Jared has my hand in his, holding it up between us before pressing his lips to the back. I watch him, preferring his rough beauty to that of the nurse poking around my bits.

While she does her thing, Jared and I stare into each other's eyes. I've never felt this close to another person before. Never felt so in tune. So accepted.

"Ok, sweetie. Can you take a deep breath for me? I'm going to slowly pull it out."

I nod quickly at the nurse's request, my eyes remaining locked with Jared's, and I suck in a lungful of air. As she draws the tube from inside me, a burning sensation makes me stiffen, and Jared wraps his free hand around the back of my head, holding me tight. Giving me the support I need.

"Ok. All done." The nurse declares, and I have to hold back the urge to slap her.

That fucking hurt.

Well, maybe stung is a better word.

As the sheets go back over my legs, I glance at the nurse, now packing up her supplies, when she speaks again.

"Drink plenty of water. You have a higher chance of getting a UTI, so drink and pee frequently. Ok?"

Nodding in agreement, I watch as she shoots a glare to the back of Jared's head before pushing her trolly back out into the hall.

"Is your hoo-ha ok?" Jared asks, smirking, and I finally relax, giving him a nod.

"It will be fine. But I really need that shower and a toothbrush."

With a low chuckle, Jared stands, pushing his chair right out of the way before holding his hand out to me.

"Cynthia and Will brought some of your things in on Sunday. Your toothbrush is already in the bathroom waiting."

Shit. Cyn and Will.

"Are they... Ok?"

Jared nods. "Yeah. They're ok. Worried about you more than anything."

"And Rhys? The twins?" I ask, remembering how they snuck from the house and hid in the park the night Adam Kerr broke in looking for me.

"They are fine, too. Everyone is fine."

I frown. "But how can they be? Someone broke into their home and terrorised them. Because of me."

"Hey." Jared frowns, tugging me to the side of the bed as I shuffle to get out. "That's not your fault."

"Isn't it?" I ask, feeling very much like it is. "If I hadn't manipulated the system so the Rogans would find me. If I hadn't come into their life, then none of this would have happened."

Jared stares at me for a long few moments, his eyes roaming over my face, a frown tugging at his brow.

"You couldn't have foreseen this, Dee. No one could. If anything, the Angels have a lot to answer for. They should have told you who they were to you. Perhaps then you would have trusted them enough to ask for their help in getting to Travis."

The Angels. My aunties.

Jesus fucking Christ. Everything is intertwined. Everything.

"Besides. I'm kind of glad you came to Fox Pines." He shoots me a sly grin.

My shoulders relax at that statement, so I decide to give myself a break for the time being, because I know deep down that what I've done to the Rogans is not ok. And soon enough, this little bubble I'm in with Jared will burst, and I'll have to face the reality of my situation.

Even though I can stay here in Fox Pines now, I know that I can't.

Not after the danger I've brought into the lives of innocent people.

Jared, being one of them.

37

JARED

$\mathcal{M}$y heart is full as I help Dee to the attached bathroom of her hospital room. For a few days there, I didn't think I'd see the old Dee again. I thought she was gone. Lost in the dark depths of her mind, never to return. Yet here she is, letting me hold her up as she walks on weak, shaky legs.

Knowing she's back and ok has triggered an array of hope to bloom in my brain. We have a real chance at a future now. She can stay here in Fox Pines. She can finish school, keep dancing, get a job, and build a life for herself. A real one that doesn't involve keeping her voice to herself or sneaking through the shadows at night and slicing someone's throat in their sleep.

Now, we can be together.

I hadn't wanted to let myself truly think about what that might look like when I knew she was planning to leave. I knew it would just make things harder for me to dream about a future that would never be. But now? Fuck, now I can let myself indulge in that.

Now I feel like I can truly breathe.

I turn the shower on, holding my hand under the spray until the temperature feels right, and then help Dee slip out of the hospital gown.

Instinctively, she covers herself, one arm held to her chest, covering the pretty pink nipples I love to lick. Another hand shifts to cover her hoo-ha, as she calls it.

"I can step out," I offer, feeling like an idiot for assuming she would want me in here while she showers, but she shakes her head, her brown eyes wide like she's scared I will leave.

"Stay," Is all she says, and I bite back a grin and nod.

"I can face the other way if you like?"

She shakes her head again. "Can you take your clothes off too?"

My brows shoot up, and she sucks her lips in, trying not to laugh.

"It would make me feel less... exposed if you were naked, too."

"Oh." I chuckle, and nod, shucking off my t-shirt before slipping off my pants and jocks.

When I look back up at Dee, her dark eyes are travelling over my body, stopping at my dick, and all of a sudden I feel like I'm the one who's exposed.

I drop my gaze to my dick, noticing that it's still slack, but a little firmer than usual, which I know has everything to do with the way Dee is looking at me. If she's not careful, my cock will be standing at full attention in a matter of seconds.

"Are you perving at me?" I ask, and her brown eyes look up at me with an air of innocence before her cheeks flush.

"No. I just haven't really paid that much attention to you when you're..." She trails off, and I chuckle.

"When I'm soft?" I ask, and her cheeks flare. Hell, I bet if I reach out and touch them, they'd be burning hot.

Ignoring my question, she slips past me and steps under the spray, giving me her back.

Shit.

As my eyes travel down her slender curves, my dick starts to rouse. Especially when I study those two perfect globes of her arse.

And there it is. My full boner.

Fucking hell.

Trying to ignore it, I step in behind Dee, resting my hands on her shoulders and slowly running them down her arms. She leans back against me, letting the spray of water cover her head completely, and she just stands there, letting it wash over her.

Using my hands, I start to run them over her body like a washcloth, squirting a few pumps from the soap dispenser into the palm of my hand before washing her soft skin.

I'm careful to avoid the waterproof patch covering her wound, and after a minute, she turns in the spray, pressing her cheek to my chest and wrapping her arms around me, so I continue to wash her, this time focusing on her back, and arse.

"Does it hurt if you don't... you know?"

Her words still my hands, and I frown as I run what she asked through my head again.

Oh.

She's talking about my erection.

"No, it doesn't hurt," I say, and then frown. "Although if we were deep in the middle of heavy teasing, foreplay or sex and we stopped, it may hurt a little, but nothing that won't go away quickly."

She nods against my chest, dropping one of her hands from my back, pressing it to my pec.

This side of Dee is so different from her assassin side. I can't believe I thought she must have been a pro at sex just because she was a killer tangled up in organised crime. Pretty fucking judgemental of me.

All this time she waited, and it was me she chose to give herself to.

Fuck.

My heart swells in my chest, and my dick seems to get harder, and I really need to stop thinking about Dee and sex, only I can't because now, Dee's hand is travelling down my abs, and my dick very much wants to feel her hand wrap around it.

But now isn't the time.

Now is the worst fucking time after everything she's been through.

I hiss in a sharp breath as her dainty hand brushes over the length of my cock and down to cup my balls.

"Dee," I say in warning, and she looks up at me, her chin pressing to my chest as the most mischievous look I've seen her wear lights up her face.

"Sorry. It's hard to resist."

I chuckle, washing the soap from my hands and reaching between us to take her hand in mine, bringing it up between us where I kiss the backs of her fingers.

"When you're out of this place, you can touch me all you want." I grin, and she nods, wearing a small grin of her own.

Hell, I can't wait for that. To be alone with her where we can explore each other even more. Stay tangled in each other's arms and never let go.

We stare at each other for a bit longer before I wash her hair, revelling in the way she lets me take care of her, and then I step out of the shower to grab her toothbrush, squeezing some toothpaste on it before handing it to her in the shower where a look of relief washes over her, and she proceeds to clean her teeth.

The whole shower experience is intimate in a way I didn't realise it could be. There's real trust here, and my mind goes back to that awful moment when Adam Kerr dragged Dee from the house. The moment she turned back and told me she loves me.

Her voice and those three words have bounced around in my head in a continuous loop ever since she said them, desperate for an opportunity to say it back to her, and scared I'd never get the chance.

Soon Dee finishes spitting her toothpaste down the drain, and cups her hand under the spray to take a drink of the hot water. I take her toothbrush and put it back out by the sink before returning to her for one last moment in our little shower bubble.

Using both hands, I brush her wet hair back, keeping it off her face, and the moment our eyes lock, I say the words.

"I love you, too, Dee."

Her brows shoot up in shock, and I grin, because she looks absolutely adorable being taken off guard like that.

"You said the words, before... You know."

Slowly, she nods. "Before I was taken."

"Yes." I agree, "And I promised myself that when I got you back, I would tell you how I really feel, too."

Her eyes turn glassy, and she starts trying to swallow like she's trying to clear a lump in her throat.

"I mean it, Dee." I brush my thumb over her lower lip. "You own my heart. My mind. My body. My soul. It's all yours. Always."

Even as I graze her lip with the pad of my thumb, I feel it quiver under my touch, and a tear pops from one of her chocolate eyes. I quickly brush it away, keeping my gaze locked on hers, and a moment later, she presses up on her toes, her eyes falling to my lips.

I meet her halfway, our lips coming together like they were made to do so, and her small hand grips the back of my neck, holding me to her.

I lose myself completely in that kiss. Our need to show

how much we care coming through in each brush of the tongue and stroke of our lips.

It's hot, heavy, and by the time we break apart, we are both desperate to be free of this hospital to have a quiet place to ourselves where we can worship each other and lose ourselves completely.

38

DEE

*T*he day I've been waiting for has finally arrived, and I wish more than anything it was still a lifetime away. Today is my eighteenth birthday. The day I'd originally planned to run away with Travis. To leave this town. To leave Jared.

Since waking up in the hospital on Tuesday, I knew I still had to leave. The only difference between my original plan and now, is that I'm not taking Travis with me.

I spent another two days in the hospital before being released yesterday, and I've felt sick to my stomach ever since.

And no. I'm not pregnant. The doctor had apparently given me an injection at Griffin's order, just in case Adam had raped me, and then on the Angels' order, a birth control implant was injected under my skin.

I'm not mad about it either, since I needed to try to get something sorted out anyway, but hell, with me leaving, I know I'll never need it. I'll never be intimate with anyone but Jared. Not when he owns my soul.

Which is why I've felt so sick, knowing I'm going to be leaving him. Leaving Travis. Leaving the Rogans.

I've kept my plan to myself, not wanting to upset anyone, but I have to go. I can't stay here and put these kind people through any more hell than I already have. They deserve better. So much better than the likes of me.

The Rogans, Travis and Jared, all deserve a life untainted by the dangers I've brought them, and may potentially bring them in the future. I'm a killer. It's in my blood, and I can't stain them with that any longer.

They have all suffered enough because of me, and will carry the effects of my stay here with them for years to come. I've already overheard Cynthia talking about the twins having nightmares, and I can only imagine the trauma Cynthia and Will try to face daily after what Adam and his thugs put them through.

When I was finally able to see Travis, it became clear to me that he really didn't want to leave his foster sister, Cassie. They are close. The way he and I should have been if we were gifted a normal life to grow up together.

Travis has built a life here and has agreed to work with Griffin and the Marx crew once he and Cassie have healed.

I just hope he means being healed on the inside as well as the outside, too.

The Angels have offered him shelter, money, and the chance to go back to school and finish his education. All the things I'd planned to offer him, and since they are his aunties too, I've decided that perhaps having them as role models for him isn't so bad.

After all, they mean well and everything they have done regarding me was from a place of love and support. My situation was far from normal, and they did what they could to steer me down a better path.

And I realise now that's exactly what happened.

I could have been a psycho killer. Probably would have been shot dead by cops by now, but the Angels taught me another way, and to me, it was, and still is, an important role in eliminating the predators so they can't cause harm again.

"Happy Birthday!" Rhys cheers for the hundredth time today as she walks past me in the main living area of the Rogans' house, dragging me out of my mournful thoughts.

I grin and shake my head, keeping silent, because I'm good at that. Especially when I'm keeping a secret.

In fact, I haven't spoken verbally much from the moment Jared and I stepped out of that intimate shower at the hospital when I woke up. Sometimes words are just too hard, so I keep them to myself, only occasionally giving them to Jared when I can't help myself.

"What did you give Dee for her birthday, Crowley?" Marcus asks, coming to stand before me and Jared as we loiter around the table covered in plates of party food.

"None of your business," Jared answers, sounding amused.

"You gave her your dick, didn't you?" Rhys asks, bouncing up to jump on Marcus' back, sliding her hands to his chest as she rests her head on his shoulder. "It is a nice sized dick."

I roll my eyes and Jared chuckles, not denying it, while Marcus reaches back and gives her an awkward backwards slap on her arse.

"Stop talking about other guys' dicks, Rhee," he whines, calling her by his pet name for her. They all seem to have a different name they call her, and I wonder how she remembers they are addressing her and not someone else. That girl has too many boyfriends for me to even comprehend how it all works.

"It's not other guys. It's Jared, and his dick belongs to my foster sister, so I can talk about it all I want."

I shake my head at her, and she shoots me a wink. "He gave you dick for your birthday, didn't he?"

"Ok, that's enough out of you." Garrett sweeps in, stealing Rhys off Marcus' back and slings her over his shoulder like a sack of potatoes.

Rhys then proceeds to pinch his arse as he walks, and he ignores her, taking her into the back part of the house towards her bedroom.

I guess Rhys is the one about to get dick.

The thought causes me to smirk, and I'm thankful when Marcus is too busy watching his girl get carried off by another guy to notice.

Rhys was right, though. Jared gave me his dick for my birthday. And his fingers. And his tongue.

God, the things he can do with that tongue!

He also got me a mood teddy. An adorable reversible octopus that's pink with a smile, but when you push it inside out, it's blue with a frown. He told me to use the grumpy side on the days I don't feel like talking, so he knows not to annoy me too much.

I love it so much.

It's the best gift I've ever received. Not that I'll get to use it with him, but I'll keep it and remember him always.

The night is nice, celebrations that I'm not used to having make me feel somewhat normal for a short time.

Travis and Cassie drop by and Jared sits with them for a bit chatting, while I stay on the sidelines, silent.

Griffin joins the celebrations, too, handing me a long velvet box and suggesting I open it later when no one can see, so I rush off and stash it in my room, knowing it's most likely something illegal.

The Angels join the fun, handing over some gift cards and a bottle of wine, which I don't bother opening.

I'm not, nor will I ever, be a drinker.

For them, when most people are out of earshot, I use my voice for simple things, before thanking my aunties for looking out for me, and reminding them that Travis needs extra support, now more than ever.

I watch from the sidelines as Griffin, his woman, Aggie, and my aunties all chat away with the Rogans like they are old friends, and I realise it's because of me that they've come together.

Or maybe it was Rhys.

Either way, I guess it's not a bad thing that they all get along. It gives me hope that if the Rogans ever need help after I'm gone, that they will get it.

Later in the night, Cynthia brings out a cake she baked for my birthday, and I feel rather emotional at the simple act. I can't remember the last time anyone baked for me.

Charlotte, my oldest foster sister who has never really given me the time of day, wishes me a happy birthday and offers an awkward smile, and yet again, my heart hurts because I really want to stay, but I know I can't do that to them anymore.

After I give in to the twins and dance around the backyard, drawing pictures in the dark with sparklers together, the guests start to leave, and my eyes find Jared, who I know has spent endless minutes watching me from afar.

Does he know I'm leaving?

Paranoia gnaws at me, so I avoid him for a bit more, helping Cynthia clean up given all the mess is in honour of me. When we are alone, I clear my throat to gain her attention, and she looks up, having just placed a glass in the dishwasher, and her eyes are soft and warm, waiting for me to speak.

"I never meant for any of that stuff to happen," I admit, and she frowns, nodding.

"I know, honey."

"It's just, I came across your file when I was looking for potential families in this area that had a link to the Archer Network."

Cynthia nods, knowing that through that program, the twins and I were placed with her.

"How did you get your hands on files from the Archer Network?"

It's Rhys' voice, which startles me, and I whip around to see her behind me.

Where did she come from?

"Uh…" I glance between her and Cynthia, and decide just to tell them the truth. "I'm good at breaking into things."

"You broke into their office?" Rhys gasps and Cynthia sighs.

"I probably shouldn't be listening to this."

Ignoring that, I nod at Rhys. "I knew Travis was in this town, and I found you guys in the files, so I filed some false paperwork which put me in the Archer Network's system, and a few months later, Cynthia and Will came into the office to meet me."

Rhys' mouth drops open, but then she smiles and points at me.

"You are more than this quiet girl. I knew it from the start. What else can you do? Because I saw that huge knife you were carrying last week when those pricks broke into this house." She claps in excitement. "Tell me everything."

Frowning, I glance over at Cynthia, and then back at Rhys.

Fuck it. I'm leaving in the morning anyway, and it will make it easier on them when they find out the truth. They are sure to hate me and want me out of their lives.

"I… um… I kind of assassinate people for a living." It comes out more as a question, but Rhys doesn't care, her eyes going wide with excitement.

"It's you, isn't it? The one who's been killing all of those sick fuckers linked to Carnal Unicorn?" When I nod, her mouth drops into an O and she rushes forward, gripping my shoulders. "Holy shit balls. You must know who Hush is. The podcaster. OMG, you need to hook me up with her details. I want to meet her. Thank her. She helped me, and she helps so many, and—"

"Ah, Rhys?" Cynthia comes to my side, gaining Rhys' overactive attention. "I think you've already met her."

Rhys' expression turns to confusion, and I glance at Cynthia, really taking her in.

She knows.

"What?" Rhys asks. "I have?"

Cynthia giggles. "Yes, Rhys. She's standing right in front of you."

It takes Rhys a moment to catch up, but when she does, her deep chocolate eyes roam my face and fill with tears.

"You're Hush?"

I nod slowly, eyeing Jared in my peripheral as he leans against the wall, watching everything transpire.

"Oh my god!" Rhys cries, lurching forward and pulling me to her chest in a hug. "It's really you."

Awkwardly, I hug her back, patting her on the back a little as she squeezes the life from me, and it isn't until Cynthia pries her off me that I can breathe again.

"I won't tell anyone," Rhys whispers, zipping up her lips and throwing away the key in an overdramatic move.

I smile at her and offer her one last piece of information.

"I was the one who killed Terence Hill," I admit, and her face drops, her normally always moving body falling completely still. "I entered through the ceiling, dropping right into the bathroom of his hospital room in the burns unit. I leaped up on the bed, startling him awake and held up a note for him." I clear my scratchy throat again, glancing at

Cynthia for any sign of horror, but hell, I get the feeling she already knows all of my secrets.

"What did it say?" Rhys whispers, gaining my attention again.

"It said, I'm here on behalf of the girl you call Kitten, to deliver you to hell."

A sob bursts from Rhys as she slaps her hand over her mouth, tears streaming from her eyes, as her chest rises and falls quickly.

When movement from the corner of my eye catches my attention, I watch Jared stop Shaun from stepping towards Rhys with his arm, holding him back as Rhys stammers over her next words.

"T-then what happened?"

Slowly, a grin tugs at the corner of my mouth, turning my expression sinister.

"Then I slit his throat from ear to ear."

Rhys' hands fly to her mouth again, smothering another sob, and this time when Shaun tries to rush forward, Jared doesn't stop him. Shaun quickly tugs his girl to his chest, wrapping Rhys in his arms before his eyes look up over her head to me.

"Thank you," he says quietly, and I know that it's from both of them.

I know everything that happened under the roof of Vixen's Lodge, and Shaun was a victim of the Feast nights as well.

Breaking free of Shaun's arms, Rhys hugs me again, thanking me over and over, and I want to say I didn't tell her to get thanks. I told her so she could get more closure, but Shaun whisks her away to her room before I can voice that, and I'm left standing with Cynthia.

"You knew all of that, didn't you?" I ask her, and she grins slyly and nods.

"Not at first, but just so you know, Dee. Will and I also do extensive research into the people we bring into our home, and even though it was after you were already here with us that we started to get the information you had hidden so well, we still chose to have you here with us."

Damn.

Now it's my turn to tear up, Cynthia's face going blurry as I try to bat away the tears that are falling faster than I can move.

Cynthia pulls me in for a hug of her own, and I swear I've never been hugged so much in my life, and since I know it's probably the last hug I'll ever have, I linger a little longer, drawing it out.

Jared steps in after that, no longer willing to share me, leading me to my bedroom where we close ourselves in for the night.

I'm nervous, and emotional, and nearly ready to lose my mind completely because this is it. This really is my last night with Jared, and he doesn't even know it.

I thought about telling him, but I'm a coward. I can't do it, and I just have to hope that the hate he feels when he finds out I've left doesn't taint his beautiful soul.

"You're amazing. You know that?" Jared asks, holding my head in his big hands and leaning down to press his lips to mine. I don't answer him, because I feel nothing but shame for the deceit I'm about to rain down on him, and instead I lose myself in his kiss, knowing this is the last time I will ever feel this sort of love.

Our clothes come off in a hurry, and before I know it, I'm flat on my back, half on and half off my bed as Jared dives between my legs, his tongue devouring me.

I let go completely, grinding my pussy against his face, searching for more and knowing how close I am to coming already. He owns my body in this moment. Controlling me like a puppet and playing me like a fiddle.

When he sinks two fingers inside me, I shatter, grabbing my pillow and slamming it to my face as I scream into it, like I seem to do each time I lose myself with this guy.

As soon as I fall slack, Jared tears the pillow from my face and his lips crash into mine as he eases his hard length inside me.

"Fuck, Dee," he rasps, moving above me, his eyes everywhere from my face, my jiggling tits, down to where our bodies join, and he grabs my thigh, lifting it as he thrusts faster.

I've hardly had a chance to recover from my last orgasm when I feel another one building. Jared must feel it too, because he watches my face, his own expression a mix of pleasure and pain, and he pounds harder and harder until my back arches off the bed and I clamp around his dick.

My cries are muffled by his lips, the orgasm prolonged as he continues to piston inside me, and when I finally fall limp, he pulls out, drags me off the bed, and I nearly topple over because of my jelly legs.

Jared chuckles, helping me to stay upright, his hands on either side of my hips, as he sits on the bed before turning me away from him.

"Step backwards and sit on my cock," he demands, and hell, my pussy throbs with more need.

How is that even possible?

Glancing at Jared over my shoulder, his blue eyes are bright with desire, his hands gripping my hips as he leads me backwards until I'm straddling his lap.

At first I figure this position is going to be awkward, given how much my legs are spread, completely opening me, but as he guides me down onto his thick shaft, filling me in the most delectable way, we seem to mould together as one.

Brushing my hair over one shoulder, Jared pulls me back firmly to his front and wraps his arms around me in the most sensual hug I've ever experienced.

From this angle we can both see down the front of my body, and as we start to move in unison, me rising and falling and him pulling back and pushing in, Jared's hands travel all over my front, grazing my nipples, cupping my tits, pressing my middle closer—all while avoiding my bandage—and circling my clit until I'm so slick, you can hear it each time he drives deep.

"I'll never get enough of you," he rasps against my ear, nipping at the lobe, and I manage to turn my head enough to kiss him awkwardly.

The sensual position is exquisite, and I feel closer than ever to Jared as his lips pepper kisses down the column of my neck and over my shoulders until I coil so tight, I erupt in a cry that I have no way of stifling.

It's only then that Jared lets himself go too, a low growl rumbling against my ear as he stills and fills me with his cum.

I'm helpless to stop the tears, and as Jared lifts me off him, planting me under the covers and slipping in next to me, I cry into the crook of his neck for all the heartache we've both already endured, and unbeknownst to him, the heartache we are both about to suffer.

Jared doesn't ask why I'm crying, probably thinking the emotion of the past days is catching up with me. He just holds me tight and makes me feel safe. And for a while, I let myself imagine that this right here, is my forever.

We stay huddled together for a couple of hours, Jared falling asleep once my tears dry up. When the first rays of light pinken the early Saturday morning sky, with a heavy heart, I quietly slip from the bed and get dressed.

I watch Jared for any sign of him rousing, but he remains still and silent, and I quietly open the wardrobe and pull out my backpack. I packed it yesterday morning when Jared went home to see his parents, so leaving would be easier for me. Eyeing Griffin's present on the bedside table, I take it and slip it inside my bag too, still unsure what it is, before staring down at Jared's sleeping form.

My heart splinters.

I know I can stay if I want. I know if I do, I can finally be happy. But staying is selfish. The danger I could potentially bring this family is too high of a price to pay.

They deserve more. They deserve better.

So for them, I will give up my chance at happiness, and I will leave them to move on knowing they will be safer if I'm not here.

A sob leaps from my throat as I let myself feel the pain of walking away, and as I bat my tears away, I move to the door and turn back for one last look at the guy who took a chance on me, and who will forever own my heart.

"Goodbye," I whisper, more tears breaking free. "I will never forget you, Jared Crowley. And my heart will always belong to you."

Then, I turn and quietly leave my bedroom, tip-toeing through the kids' zone, before placing a letter on the kitchen bench before I leave the Rogans' house for good. The only house that's ever felt like home.

39

JARED

She actually did it. Fuck! She actually did it!

Dee didn't know I was awake. She didn't know I felt her slip from the bed. Or that I heard her moving around her room as she got dressed and then got something from her wardrobe.

I knew it. I fucking knew something was up with her. She'd been quieter than usual after that first day waking in the hospital. She even retreated back to not talking most of the time, only occasionally sharing her voice with me.

Deep down I knew what she had planned, but denial was a motherfucking bitch setting me up for nothing but fucking grief.

And fuck. Her sob. It nearly made me blink my eyes open and beg her not to leave. But I couldn't do that. I can't ask her to stay if she really wants to go. She has to stay because that's what she wants, and even after the Kerrs were eliminated, and her brother chose to stay here, I'm not enough for her to want to stay and build a life.

Fuck. My chest hurts. It feels like it's being sliced open by that big fucking knife she carries.

It's her whispered words that really fucking broke me, though.

"I will never forget you, Jared Crowley. And my heart will always belong to you."

I stay there in Dee's bed, my heart aching and tears streaming from my eyes as I clutch onto her pillow like it's the last bit of her I have. It smells like her, and I can't help it. I torture myself for what seems like days, but is merely an hour or so before I drag myself up and get dressed.

I'm a mess as I dress, my hands trembling, my eyes red raw, my heart shattering like Dee just died.

That's what it feels like, too. Like she died. I remember that pain when my brother was killed. It's excruciating. Unbearable. Like it might actually kill me, too.

Maybe I should have gone with her? I've thought about that before, but the idea of leaving my parents when they have already lost one child is what's kept me here. Besides, as fucked up as this town seems to be getting, it's still home. I just wished Dee would have given it more of a chance because it could have been her home, too.

Taking one last look around Dee's room as the sun rises higher in the sky, filling the space with light, I turn my back on it, hoping to sneak out of the house unannounced.

When I step through the door to the living area, I pull up short, my eyes landing on Cynthia and Will as they read something.

A letter.

When Cynthia glances up, I notice her eyes are red, tears falling from them in rivers, and I know they know too. They know Dee has gone. She must have left them a note.

"Jared," Cynthia cries, dropping the piece of paper on the benchtop as she makes to move towards me.

I hold up my hand, shaking my head.

"I know she's gone. I heard her leave," I say before I can't say another word, tears choking me.

"She thinks she doesn't deserve to be here. That she's to blame for everything bad happening, and that we are all better off without her," Will states, his voice cracking as he fights his own emotion.

"We have to stop her," Cynthia cries and I frown.

"How? How can we ever make her want to stay? She's never going to stop blaming herself."

"Fight for her." It's Rhys' voice coming from behind me this time, and she steps into the room looking frantic. "Think about it. The only person who ever fought for her was her dad. No one else did. She's always been the one fighting for everyone else, even when they pushed her away. She knows we care about her. Hell, she knows she wants to stay, but she thinks she can't burden us with what she brought into our lives. We need to show her that it doesn't matter. That no matter her past or her flaws, we will always fight for her."

"You're right." Cynthia nods, her worried eyes turning to Will.

Shit.

Fight for her.

Had I fought for her?

Sure, I fought to save her life. I fought off others to protect her, but have I fought for her to stay?

I've told her how I feel. Shouldn't that be enough?

No.

Rhys is right.

She needs more.

She deserves more.

I turn and charge for the front door, not even knowing where to look first but knowing I have to start looking regardless, because I'm going to find her and beg her to fucking stay.

I hear my name called by Cynthia and Rhys, but I ignore them, pulling the front door open and screaming at the top of my lungs.

"ELODIE!"

I bolt down the front path and scream again. "ELODIE COME BACK!"

I don't fucking know what I think I'm going to achieve by doing this. She left over an hour ago so she's probably long gone by now, but it's the faint sob I hear from my left that turns my attention that way, and my eyes widen as I take in the small frame of a dark-haired girl wearing a black hoodie and black jeans, sitting on the corner curb three houses down.

"Dee?" I ask, even though she probably can't hear me from this distance.

She gets up, sobs flying from her as she starts running towards me. I don't fucking hesitate. I bolt towards her twice as fast, ignoring the calls of the Rogan family behind me. My sight set on the only thing that matters in this moment.

"Dee!" I call, her tear-stained cheeks flushed red as she nears and at the last minute, like the little acrobatic monkey she is, she leaps at me, wrapping herself around me as she crashes to my chest and cries into my neck.

"Fuck. Dee. I thought you'd left." I squeeze her to me, my arms around her like a vise, never wanting to let go.

She tries to speak, but she's in such a distressed state that all I pick up is babble.

I hug her tighter, pressing kisses to her hair before another body slams into us, and Rhys speaks into Dee's ear.

"Don't leave us. We want you to be a part of our family."

"We all want you here," I add, holding her tight and not willing to let her go. "You are ours and we are yours and we will fight for you no matter what."

Another loud sob escapes her, and then I feel someone

rubbing her back. Prying my eyes open, I see Cynthia, still crying, but her focus on Dee, trying to let her know we are all here for her. No matter what.

Slowly, as we all surround the small girl who came into our life only weeks ago, her silence louder than any voice has ever spoken, her tears start to subside and her sobs ease off.

"I'm sorry," she whispers, but we all hear it. She pulls back from me, using the sleeve of her hoodie to clean up her tears. "I couldn't do it, even though I should. Everyone would be better off without me. But I just can't leave."

"Fuck, baby." I shake my head, cupping each side of her flushed face as I stare into her red-rimmed eyes. "You don't need to leave. No one wants you to leave. Your home is here with me. With the Rogans."

"Jared is right," William adds, and I release Dee's face so she can glance around at her foster parents. "This is your home now, Dee. If you'll have us."

Cynthia nods. "Remember what I said last night? Even after we found out everything, we still wanted you to be a part of our family. Please let us take care of you for once. Let yourself have the happiness you deserve."

Another sob escapes Dee as she nods, and I'm swarmed again by the Rogans as I'm put in the middle of a group hug.

After another few minutes of hugs, Rhys and her foster parents leave Dee in my arms, returning to the house, and I walk to the corner, still carrying Dee wrapped around me so tightly that I know she's not going to let go anytime soon, and I bend and pick up her backpack before returning to her house.

Yes. HER HOUSE.

No one says anything when I carry her back into her bedroom and close us in. They know we need some private time and give us the space we need.

Slowly, I manage to peel Dee off me and sit her on the

bed. She won't look at me, and I know she's feeling ashamed or embarrassed, but if she thinks I'm not going to say anything about the stunt she just pulled, then she's sorely mistaken.

Falling to my knees in front of her, I gently grip her chin and lift it until her eyes meet mine.

"I heard you, Dee. I heard you get out of bed, get dressed and whisper your goodbye to me."

Her eyes go round in panic, but I continue.

"The mistake I made was not jumping up right there and then and begging you to stay. I'm sorry I didn't do that. I had it in my head that I couldn't make you want to be here if you really didn't want to. I didn't consider that perhaps you just needed to hear it. That you just needed me to fight for you so you'd know that no matter what, I will always come looking for you. I will always chase you. And you know what?"

She shakes her head, so I continue.

"I will always find you."

Her bottom lip wobbles, but I'm not done.

"I fucking love you, Dee. Like really love you. The type of love that fucking hurts when you try to leave me, to the point that I thought I might just fucking die." I punch my chest, letting my emotions control me as I remember the agony I felt not that long ago.

"I'm sorry," she cries, more tears springing free.

"I know you are. I know you haven't had this before." I gesture to her room, meaning a home. "I know you're used to only looking out for yourself, because you are the only person you can trust, but that's changed now. Here. In this house. In this town. With me. You can finally trust that we will all always have your back."

She nods, swiping at her tears.

"Fuck," I lean forward, gripping each side of her head, not

able to go long without touching her. "You mean everything to me, Elodie Porter. Fucking everything."

She nods, smiling through her tears, and I don't give a fuck that she's probably all snotty right now. I kiss her anyway, because I'm starved to have her close.

We kiss frantically, clawing at each other like we are trying to dig under each other's skin, and when we break apart, Dee's tears have dried, and her cheeks are flushed with arousal.

"Jared," she says quietly, her husky tone the sexiest thing I've ever heard. "I really love you, too. It's why I couldn't leave. Sure, I didn't want to leave Travis, and I really wanted to stay here and see what it would be like to have a family that cares, but it's you. I couldn't leave you. I couldn't take a step further than the corner house, because I actually thought I was about to die from the pain tearing through my chest, too." She shakes her head. "I'm so sorry for putting you through that."

Her words mean everything. To know she felt the same agony as me tells me that she really does love me with the same ferocity as I love her.

That's how I know that we are going to be alright. No matter what this fucked up world throws at us.

DEE

EPILOGUE PART 1

*I*f I thought the drama of me leaving Fox Pines on my eighteenth birthday was all I was going to have this year, I was dead wrong. Only a few weeks after I realised my home really was here in this regional area in South Eastern Australia, a virus spread across the world, and our government put us in lockdown.

I swear Cynthia Rogan can handle anything. After all the drama her foster children bring into her life, me included, she then had to deal with setting up something they started calling remote learning, which is how I finished my final year of school.

Of course, the Rogan house was still bustling with boys sneaking in at all hours of the night for secret visits that Cynthia and Will turned a blind eye to.

I'm thankful for that, because not seeing Jared daily just wasn't an option for me, but I don't think they chose to look the other way for my benefit.

It was all for Rhys. She has needs that no one but her guys can give her, and her foster parents recognised that taking away access to her guys would have led to dire consequences.

Cynthia and Will really are the most understanding adults I've ever come across, and being stuck in their home while on lockdown was a trillion times better than any of the other homes I've ever lived in.

I didn't really hate staying home to do schooling. It suited someone like me perfectly, but what was hard was not being able to go to dance classes.

Eventually, Miss Adele started holding remote dance classes online as well, and Will moved the lounges out of the theatre so I'd have a space to do the classes online.

For that, I was extremely grateful.

Unfortunately, with no in person dance classes, Ruby went off the radar. I haven't heard of her or from her in months, so I reached out to my aunties, the Angels, to track her down and do a welfare check.

They haven't been able to find her either. Nor her little sister.

"Are you ready, beautiful?" Jared asks, bringing me out of my thoughts as I stare at my reflection in the mirror.

I'm pale because I feel like I'm going to hurl.

"I can't do it," I whisper, and he grins, already knowing I was going to have this reaction today.

"Yes, you can. Because of the virus, the audience is only at half capacity. And you probably won't even see them past the bright lights."

Bright lights?

Jesus, that doesn't help the nerves!

I buckle forward, my hands on my knees as I breathe through the wave of nausea. Why did we have to come out of lockdown already? Perhaps I should have feigned having the virus. Played sick and stayed home in bed.

"This is a bad idea. Why did I think I could perform in a dance concert? I can't go out there. I don't dance on stage for people to watch me. I dance for me. I dance to feel, and that's it," I mutter in panic, and Jared offers me a warm smile.

Helping me stand upright, he turns me to face him, his hands rubbing soothingly up and down my arms.

"Don't you understand? When people watch you dance, you make *them* feel too."

Shit. Why does he have to go and say things like that? It just makes my heart squeeze and my chest feel warm and then I want to kiss him, which will likely turn into us getting naked.

Hey, there's an idea.

Maybe I'll miss my spot in the end-of-year showcase while I'm getting busy with Jared.

"Whatever you are thinking, stop." Jared grins, and I roll my eyes. "Come on now. You can do this, Deranged. You've been practising like crazy for today, and you made that beautiful costume in textiles class. It would be a shame not to show it off to everyone."

Damn it. My costume *is* good. Like *really* good. People *do* need to see it.

"Maybe one of the other girls can wear it?" I suggest, looking hopefully up into Jared's amused blue gaze, and he chuckles.

"Nope. It was made for this sexy little dancing assassin. Now go and get ready." Gripping my shoulders, he spins me around and slaps me on the arse, and I squeal before going to do what he said.

As I get ready, my phone lights up with a message from Travis, and I open it to see a photo of him, Cassie, and Tillie, poking their tongues out. He looks so happy, something he's been since being freed from the Kerrs' grasp. He never did go back to school, though, lockdown making it hard, but Griffin has taken him under his wing, and even though I'd rather him live a crime free life, I just don't think Travis has it in him to live that way. So better the devil you know and all that.

Our aunties, Bec and Amanda, purchased a house not too far from the Rogans, which is where Travis and Cassie are living, and my aunties stay there whenever they come to town, which is pretty frequently.

It's nice to see Travis growing closer to them, and when I go around there once a month for a family dinner, it feels less awkward than it used to, and we rarely bring up any bitterness of the past anymore.

After the dust settled from my attempt at fleeing, I spent quite a bit of time with Bec and Amanda. I was angry at first. I had so many questions, and they filled in the blanks, but at the end of the day, they did what they thought was best given my killing tendencies and their ability to help me. Which became easier with each year that passed as they dominated the organised crime industry in this country.

Now, we have a more personal relationship, more befitting of a niece and her aunties. Our time isn't spent talking about who needs to be assassinated, or what crime lords need to be taught a lesson. Now, we talk about clothes, songs, and dance. A lot about dance. And Jared. There's a lot of discussion around that topic. Mainly them asking if he's treating me right. Which is something they'll never have to worry about.

Jared Crowley treats me like a queen.

Sometimes a naughty queen that needs to be taught a lesson through some edging, but they don't need to know that.

Closing Trav's message, I put my phone away and stare at the costume I made in my textiles class. Really, I made it at home, but it was for that class, and I spent way longer than I probably should have hand stitching some lacy motifs on it before teaching myself how to bling the fabric using hot fix rhinestones.

That shit is addictive. Like, to the point that everything you look at around you makes you consider if perhaps it would look better blinged. And I guess most things would look epic, all sparkly and stuff.

As I slip into the teal and black costume I made, I grin at how much my life has changed since I turned eighteen. I haven't killed anyone since I slaughtered Bianca, stabbing her the same amount of times I did her sister. Griffin hasn't asked me to do any more kills either, upholding our agreement.

Sometimes I feel sad for Thana, wondering if she's lonely hiding at the back of my bedhead. Although she's not alone. The birthday gift Griffin got me was a new knife. A small yet just as deadly one, and a lot prettier than Thana. I called her Princess after the little chihuahua that enjoyed eating sausages, both the food source and the one attached to her previous owner.

Maybe one day I'll let Princess bathe in blood like Thana did.

Maybe.

Once the costume is in place, I stare at my reflection in the mirror.

Who are you?

Leaning closer, I stare into my own eyes.

"Are you still a killer?" I whisper, and the smirk that lifts the corner of my mouth tells me everything I need to know.

Yes, I fucking am.

Ahhh, there she is. Hush. I summon that beast, knowing the only way I'm going to be able to get on that stage and not puke my lunch up, is if Hush is here with me.

Yes, I know Hush and Dee are the same person, but I'll use whatever I have to in order to get through this situation.

So, if I believe I'm the lethal, invincible, confident Hush, then that's who I am.

Stepping out of the change room, Jared's blue gaze lifts to meet mine, going wide as I approach.

"Fuck," he whispers, his eyes raking over me before settling on my face. Then, with a frown, he tilts his head to study me. "Hush?"

I grin.

Yeah, he knows.

He likes to visit this version of me on occasion, driving me out to the lake and letting me hunt him instead of the other way around.

It's fucking hot.

I smirk at him, and he rearranges his dick in his pants before looping his arm around my back and pulling me flush against him.

"Hush needs to stay until I've fucked her after the concert." He breathes against my lips, and my brows shoot up.

"You've already fucked me today."

He shakes his head. "I've already fucked Dee today. Now that Hush is here, I want to fuck her too."

I snicker, and Jared grins back, nipping at my lips before he pulls back and frowns as his phone buzzes in his pocket. Releasing his hold on me, he pulls it free and reads the message.

"Damn." His eyes dart up to mine. "Griffin found the leaders of Carnal Unicorn, and they are local. Later tonight, our team is going to surprise them."

Shit.

I'm actually jealous.

Jared has remained working for Griffin even though I asked him not to. He told me that working for Griffin is the first time he's ever felt like he has a purpose other than pleasing my pussy.

His words, not mine.

I can't force him to stop working for Griffin, but I can sure as shit make sure Jared is protected.

I may have visited Griffin's house in the dead of night some months back, much like the first time, reminding him how easy it is for me to get in undetected, reiterating that he'd better not let anything happen to my guy or he'll be dead before he even realises I've broken in.

He assured me that he'd keep Jared safe.

Time will tell.

"Griffin wants to know if you want to come? You know, since they were the ones that ordered the hit on the farm-house the night we were ambushed."

Shit.

Yeah.

The night I killed Ruby's parents.

An ache blooms in my chest when I think about poor Ruby again.

She deserves more than having scum parents wrapped up in the sick shit that Carnal Unicorn promotes. Which is why I nod.

"Yes. I'll be there."

A sexy smirk spreads Jared's lips. "I'm so fucking hard right now."

I roll my eyes as Miss Adele appears from around the corner, shooting me an excited smile.

"It's nearly your turn, Dee."

I nod, butterflies having a party in my belly, and as Miss Adele hurries back into the concert hall, I suck in a deep breath, summoning Hush to shake off my nerves.

"You've got this," Jared insists, leaning forward to kiss me before giving my arse another audible slap.

He's so feisty these days, and I can't wipe the grin from my face as he strides out of the room to go into the auditorium where his parents are already seated.

His relationship with his mum and dad has improved over the last few months. Janine enjoys it when I come over for dinner, spending girl time together. I still don't talk all that much to people, but I make an effort to talk to Jared's parents.

There's been less and less signs of empty wine bottles of late, and more signs of them going out on dates and having a social life, something that pleases Jared a helluva lot.

My nerves rear up again as I refocus on the fact that I have to get on stage soon, and I call on Hush to do a better fucking job at calming me.

I can do this.

I can do this.

I chant encouragement in my head as I make my way backstage, letting the song I'm about to dance to fill my mind as I practise the dance for the millionth time in my head.

I can do this.

Once I'm side stage, I stand in the wings with Miss Adele as she watches a little dancer, probably only eight years old, smash out a jazz routine that involves flips, turns, and a lot of sass.

Man, I wish I could have that sort of confidence.

I swallow thickly as I look past the wings to the darkened audience beyond. You can barely see any faces with the lights shining so brightly on the stage.

I can do this.

As the little dancer's music ends and she death drops to the floor, the audience cheers loudly, whistles piercing, and applause stretching out as the dancer rolls out of her end pose to stand up and give a sassy bow before running off stage the way only a dancer runs. With pointed toes.

I can do this.

"Ok, Dee. Your turn," Miss Adele whispers from behind me, giving me a gentle push towards the stage.

For a fleeting second, fear rushes through me and I think I can't do this.

Then I remember Jared's words.

"When people watch you dance, you make them feel too."

I CAN DO THIS!

I step forward as the lights fade to black, running on stage to take my starting position, my heart thundering in my ears as I call on Hush to give me courage.

If I can slaughter a person, then I can dance on a damn stage.

When the lights slowly brighten, I close my eyes and wait for the music to begin. The moment Knife by Mary Lambert starts to play, I don't even have to think. My body just moves, like I'm a puppet, controlled by the music and emotional lyrics.

Right now, I'm not Dee *or* Hush.

I'm Elodie Porter.

I barely register the bright lights, or the audience beyond, my mind completely engrossed in the emotions in the lyrics as I let my body tell a story. It's a story of grief. Of loss. And it hits home so rawly, that as I dance, tears fall from my eyes, letting myself feel the pain I need to leave behind forever, and move on.

It's not until I'm in my end pose, curled in a ball of emotional suffering, that I snap out of the zone I was in, and all I hear is complete and utter silence.

Shit.

Did the audience leave?

A heartbeat later, I jolt from the startling cheers that sweep across the audience as if they've only just snapped out of a trance, and I roll out of my ball, slowly standing before doing a small curtsy that Miss Adele showed me how to do a couple of days ago.

"Yeah!" Jared cheers over everyone. "That's my girl!"

I suck in my lips, trying not to laugh even as I cry. And for some reason, the lights in the auditorium brighten, allowing me to see the audience.

Although everyone is spread out, sitting mostly in family groups due to social distancing rules, there are more people here than I realised.

And they are all standing.

For me.

They keep clapping, and I notice some people wiping their eyes, or dabbing the corners with a tissue.

Damn. Did I do that?

I find the Rogan family in the audience. My family. I see Cynthia sobbing yet still smiling as Will beams at me. Rhys is a mess, black mascara running down her face as she claps and I'm pretty sure her claps are louder than anyone else's.

The twins are there too, clapping in unison while jumping on the spot, and Charlotte stands next to them with her girlfriend, both wearing huge smiles as they clap too.

My eyes find Griffin and Aggie a little further back, and my auntie Amanda and auntie Bec are next to them, dabbing tissues to their eyes as they smile broadly at me, not looking like the lethal women they are in the least.

Travis is closer to the front of the audience, with Tillie on one side and Cassie on the other, both of them leaning in to hug Travis as he wipes a tear from the corner of his eye.

Jared is right there behind Travis, standing next to his parents as he claps with vigour, his blue eyes bright with happiness and his smile beaming, which just makes me feel all sorts of emotional. Above all else, I love seeing Jared happy.

My heart feels so full as I smile back at all the people who have come here to support me today, all of them meaning so much. I blink back more tears, and just as the auditorium's lighting over the audience starts to fade, I lock onto familiar green eyes, framed by fiery red hair tumbling from a cap.

Ruby.

Shit. I can't be sure it's her though, the audience fading black before my eyes could make sure.

I give another quick curtsy as the applause dies down before running off stage and Miss Adele is there, her arms open wide as I throw myself into her embrace.

She's crying too, and she squeezes me so damn tight that I'm not sure I ever want to leave.

"I'm so incredibly proud of you, Dee," Miss Adele cries quietly as another dancer takes the stage, her teacher shifting in front of us in the wings to watch her student perform.

I pull back, offering Miss Adele a warm smile, and thank her for never giving up on me.

As I turn back to the stage to watch the next dancer do her thing, I feel proud.

I feel pride in myself unlike I've ever felt before.

Coming to Fox Pines was both the hardest and best thing I ever did.

I got my brother back. Found out I had aunties. Found a family willing to accept my flaws. Made friends. And found the love of my life.

Jared.

For the first time ever.

I feel whole.

JARED

EPILOGUE PART 2

*R*unning through the scrubby bushland, my heavy feet give away my location as I choose speed over stealth. I've tried the slow quiet approach before and compared to Hush, I suck.

So, speed it is.

I know she's fast, but I'm going on the theory that my stride size will get me over the line, for a little while at least. But fuck, just knowing that Hush is out here in the dark with me somewhere, stalking me, has my dick as hard as a rock.

Dee has two versions of herself. One that's quiet, chill, and smiles with sweetness. The other side smirks with sinister desires and takes what she wants. Sometimes, when I have Dee writhing under me, the two versions collide, giving me a feisty little brat. And fuck do I love that version of her where she's stuck in between her two personas. It's honestly who I think she really is. The real Elodie Porter. And it's a side of herself that only I ever get to see.

Tonight though, Hush is on my tail and an exciting shiver of fear travels up my spine in knowing that.

She could kill me if she wanted to. It would be so easy for

her, but she never seems to go completely to that dark place anymore. Not since waking up in the hospital days after killing Bianca Kerr.

Since that day, she hasn't killed anyone.

Or hadn't until earlier tonight.

After Dee's dance concert earlier today, we geared up and went with Griffin and his men to a small, yet popular local church.

The Valley of the Trinity and Merciful Fellowship.

Sounds like a fucking cult, if you ask me, but the name is not unfamiliar. I've heard kids at school talk about this church that their parents go to, and now I have to wonder if Carnal Unicorn isn't even bigger locally than we originally thought.

The Priest and Minister, two brothers, were lucky enough to meet Hush in person, and Griffin stood back, letting her show those sick fucks just how unmerciful she can be. While it was a sight to behold to see Hush back in action, it was also brutal. She didn't hold back, making sure the two men suffered excruciating torture before they finally stopped breathing and Griffin's men set the church alight in an inferno that is likely to cause a stir in the Timber Valley district.

A rustling in nearby bushes has me forgetting all about everything that happened as I pick up my pace, knowing my stalker is getting closer.

I skid to a stop as I push through the bushes, my feet sinking in the sandy bank of Lake Woodall, my head darting around under the moonlit shore to try to spot my predator.

Air shifting behind me has me whipping around, only to see nothing but the bushes I came through.

Then something taps my shoulder.

My heart lurches as I dart around, coming face to face with Hush.

Her grin is sinister as fuck, and her blade, Thana, is now at my throat as she flashes her teeth in satisfaction.

"Tell me to stop," she hisses, and my heart flips.

She's using my tactics.

Naughty little pocket rocket.

Clamping my lips shut, she grins wider, excitement flaring her dark eyes wide as she shifts closer as she presses Thana a little harder to my skin, so much so that it starts to sting.

Shit. She just cut me.

Her dark hair swirls out behind her as the breeze picks up, and if I didn't know who she was, I'd almost say she was inhuman. A creature of the night, ready to make her kill.

My dick jerks.

"Tell me to stop," she hisses again. And again, I stay quiet, giving her back her own treatment.

The blade bites deeper into my skin, and for a flash, I wonder if perhaps she might actually kill me.

Lightning fast, I find myself tumbling back, my feet being kicked out from under me as Hush ninjas me, and before I know it, I'm flat on my back on the cool sand with an assassin straddling my lap.

My eyes widen in surprise, but she doesn't give me much time to react before she tosses Thana to the side and drags her tongue over the cut she made, licking up the trail of blood.

Fuck, that's hot, and all of a sudden we are both lost to the primal need to claim each other.

Hush tears my t-shirt right down the centre like she has superhuman strength, all while grinding herself against my hard length.

We roll in the sand, a battle to get naked as our lips collide and our tongues devour each other. It's raw and primal and fucking perfect.

Somehow, Hush ends up back on top of me, our clothes shed, some in shreds, and she lifts herself while lining up my cock before slowly lowering herself down on me.

My fucking eyes roll in the back of my head as her tight cunt squeezes my dick like a hot, moist vise. Her hand roughly grips my chin, sending my lips open again, and she sneers at me.

"Don't ever tell me to stop. You're mine."

Fuck.

I grin wickedly, thrusting my hips up, driving my cock deeper even while she tries to maintain control. It's heaven feeling her hot silky cunt with no barrier, something which has been a constant since she got out of the hospital back in March. There's just something about shooting my cum deep inside her that has me feeling primal, and I know she loves taking it, making her feel like I am marking her, claiming her, each and every time we come together like this, whether it's Dee or Hush.

And hell, right now I have Hush and I love fucking her. It's a battle for dominance that I'm here for. It lets her release some of her demons as well, and I'll always be here to help her do that. I'll never stop loving her and helping her see that she really is worth fighting for.

"Fine," I hiss back in response, gripping her hips so I can get better momentum as I drive up harder and harder, watching Hush slowly lose her battle of remaining in control. "As long as you never tell me to stop, either!" I grunt, my lip curling with pleasure and pain rushing through me. Her gaze is molten, but she doesn't argue, so I continue as I glide my hand up to cup her full tit and roll her nipple. "And don't forget that you're mine, too!"

"Yes!" she gasps, throwing her head back as she gives herself over to the dance our bodies evoke.

She's a fucking beauty. The way the moonlight makes her

skin glow is otherworldly, and as she presses her own fingers to her needy bud, her hips rising and falling in sync with my thrusts, I feel her start to clamp around me.

The moment she starts to convulse, my nuts tighten and a wave of pure ecstasy rushes over me.

My roar is loud, but nothing like the sound that flies from my girl's lips. Lips that were once silent, not making a sound for anyone.

It's the most beautiful sound I've ever heard, and I know I'll spend the rest of my life worshipping Elodie Porter and hoping to hear her make that sound again.

It's pure animal. The war cry of a warrior princess.

It's a truly beautiful *savage scream*.

THE END

IF YOU ENJOYED SAVAGE SCREAM

PLEASE LEAVE A REVIEW

BREAKING THE SILENCE DUET

SILENT HUSH – BREAKING THE SILENCE BOOK 1

AMAZON: https://books2read.com/BTSbook1
GOODREADS:
https://www.goodreads.com/book/show/62852392-silent-hush

SAVAGE SCREAM – BREAKING THE SILENCE
BOOK 2

AMAZON: https://books2read.com/BTSbook2
GOODREADS:
https://www.goodreads.com/book/show/62926130-savage-scream

STAY CONNECTED

To stay connected and be in the know about future works
that may include some of the side characters from my books,
join my reader's group:

Sarah JD's Vicious Kittens – a Sarah JD Readers Group
https://www.facebook.com/groups/
sarahjaneduncanreadersgroup

Visit Sarah JD at
https://sarahjaneduncan.com
for updates!

STAY UPDATED

Join my VIP Readers list and receive monthly newsletters
jam packed with updates about your favourite Fox Pines
characters!

SIGN UP HERE!
https://sarahjaneduncan.com/newsletter/

ALSO BY SARAH JD

THE HEAVY HEARTS SERIES

https://books2read.com/HeavyHeartsBook1/

https://books2read.com/HeavyHeartsBook2/

https://books2read.com/HeavyHeartsBook3/

or

https://sarahjaneduncan.com/my-books/heavy-hearts-series/

THE INSATIABLE SERIES

https://books2read.com/KittenBookOne
https://books2read.com/Kitten2
https://books2read.com/KittenBookThree

or

https://sarahjaneduncan.com/my-books/the-insatiable-series/

SUBBING FOR SANTA

SUBBING FOR SANTA – Standalone

https://books2read.com/subbingforsanta

or

https://sarahjaneduncan.com/my-books/subbing-for-santa-2/

ABOUT THE AUTHOR

SARAH JD

Sarah JD, also known as Sarah Jane Duncan is a dark romance author, living in the beautiful Gippsland region in Victoria, Australia, with her high-school-sweetheart-turned-hubby and three grown children.

When she's not busy writing, Sarah can be found sewing dance costumes for her daughter or helping her hubby in their family business.

Sarah writes about females who have to fight against the odds to find their power, find their voice, and find their truth. The heroines in Sarah's stories possess the strength that only comes when you have to fight for your life!